AT ATHENA'S GATES

AT ATHENA'S GATES

BULLETFOOT™ BOOK THREE

MARSHAL RUST

Copyright © 2020 LMBPN Publishing
Cover Art by Jake @ J Caleb Design
http://jcalebdesign.com / jcalebdesign@gmail.com
Cover copyright © LMBPN Publishing
A Michael Anderle Production

LMBPN Publishing
PMB 196, 2540 South Maryland Pkwy
Las Vegas, NV 89109

First US edition, December 2020
(Previously published as a part of *Bulletfoot*)
ebook ISBN: 978-1-64971-348-3
print ISBN: 978-1-64971-349-0

THE AT ATHENA'S GATES TEAM

Thanks to the Beta Team:
Nicole Emens, Timothy Cox, Mary Morris, Kelly O'Donnell,
Rachel Beckford, John Ashmore, Larry Omans

Thanks to our JIT Team:
Billie Leigh Kellar
Dave Hicks
Deb Mader
Debi Sateren
Diane L. Smith
Dorothy Lloyd
Jackey Hankard-Brodie
Jeff Eaton
Jeff Goode
Larry Omans
Misty Roa
Paul Westman
Peter Manis
Veronica Stephan-Miller

Editor
Skyhunter Editing Team

Lightning flickered vividly across the sky once more—or, possibly, it flared from the bunker tower in the distance. Jessica13 wasn't sure which but decided it didn't matter in the bigger scheme of things. It faded into relative insignificance when she focused on Athena, who marched at the front of her army toward the town of Auburn.

Mini pinged the HUD of the Minato and caught her attention almost immediately. "Your raised heart rate and dilated pupils indicate that you are currently in a state of choice between fight or flight."

"We can't fly. Right?"

"The Minato is incapable of flying, yes, but in this case, flight means running away."

She settled into the controls of the mech. "Flight means running away?"

"It's likely an indicator of the fastest way for someone to run away, although not for everyone. It's not important as the fight or flight instinct was what I referred to rather than the action itself."

She scowled at the indicator on her HUD. "I won't run away. The Knights Mechanica still need me to stand by them, especially in the face of this…"

Her voice trailed off for a few seconds as she stared at the approaching army.

"I didn't think you would. But the instinct would be there. Fear and terror are indicative of a human's response to impending danger."

"How does that help us now?"

"It doesn't, but it should be noted that your heart rate has dropped over the duration of our conversation, so I would say there was at least one benefit from the discussion."

Jessica13 stared forward and realized the AI was right. A hint of terror remained in her gut, but the heart-wrenching knowledge that she would probably die in the coming battle was gone. She stood beside some of the best fighters on the planet, as far as she knew.

They were led by Hammerhand, who manned one of the few Excalibur mechs in the world.

Those two facts provided a little hope, at the very least.

"What do you think our chances are of surviving this?" She was determined to stop herself from descending into panic like she had been before.

"Do you want to know the actual odds?"

She shrugged. "Sure, why not?"

"I would put the odds of surviving the night at around seventy-eight point three-two to one. That is slightly worse than those for the battle we recently fought. I could inform you of the variables that went into the calculation."

"How… No, I don't think that would be a good idea. Merely knowing we are in a worse position than we were in earlier today is enough. Honestly, I'd rather not test the fight or flight instinct you mentioned."

"Understood. Although it would probably be best for you to do as Windchime has repeatedly told you to do and stay away from the fighting. At least now, you have a way to inflict damage from a distance."

Jessica13 checked the rifle she carried. She still had sufficient ammo and she didn't need to head to the Beast to reload yet. Besides, the chances were that she would have to access their supplies to take ammo to the team on the front lines before she ran out anyway.

Hammerhand seemed to have snapped out of what she believed was a moment of speculation. With the mech, it was impossible to read his reaction but she had wondered if he felt the same thing she did. In her case, it was all-encompassing terror, but she wasn't sure if he was even capable of something like that at this point in his life.

"They'll arrive by nightfall." The man's booming voice had a calming effect on the other knights. They had all communicated between themselves and the entire team suddenly came to a standstill when his voice thundered through Auburn. "We will be prepared for their arrival. Get those barriers working again, and I want to see all the battle lines drawn up within the hour. Go!"

The last syllable was enough to snap both the Knights and the Auburn townsfolk out of the fear-induced stupor they had apparently all slumped into. They jerked into action and immediately set to work. A large part of the town had been destroyed in the combat, but the overall sentiment among the people and the knights alike appeared to be that reconstruction and mourning could wait until a time when they didn't face an impending assault.

Mayor Edgar Jones had already gathered the people and now organized them into workgroups that would collect the rubble, chunks, and pieces and arrange them into defensive constructions. He called on those knights who could be spared for help to carry the heavier loads.

Jessica13 noted that, in the meantime, Tinker had moved to where Hammerhand stood. The older man climbed out of his hybridized mech and began to work on their leader's Excalibur. Being struck by lightning was no small thing, even for a mech that size. By the looks of it, they were running a handful of diagnostics to make sure none of the vital functions were permanently damaged by the strike.

She understood their concern. Their chances were already slim against Athena and her army. If Hammerhand wasn't able to fight at full capacity, their fate was all but sealed.

With the other mechs quickly engaged in preparing the town for the fight, she proceeded toward the two men with the intention to offer her help.

Tinker turned to see who was approaching and waved her closer. "Jessie, fantastic. I need to perform a miracle or two to get this damn thing working again, and you'll have to help me. Come on up, lassie. Don't be shy. And bring those frequency adjusters on the way, would you?"

She climbed out of her Minato and collected the tools the man had left at the boot of the Excalibur.

"Why will they only attack at nightfall?" she asked once she was halfway up the leg and handed the pieces to Tinker.

"Well, I assume they're not here for a friendly chat. Now hand me the…tumblers, yes."

Jessica13 knew what was needed to install a frequency adjuster and had the tool waiting for him. "Well, by the looks of it, they'll reach here at least an hour before sundown. Why would they wait until nightfall to attack?"

"It's her way." Hammerhand's voice boomed again and almost shook her free from her perch with the vibrations alone.

"That...doesn't explain much," she muttered and hoped he wouldn't hear her.

He did, though, and chose to explain. "Observe the way she has her forces marching in formation like it's some kind of a parade. They have the intention to instill fear and terror prior to the attack. Besides, fighting at night only serves to enhance the feeling of fear for those under attack. Athena sees terror as a weapon to be used to advantage and takes it very seriously."

While they spoke, Mayor Jones rushed to where they stood and maintained high ground to enable him to keep an eye on the approaching enemy.

"Master Hammerhand, if I could have a word?" The man looked tiny compared to the massive Excalibur, which was why he shouted to get the knight's attention.

"There is no need to raise your voice, Mayor," the Knights' leader replied, careful not to move the mech.

"The preparations for the fight are underway. I would like to discuss the battle plan with you."

"Our best chance would be to prevent the enemy from reaching the city," Hammerhand asserted. "We will need to control the access points to the town to keep the invaders at arm's length and away from where they can do the most damage."

"If I may offer another plan?" Mayor Jones looked timid at the prospect of even suggesting any changes, but when there was no response from the knight, he grew a little bolder.

"There are those among us who feel the battle will be better suited to our particular situation should Lady Hoot's fighters be drawn into the town."

Hammerhand's head twisted to look more closely at the mayor. "Your people would be willing to risk their homes in such a fashion?"

"They feel there will be no homes to risk should we suffer defeat."

Jessica13 and Tinker continued to work as their leader paused to think about the suggestion.

"Using the narrower streets of the town would allow us to funnel them in and counteract the advantage of their numbers."

"You will notice as well that they appear to be armed with weapons better suited to a pitched battle out in the open," Tinker interjected and continued his efforts to restore the Excalibur to full functionality. "Drawing them into a situation where their longer-range weapons would be useless could also prove effective."

She could almost see the gears turning in Hammerhand's head as he inspected the fighting force that approached. "This is true. The rifles, launchers, and artillery would be better suited for a fight out in the open but would be almost fully inhibited by the tight confines of the town's streets. Make it so."

The mayor appeared excited that his plan had been accepted. "Fantastic. We have already begun to plot choke points and set up traps and the like to funnel their numbers even more."

"If I may suggest something, Mayor," Tinker called from where he closed the panels on the mech. "I don't suppose you would have any fertilizer available?"

Jones paused and glanced quickly at the strange old man. "Literally tons. Why do you ask?"

"It can be used to make potent explosives, and if you hold none back for planting, we should be able to give Lady Hoot's men quite a greeting when they arrive at our doorstep."

The mayor nodded resolutely. "I will order that all of it be gathered."

Tinker finished with the last of the repairs and climbed down. "I would advise not to get hit by lightning again, but should it happen, I think you should be protected from all except for a direct hit."

Hammerhand ran another quick diagnostic on his mech. "Tell me, Tinker, if you see as I do. The mechs out there are not the same kind Athena put in the field before. They are untouched by the modifications and paraphernalia the others bore."

The two returned to their mechs and turned to study the enemy force. Jessica13 zoomed into the parade Athena had arranged for their benefit and identified a few mechs with the same kinds of additions and capes as those that had attacked before them. Most, however, looked like they had come out of the box. They were gray or white and possessed none of the ornate decorations their adversary's raiders usually displayed.

"It could be that these are the better fighters," Tinker suggested. "Perhaps the ones we killed were merely the pawns —the chaff or the disposable pilots."

"That's a comforting thought," she grumbled. She knew for a fact that Hammerhand couldn't hear her this time but when the massive Excalibur twisted easily, the repairs and diagnostics apparently effective, her heart jumped to her throat.

"Actually, these are the Citadel's forces," Mayor Jones explained as he paused from sending orders through the radio. "They are not Lady Hoot's men. The Citadel's forces prefer to remain underground, while Lady Hoot fights on the surface as their auxiliary. That they have stepped in now is worrying."

"Either way, we will be ready for them," Hammerhand said and his voice thundered through the town as he and the mayor marched back to inspect the preparations.

"What do you have going on in that mind of yours?" Tinker asked, having obviously waited for the men to move on before he spoke.

Jessica13 scowled. "Remember how we used to set up the comm jammers over Sanctuary's entrance to make sure attackers had no way to communicate with each other?"

"Remember? I still hold the record for setting it up in seventeen minutes."

"Used to hold it. I put it up in under fifteen minutes."

"No shit?"

"Sorry. Anyway, as I was saying, I've thought about setting one of those up at the edge of Auburn. Of course, it would mean that we don't have comms either, but given that there are more of them to coordinate and they're entering our territory, they would be the most crippled if they didn't have any comms."

"That's an interesting idea but how would you power it? We don't have any power cores to spare, not even in the Beast."

"I can power it with the generators we used to collect the lightning."

"How quickly can you set it up?"

She snickered. "Come on. Under fifteen minutes, remember?"

"Make it so. I'll talk to Hammerhand so that we can organize a low-tech comm system. Maybe we can use physical runners to relay messages."

They moved into the town, where she could already smell the fertilizer being moved from the farming areas and into where Tinker could use it. The man was immediately called away to direct the construction of the bombs created from it, leaving her to start work on the jammer. She picked out the bits and pieces that were needed from the Beast and climbed to the top of the tallest building in the town.

It would be slow work, but with Mini to man the heavier aspects while she worked on the circuitry, it would go quicker than it would otherwise.

"Take cover!"

Someone shouted it from below, and she flung herself prone and covered her head at the sound of rockets fired in the distance.

Mini moved quickly to stand over her body to protect her. The seconds ticked past and she couldn't understand why the town wasn't rocked with explosives yet.

"Look."

The AI directed her gaze to what had been fired from Athena's Artillery mechs. They weren't shells at all. Halfway to the ground, bright white parachutes opened and what looked like cases drifted slowly earthward. At ten meters up, the bottoms opened and a shower of leaflets fell like snow.

"What is that?" Jessica13 asked, scrambled to her feet, and brushed the dust from her clothes. "Why leaflets?"

Mini pivoted and scanned the papers strewn around them.

"It's a message from Athena, or Lady Hoot. The paper states the following—surrender peaceably and you will be spared. Resist and no mercy will be shown."

"Bullshit," she snapped. "She'll kill everyone here like she did in the other town."

The AI turned the mech to pick up the jammer that had fallen when they had taken cover. "Agreed. And yet…if they are within range to strike, why haven't they done so?"

"That…uh, is a good question."

The townsfolk began to retrieve the flyers and read and discuss them. She didn't need to hear what they were saying to know what they were feeling.

Despair, probably, and a hint of hope in the thought that if they simply followed Lady Hoot's orders, they would live to see another day. They weren't soldiers and they didn't know the kind of woman they were dealing with. Or maybe they did and refused to face it. They wanted to survive.

Hammerhand knew Athena, though. Based on his knowledge, she knew the woman would kill everyone in the town and make another example of them if she could.

There would be no way to avoid this easily.

"The question," Mini said and sounded pensive, "is why they have sent this kind of message if they intend to kill everyone anyway? Why not simply start shelling the town?"

Jessica13 turned and noticed that Tinker and Hammerhand both inspected the papers.

"This is their way to show that they are close enough to start shelling the town," Tinker said and held the page up for his leader to see. "They're close enough to start attacking. That means they're putting themselves in an attack formation."

The Excalibur zoomed in to see what the papers contained. "Agreed, but if they are close enough to shoot these letters, they're close enough to shell the town. Why haven't they?"

"Do you think the offer could be genuine? That she would leave Auburn intact in case someone else wants to settle here?"

"You know Athena better than I do," the Knights' leader countered. "What the hell do you think?"

All Tinker could do was shake his head.

"No, I think she wants to leave the town intact for some reason. She'll kill everyone here but the structures are not to be damaged. Or maybe something in the foundations. Those waterways, maybe?" Hammerhand turned the Excalibur almost full circle to survey the town.

"I really wish we had something better than your reasoning to go on for this leg, laddie. Basing all our defenses on assumptions is a good way to get ourselves killed. You know that better than I do."

"What do you suggest we do, then?"

"You won't like this." Tinker looked like he didn't like it either but pressed on. "We could leave Auburn. It would draw Athena away from the town and we would be able to engage in tactics that suit us best. Hitting and running and staying mobile is what has allowed us to stay alive this long, laddie. Entrenched defenses, open warfare...the Knights were not built for this."

"And yet, we must stand our ground," the other man snapped. The people around them had begun to listen and some muttered about the Knights abandoning them. "We will not leave the town of Auburn to the fate this Lady Hoot doubtless has in store for them. We will fight and we will win and take this land back from those who would see them ground under their heel."

Many of the townsfolk had paused their work to listen to him, and a couple of them now moved closer. The despair she had seen before had begun to fade, replaced by a faint glimmer of real hope. The assurance told them they would be able to fight for their town without having to kowtow to the likes of Lady Hoot. The efforts of the various groups resumed with more determination than before.

It was odd how Hammerhand had that effect on the people around him. Only a few words from the man could turn the tide of their drooping morale.

Jessica13 finished working on the device as quickly as she could. It would interrupt comm signals broadcast from the kinds of short-range devices most mechs used.

She clambered down with Mini guiding her using the grappler she had used to climb to the top.

When she reached the bottom, she noted that three of the townsfolk hadn't involved themselves in setting up the preparations.

No, they weren't locals. The tanned skin and the darker hair indicated that they were peddlers from outside and recent arrivals too. They were seated in a circle and spoke softly in a language she didn't understand.

"What are they saying?" Jessica13 asked.

Mini scanned the audio of their speech. "The language itself isn't in my databanks, but it does share some similarities with the desert folk. If I have translated it correctly...they appear to be praying."

"Praying? Like we do to Sagan?"

"Well, you mostly quote the words Sagan left behind but no, this is something different. They appear to be appealing for help from a higher power."

"What higher power?"

"None that I know of. And I know of none that would help us in the coming battle."

"How do you know?"

Mini displayed a small spike in processing power as he accessed his core for more data. "They have faith that something or someone will come to help. Faith ends up as a crutch to many and allows them to delay acting in hopes that something more powerful will intercede."

Jessica13 trudged to where the men continued to chant in their language. "I'm sorry, I don't want to interrupt but..."

The three turned to look at her with soft, inviting smiles.

"How can we help you, my child?" The man's accent was foreign to her, yet he still had a good grasp of the language.

"We'll need all the help we can get."

"And we are providing help," one of the others stated and his smile remained. "We ask for the Prophet to come. He always does. When there is imbalance, he will right it."

There didn't seem to be any real answer to that, and they returned to their prayers, lowered their heads, and muttered again in the language she didn't understand.

She turned away, and Mini came alive on her HUD again. "Like I said, a crutch. And it can be spread like a disease, so I would suggest not catching it."

With so much still left to do, there seemed little point in continuing a fruitless discussion. She moved to join the fortification effort as the sun began to sink toward the horizon and cast a broad wave of reds and purples across the ever-darkening sky.

"It won't be long now," she said softly and gave the gorgeous expanse of color one last look before she focused on the work needed.

CHAPTER TWO

The last of the sunlight faded from the sky. The clouds from the summoned storm in the first battle for Auburn still lingered, but they had begun to disperse. Their slow withdrawal gave her a view of the stars that had entranced her so much the first time she had been out of Sanctuary.

It felt right that they would be present for the second battle of Auburn.

Jessica13 settled herself beside the jammer and looked through the scope of her rifle.

For now, there wasn't much to see out there. The flickering light of the spire in the distance no longer illuminated Athena's fighters. If anything, it made it more difficult to peer deeper into the darkness.

The silence around them was palpable. All the preparations that could be completed were already in place. Those that needed more time were handled by some of the townsfolk, but most of the attention was focused outside the town. Everyone watched and waited for something to happen.

Despite the pervasive sense of expectancy, the moment still came as a shock.

The night sky's darkness was shattered when dozens of flares were launched, arced high above them, and hung there like gravity had no effect on them. Their brightness illuminated the town.

"Activate the jammer on my mark," Hammerhand shouted into her commlink. "Not a second before and not a second after, do you understand?"

"Roger that."

The flares began to descend slowly. Mini hastily adjusted the light filters in the HUD to provide her with a better view of what approached. The lights were meant to expose and illuminate the Knights and the town, but she could see them move into the trees around the town to use them for cover.

More rockets fired from the Raptors set up in the distance —not flares this time, and when they picked up speed, an unpleasant whine accompanied them. As they approached, it sounded more like screams and the deafening noise filled the air. Jessica13 couldn't do much except cover her ears as they soared over her head.

Mini was already working to filter the noise out, but it took a few seconds.

"Are you all right?" The AI ran a quick scan of her body.

"My ears are ringing but..."

Her voice trailed off when the missiles collided with the hills behind the town and set the trees on fire.

Hammerhand laughed into the shared comm channel. "Like I said. They have no intention to cause any harm to the town."

"And we all know that's the last time we'll hear of that," Tinker snapped.

"Stay steady. Activate the countermeasures on my mark and on my mark only," their leader continued without acknowledging the comment. "They're coming now and hope we'll be distracted when they arrive. Let's prove them wrong."

The blood rushed in her ears, louder than the ringing in them.

"How the hell does he do that?"

Mini popped up. "Who do what?"

"Nothing. Can you locate targets for me? I can't see anything."

The brightness from the flares played hell with her night vision and left almost nothing visible on the ground.

The AI responded immediately, brought up a handful of other protocols quickly, and within seconds, the vision from the HUD was improved and a handful of targets presented themselves. Most seemed to be Lancers, but a couple of Balthazars caught her attention. They would be the most dangerous to her once they realized their communications were down.

"Hammerhand, I have targets. Am I clear to engage?"

"Roger that. Fire at will. Give them something to think about as they advance."

She took a deep breath, exhaled slowly, and relaxed into the controls. The Balthazar that was closest activated the rockets on its back and prepared to take off.

"Fire when ready," she whispered and pulled the trigger.

The head of the target mech snapped back and it overreacted to the jerking motion of the human within. It continued to rise, but the pattern soon became erratic when the AI failed to pick up that its pilot was dead. A few seconds later, it twisted and flared earthward. The crunch could be heard even in the town as the rocket on the Balthazar's back deactivated.

The other long-distance specialists fired on the command to eliminate a handful of the advancing mechs. They continued to move, but slower and with jolting motions.

Those that were closer opened fire on the town. Rockets and grenades impacted the walls of the buildings at the edge.

"No one else open fire until they're within the city perimeter. They'll probe for our defense points. There's no sense in letting them know before they're inside."

Athena realized what was happening and ordered them to increase the pace. More of the rockets rushed overhead and filled the air with the ghostly screams that chilled Jessica13 to the very bone. She maintained her position and pulled the trigger in a continuous rhythm.

A few of the rounds didn't find their targets. It came from having to choose them and shoot quickly. Mini helped with the aim but even then, a couple of the shots struck the shoulder pauldrons and bounced away into the darkness while the mechs moved on.

There were too many of them. Those she did manage to eliminate were merely a drop in the proverbial bucket. Dozens more broke through the tree line and savaged through the defenses that had been set up for the first battle using rockets to obliterate them and create them more openings to attack through.

"Jessie, are you ready to kill comms?"

Hammerhand sounded like he was under stress, a far cry from the full-blooded confidence he had filled the commlinks with.

"Ready for your mark." She pulled the trigger again, focused on two Sherlocks that attempted to set up a firing position from beyond the tree line. One dropped quickly with no AI to keep it up. The second realized what had happened and jumped out of the way in time to take cover behind the trees.

Her rounds could punch through the trunks easily, of course, but there was no way to be sure she could hit him where she needed to. She had no desire to waste the bullets.

"Put a highlight on that tree," she snapped at Mini, who quickly did as he was told. "Blink it if the Sherlock moves out from behind cover."

"Understood."

Athena's men had breached the perimeter of the town and now funneled into the kill zones, where the Knights and the townsfolk were more than happy to greet them. Hammer-hand gave them the signal and they opened fire to decimate the front lines.

Jessica13 let the others deal with those who were already in the town. Her gaze turned to those mechs that weren't marked like Athena's raiders. They held back and while they opened fire here and there, they didn't join the initial attack.

Unlike the raiders, these likely realized that they were being pulled into a location where their numbers advantage would be irrelevant and their weapons would be less effective. They would likely charge in anyway, but only after they had a quick discussion about it.

"Since when do raiders and pirates take the time to discuss tactics?" Jessica13 asked no one in particular as she pulled the trigger. "I guess these are from the Citadel."

One of the Lancers, looking oddly intact, snapped back a few steps and the gyros inside worked smoothly to keep it on its feet despite the death of the human inside. The other mechs quickly reorganized. A couple held what looked like shields above their heads in an effort to provide cover.

Their attempt was doomed to failure. Jessica13 selected

another target and fired. A few of the other Knights chose the same ones, and five of them were killed almost instantly.

It seemed the meeting of the Citadel mechs was over. Tactics had been decided, and the newer, cleaner mechs began their advance toward the town.

The push forward had no sooner begun when Mini highlighted the tree he'd marked before and pinged it once. Jessica13 immediately swept her gaze to the Sherlock that now tried to sprint to join the ranks of his comrades.

Her single shot was perfectly placed. The mech stumbled and landed hard enough to spray a wave of dirt around it.

Almost immediately, something moved in the scope line. She zoomed out and narrowed her eyes to locate the mech illuminated by new flares shot into the sky. Even profiled like that, she knew what she was looking at—the largest mechs she'd ever seen aside from the Excalibur.

"Hammerhand, we have Guardians incoming," she advised their leader.

"Not yet. Windchime, bring them in!"

Windchime burst out of hiding where he and three of the Auburnites had taken cover behind a number of wells in the farming fields. The group that raced to take cover in the city skidded to a halt and stared at the four-armed mech that confronted them. He opened fire and swung his swords viciously.

It was mostly for effect, but what an effect it was. Jessica13 wasn't sure what she would do if she was attacked by something like that.

The other knights took firing positions behind him and moved smoothly as he cut through two of the mechs on his first swing. The vibroblades sliced through the steel armor plates and into the pilot inside and released a spray of blood from the newly created opening.

A couple of rounds hit Windchime, but he shrugged the impacts off. The arms with assault rifles continued to fire at the mechs around him and they staggered back.

"Fucking hell."

Jessica13 swung her rifle to locate the targets that withdrew from her teammate's attack and tried to set up a counter-offensive.

"The downside of surprise attacks is that if your enemy survives the surprise, they can retaliate," Mini commented.

"Well then, we'd better give them a couple more surprises to keep them on their toes."

"A fine idea, Jessica13."

She fired, thankful that the mech absorbed the kickback of the rifle against her shoulder.

There were many targets to choose from. The gunfire from the streets had increased in intensity. More of Athena's men now swarmed the city. The raiders didn't seem to care and willingly offered themselves as cannon fodder. Those in the clean mechs were more careful and used the buildings around them for cover once they realized what they were facing.

"Look out!"

She looked up. Hammerhand's warning was meant for the Knights supporting Windchime.

One of the Guardians broke through the tree line, the plasma cannon in its arm raised and glowing. The blast was blinding in the darkness, and the plasma bolt streaked forward faster than she would see if it wasn't for the telltale smoke trail.

All that was left was a smoking crater where one of Windchime's fighters had been. The pieces had been melted by the heat of the bolt and vanished into the soil.

"Get the fuck out of there!" their leader commanded

"There are only a few!"

Hammerhand would have none of it. "I said get the fuck out of there—now!"

Windchime pulled back and Jessica13 took the opportunity to eliminate the mech that stood in front of him.

"Retreat."

The order was clear. Those remaining had done what they were supposed to do, which was to draw the Guardians out of the tree line and closer to the town. They needed as many of Athena's heavy hitters in range of the jammer as possible.

The mechs moved forward and tried to choose their targets from the three that now hurried to safety. The invaders no longer fired at the buildings.

"Jessie, are you ready?"

"On your mark, Hammerhand."

Another shot felled the last of the squad Windchime had engaged. The others had made their way to cover and a few even used the bodies of their own fallen as a shield.

Windchime and his two remaining men slipped into the streets as dozens more of Athena's clean mechs rushed in behind them. The Guardians marched forward, sensing weakness and looking to exploit it.

Jessica13's mouth was dry. Sweat made her hands clammy and she cleaned them quickly on her shirt.

"Come on, Hammerhand," she whispered.

CHAPTER THREE

"Jessie!"

"I'm here."

"Hold..."

She had held for what felt like forever but resisted the temptation to tell him that. While she waited, she dealt with a few more targets here and there and was mostly ignored by the return fire from Athena's mechs. There were other sharpshooters and it would take too much time for the invaders to locate and kill them all. They intended to attack the town anyway and probably thought the nuisances would be caught up in the battle.

There seemed to be no end to the marauders and the mayhem. Rockets screamed overhead and the earth shuddered from the explosions when they landed. They were all for show, of course, but the knowledge didn't stop the cold sweat on her hands or the warm tears running down her cheeks.

Jessica13 cleaned her palms on her shirt again and brushed

a few of the tears away. If she simply continued to target, aim, and fire, she could hopefully distract herself.

"Jessie…mark!"

She released the breath she hadn't realized she'd held, turned away from the battle, and connected with the jammer to bring up the rudimentary controls she'd set up and started the sequence.

It seemed like nothing happened at first. Shots, explosions, and the screams from above continued.

The chatter had died down, though. She tilted her head and checked all the comm signals that had rushed across the battlefield. They were all dead.

"Huh." She grunted and locked the controls in.

"Did you not think it would work?"

"I had my doubts. That much power rushing into the wiring could have fried all the circuits."

"I won't tell anyone of your doubts."

"That would be appreciated."

There was no word on how the battle was going, obviously, but she could see a fair amount from her position at the top of the building beside the jammer. Athena's men looked around as if to work out why orders were no longer coming in. The Guardians stopped their march toward the city and displayed clear signs of confusion over what was happening.

That was all the signal the Knights needed. Most had remained out of sight and inside the buildings Athena's men had likely been ordered not to damage.

Windchime was among them and his blades slashed into the two mechs that were closest to him. There was more frenzy in his movements than before. She didn't need to see the man to know he was angry beyond words and the only thing that would sate that rage was killing the fuckers who had killed one of his comrades. The pilot who had been killed wasn't one of the Knights but he had fought side by side with him and that would have been enough to earn his loyalty.

More joined the assault and used their blades to hack into Athena's fighters up close where they milled in the streets of Auburn, unable to move away from the attack and trapped in a situation where their greater numbers had no value. They were unable to find cover, and even if they did, the blades would still find them. All they could do was try to shoot the Knights before they pushed in too close.

But they were well-trained and despite their difficulties, they seemed about to recover from the surge by the defenders when the townsfolk made themselves known. Jessica13 hadn't seen where they had been hiding, but it was impossible not to see their fervor. The Cinders they had commandeered—both from retaking their town as well as the first battle of Auburn —entered the field of combat. The loud reports of their shotguns were hard to miss and they filled the air around them with white smoke before the flames erupted. The fire shone in the darkness and quickly covered the mechs closest to them.

The pilots withstood the barrage for a few moments longer before they turned and flailed wildly. They didn't realize that they spread the fire in their attempt to put it out. Their line wavered but held, strengthened a moment later when those who were on fire were quickly cut down by the Auburn rebels and Knights alike, only to be replaced by those who pushed in from behind them.

Jessica13 settled into her position and kept watch on the Guardians who began to advance into the city as well, but from a different angle. They could see the smoke and flames rising from their own ranks and knew that if they followed the same route, they could be caught in the trap along with their comrades.

There was no way for her to inform Hammerhand of their approach into town, but she doubted she would need to. The townsfolk who didn't actively participate in combat sent messages between them and to the various fighters who still waited for their turn to join the fray.

She highlighted the heavy mechs as they entered but chose different targets. Balthazars still attempted to gain height to find out where the jamming signal originated so they could disable or destroy it. She selected the mech closest to her, tilted her head, and pulled the trigger.

Once again, the rocket on its back kept it in the air for a few seconds before it lost altitude and finally impacted hard into one of the nearby buildings.

Hammerhand knew the Guardians were coming in closer and that they likely already knew where the signal was coming from. Whether they merely ignored the danger of not being able to contact their troops or if they were en route to her to put an end to it, she didn't know. Either way, it was another distraction for them to have to deal with.

It was like Tinker said. The Knights were best able to fight a guerrilla-style battle, and that was how they currently fought.

The ground shook and smoke billowed from the buildings at the edge of the settlement. Bright flashes of light followed quickly when the fertilizer exploded and debris flurried from the blasts while the buildings began to topple and fall into the streets below.

One of the Guardians at the back of the line twisted and tried to take steps back to avoid one of the falling structures.

Its size made for slower movement, and the building collapsed on top of it and brought the mech down with it.

The pilot was probably not dead and the mech would be able to pull itself out from under the rubble. But, as the dust started to settle, Jessica13 noticed smaller figures move within the wreckage with determination and hurried focus. The townspeople had gathered to make the most of the opportunity. Tinker had given them tools and they now took the mech apart to reach the pilot inside and kill him.

"It's not a good way to go," she whispered as she trained the scope on the other Guardians, who now realized they were almost completely trapped.

Once they halted, more people began to appear from the buildings around them and threw what appeared to be heavy tanks of gasoline, alcohol, or other flammable liquids that quickly caught alight. The flames had less of an impact as their armor was thicker than the other mechs, but it was still a nuisance and one that could prove deadly for the pilot inside. The heat could build to a level where it would broil anyone caught within.

In their distraction, Hammerhand appeared. The Excalibur was almost a quarter again larger than the Guardians, and they lacked the same kind of close-quarters weapons.

Of course, he had no plasma bolt cannons either, but when they were up close and personal, it didn't matter.

The first Guardian was struck across the side of the head when the knight stepped out from where he had hidden. He swung his hammer in a high arc that knocked the mech closest to him aside as the rocket on the back of the hammer lit up. The side of the target was left dented and the gyros struggled to cope with the impact until it crashed heavily into a building on its right. More rubble avalanched onto it to drive it to the ground as Hammerhand moved forward and brought the hammer into another overhead swing that continued in a powerful downward blow.

The rocket flared and the weight of the weapon bore down on the top of the Guardian to leave a massive dent and almost fully crushed its head. It was impressive and painful to watch.

The three Guardians that remained realized the danger they were in and tried to back away from the massive mech that now moved inexorably closer. Their plasma cannons flared and fired, but Hammerhand was ready for them, his shield up and active. He pushed forward as the super-heated slugs pounded into the pale blue film and went no farther.

The Knights' leader advanced with heavy steps that made the earth shudder around him. The shield thrust into contact with the Guardians in front of him and drove them back into the ruined buildings.

All three struggled to retaliate but their smaller mechs weren't capable of producing even a quarter of the power the Excalibur could. They nevertheless stood their ground and locked themselves in place to try to fight back.

The shield dropped and they almost fell forward when the resistance vanished. The hammer rose and the rocket flared behind it. It swung relentlessly and bulldozed most of the closest mech with it. A wave of dirt was dislodged when the weapon connected with the earth and the damaged mech slowly lost power and remained on its knees.

The other two seemed uncertain as to whether to run away or keep fighting, and both expected the shield to come up again. It didn't, but the hammer did and catapulted one to the side. Hammerhand quickly reversed the weapon in his grasp and activated the rocket again to launch it into the last of the Guardians. It stumbled over the rubble of the fallen buildings behind it and fell.

The Auburn rebels rushed in to deal with the second mech and began to remove pieces. The hammer had caused too much damage to allow it to fight them off.

The second was still active and tried to pull itself slowly to its feet, which left Hammerhand no option but to deliver a killing blow. The hammer swung into the area of the cockpit and crushed the man inside.

More explosions now rocked the battlefield, and Jessica13 stared as other buildings fell to block any chance of escape by the raiders who were still in the town. They attempted to withdraw and clearly hadn't expected the opposition to be this fierce. None of Athena's fighters remained. All the mechs that had worn her colors and adornments had been felled early in the fight, and the newer mechs were quickly disposed of as well.

She raised her rifle to study the edge of the hamlet. The elation that had begun to rise in her chest slowly stopped its swelling when she saw additional companies of the clean and newer mechs begin to assemble on the perimeter.

With her jaw set, she pushed her mech into motion and motioned to the Auburn rebels to indicate that more attackers would soon be incoming.

"I hope the word gets to Hammerhand soon," she said softly.

"Assuming he doesn't know already," Mini replied.

This wasn't how it was supposed to go. Not at all.

While he knew military operations never quite went

according to plan, this now bordered on the ridiculous. Athena had insisted that the operation was necessary and had forced them into an action he hadn't agreed with. Of course, when the hell did the higher-ups ever give the officers on the ground any kind of say over how anything was run?

Commander Maxwell2 had been the leader of Delta company for a while, but he hadn't seen anything that could compare—ever. Casualties like this were unheard of.

"Fucking Epsilon dumbasses," he muttered. He knew the comms being jammed the moment they had begun their offensive was not a coincidence, but any attempt to reach the location of the signal jammer had ended in disaster.

What should have been a simple invasion seemed set to become a massacre. Their people were being slaughtered inside Auburn.

He'd warned them that heading in would get people killed. Their troops would be funneled and their numbers would mean nothing.

There was nothing they could do to make up for the mistakes of the past. All they could do was look to the future.

Maxwell2 picked up the controls of his mech and marched toward the front lines of his squad. Delta Company was one of the finest groups of men he'd ever had the opportunity to serve with, much less command.

Small groups had begun to pull away from the town and managed to find a way over the rubble of the buildings that had been demolished to beat a hasty retreat.

"Fuck," he snapped. "All right, Delta Company, form up. We'll head in to fight!"

One of his lieutenants stepped forward. "Sir, we were ordered to hold Delta company in reserve."

"FEMA City Command gave us the orders to stay in

reserve until we were called in to help. If that isn't a cry for help, I don't know what is."

He directed their attention toward the stragglers retreating toward them.

"But sir—"

"Was I unclear, Lieutenant?"

The man took a step into the ranks. "No, sir!"

"Then form up. We'll engage the enemy. Send the signal to the rest of the companies and let them know we'll probably go dark once we get there."

CHAPTER FOUR

They hadn't expected this, although the Knights had filled them with some confidence. There was something about their leader, Hammerhand, that inspired them to fight when the thought of running had felt more enticing. It was impossible not to feel heartened after hearing that man talk.

"They're retreating!" one of those close to him stated and the others cheered.

Cameron couldn't bring himself to cheer alongside them. They might have beaten back the first wave of Lady Hoot's attack but that didn't mean they wouldn't bring in more. Even with the downed buildings blocking most of his view out of Auburn, he could still see the numbers gathered beyond the town limits where they waited for their chance to launch a new assault.

He adjusted his grip on the Cinder's controls and took a deep breath. Maybe he was a little too pessimistic. They possibly needed to celebrate the small victories, so why not let them take a deep breath and enjoy it while it lasted?

There was nothing else to say. He was in the fight with them.

The cheering stopped when they saw those who had retreated vanish quickly into the tree line. They were immediately replaced by another line that displayed none of the same scorch marks or battered armor plates that had been present on those that had withdrawn. The group sobered quickly, celebration already forgotten in the need to prepare to face the next wave.

No orders were incoming, which meant they had no choice but to simply fall back to their previous defensive positions and start the combat all over again from the beginning.

"Do you think the buildings will be safe?" one of his comrades asked. The man also piloted a Cinder and they moved inside together and out of sight.

"There's nothing we can do except trust that the plan will work again," Cameron replied. He used the wait to make sure his shotgun and flamethrower still had enough in them to face another wave of attackers. "Hammerhand said they would not attack the buildings and we have to believe him."

"Incoming!"

The airborne screaming started again but this time, it sounded closer and more intense. He covered his ears and ducked instinctively, even though he knew the rockets would streak overhead.

To his horror, his assumption proved incorrect. The earth shuddered powerfully, the strike too close for them to have fired at a point beyond Auburn.

"I stand corrected," he said and braced against a wave of shaking as another barrage of screamers assailed their ears. The building around them rumbled and cracks appeared in the concrete foundation when another strike made impact even closer than the previous ones.

It was followed almost immediately by a third.

The building began to crumble and something pounded into his chest to hurl the Cinder on its back as the structure collapsed onto him.

They no longer held back on the buildings. The Raptors had come in closer to the town and established their positions. Jessica13 could barely make them out in the flares that were continually fired into the darkness.

They were mostly shadows, but even those were impossible to mistake for any other kind of mech. She grasped her rifle and frowned at the enemy groups that now advanced on the town while more of the shrieking missiles careened overhead. This time, they were aimed into the buildings where the Knights and rebels took cover.

The enemy had clearly lost patience with the resistance they had encountered and intended to level the town in order to destroy them.

"Shit. Hammerhand needs to know about this," she said and tried to turn the radio on again.

Mini appeared on her HUD. "It would seem he's more than intelligent enough to know what the current situation is and is also spreading the word among the rest of the fighters."

"Fuck."

The new mechs that pushed forward initially marched in formation, but from the moment they reached the range of the jammer, they separated into smaller groups. Assault mechs formed up quickly around the support mechs. The heavier mechs—Guardians for the most part, although she could make out a couple of Argonauts—held back and fired from a distance.

"We need to change our tactics now," Jessica13 snapped. "It's only a matter of time before they hit this building and our jammer is history."

"That might be moot." Mini highlighted a handful of the squads that had begun their assault on the town. "They appear to have found low-tech forms of communication of their own."

Sure enough, when he zoomed the imaging in, lights flashed between the squad leaders. They flickered quickly and with good effect to guide each other through the fire and rubble-covered streets in a hunt for those who had survived the bombardment. From that point, it was mostly a massacre, although she could see that Hammerhand had already gathered most of the survivors and fighters and begun to coordinate a counterattack.

"We've lost the element of surprise and the advantage that came from not letting them use comms. What do you think we have to fight back with?"

"Hammerhand?"

"And they still have Athena, who hasn't been involved in the combat so far."

"That is a good point."

Jessica13 peered down her scope again and studied the troops moving forward. They held their formation as they pushed into the openings the bombing created for them. Their lights blinked at the Argonauts and Guardians, who likely communicated with the Raptors in turn, who continued to launch the airborne strikes into the structures around her. The building she was on began to shake.

"I think we need to get out of here," Mini suggested.

She tensed, unwilling to relinquish her position. The AI was right, but there wasn't a reason to move yet. While Athena's mechs had found a way to communicate, it was rudimentary and used the old Morse codes, which delayed them.

By seconds only, she acknowledged, but it was still a delay that would buy Hammerhand much-needed time to prepare his counterattack.

"Jessica13, I must suggest that you make your way off this rooftop immediately."

"Not yet," she snapped and raised her rifle. The squads were still moving forward, but she had noticed that only one member of each flashed the lights that communicated between them. She zoomed in on one of them. The mechs themselves appeared to be the same models she had worked on her whole life, but the heavier armor around the midsection and shoulders meant she needed to place her shots more carefully than before.

She pulled the trigger and identified the telltale signs that the pilot was dead and the AI had taken the controls. An AI couldn't send messages, though.

"Jessica13, we need to get off this roof now!"

Whether it was because this was the first time Mini had ever raised his voice at her—if only by raising the volume of the internal speakers—or because the sound of the screamers was now perilously close, she quickly surrendered control of the mech to the AI.

He was quick to act, strapped the rifle to their back, and immediately launched the grappler to embed it in the building across the street.

As they were dragged over the edge of the rooftop, she looked over her shoulder. Missiles pounded into their previous position. Perhaps they had identified where the jammer was or maybe seen where her shooting had come from, but the strikes were too accurate for it to have been a random assault.

The impact of the high explosives thumped into her back as they hurtled to the other side of the street. The shockwave threw them faster than the grappler could pull them in, and she braced herself for the impact with the building.

They punched through the thin walls almost without effort, and the Minato fell through the floor as well to land heavily about three floors down from where they had intended to be.

Her chest had difficulty dragging breath in, and the dust and smoke around them made the blaring alarms in the cockpit that much more obvious.

"Shit… Mini, are you still there?"

"I am here, Jessica13." The AI's voice was back to normal volume and as soothing as ever. "Are you all right?"

"I might have bruises or nicks, but I should be fine."

"My diagnostics tell me that you have pulled a handful of muscles in your back. I would recommend stretching to relieve eventual pain."

"Maybe later. For now, we need to get the hell out of here."

"Agreed. I would suggest using one of the windows?"

Jessica13 had no better ideas and besides, the last time she tried to get creative, she'd almost got them blown up. "This is your show, Mini."

"Affirmative."

He still had control of the mech, and after a few corrections were made to the electronics, they were on the move again. She braced herself as the Minato pushed out of one of the nearest windows, almost removed the whole frame, and launched the grappler to the top of the building which allowed them to climb down smoothly.

Speed was of the essence, as one of the squads already advanced on their position.

"Jessie, are you there?"

Tinker's voice spoke through the comms.

"I'm here. Still alive for the most part. I guess the jammer is down."

"We were worried when we saw them target your position and the comms came back a few seconds after that. Head on back. We've created barriers and defensive positions for the rest of the Knights and rebels to rally behind. Get back here now!"

"I'm on my way." She cut the connection instantly to be sure that none of Athena's fighters could key in on their commlink and trace her.

Even so, the same squad she'd seen earlier was now even closer and despite the fire, smoke, and dust kicked up, they saw her quickly.

"I suppose their comms are back too." Jessica13 hissed through clenched teeth as she took control of the right arm and drew the rifle from where it was held magnetically. She'd felt a definite twinge of pain in her back with the movement.

There were four of them, she realized as she studied them quickly. Three assault mechs worked together like they had done so forever. They circled and checked corners to make sure no one else was in this part of the town. At the same time, they tried to maintain formation as they advanced and all remained tightly positioned around what looked like a Watson. It carried two crates, ready to resupply them when they needed it.

"What are you thinking, Jessica13?"

"I think we need to get out of here as quickly as possible."

There wasn't any other option. They wouldn't fare well against three assault mechs, and that was assuming others wouldn't be drawn in by the shooting and decide to join the fight. They needed to return to the fortifications Tinker had told her about.

But still, there was something to be said for slowing the bastards if she could.

She looked down the scope as Mini turned the Minato and pulled the trigger. The round struck low and hammered into the hydraulic junction on the knee of the Lancer at the head of their squad. It almost doubled over, tried to right itself, and as hydraulic fluid began to spray from the hole, settled slowly on the ground.

The other in the group took a moment to make sure their comrade was all right before they trained their rifles on the position Jessica13 and Mini attempted to move away from.

"Any time now, Mini!" she shouted. While she didn't want to sound annoying, she also knew their shooting wouldn't create a defensive area around the Minato for long. She fired another shot but this one ricocheted off one of the armor plates on another of the Lancers.

Mini pulled back, the grappler still attached to the building, and she finally realized what he was doing. A crack appeared in the concrete of the wall above them and the Minato strained for a moment before a massive chunk fell free. He immediately disengaged the dart from it.

The wall tumbled to land with a massive thump on top of the enemy squad and generate another cloud of dust.

It was likely not enough to kill all of them but certainly enough to slow them down.

The mech pivoted in place before it twisted and altered its

shape until they were on all fours. The AI needed no adjustment period and raced them away from the other squads that had begun to converge on the position of those buried by a wall.

The inertia dampeners in the Minato were still not quite in perfect shape, and Jessica13 needed to hold on tightly to avoid feeling every jolt and bump that resulted from their headlong race across the town. Mini hurdled or dodged the chunks of building and mechs that still littered the roads and made it difficult to navigate but certainly not impossible.

It wasn't long before she could see the barriers that were already being thrown up to slow the advancing forces as well as to provide the Knights and rebels with some cover.

Of course, that barrier would do little to no good once the Raptors and Quadrupeds came into firing distance. It was a delaying tactic, at best.

Hammerhand gestured for more to be erected as they set their defenses up in a tighter formation to block access points and build more traps with what remained of the explosives they had.

At the center of it all stood the Beast, which was apparently their last line of defense.

Mini skidded closer to the blockade and proceeded to vault up the rubble until they were finally over it.

Tinker saw her immediately and rambled over to where the AI brought them into a bipedal stance.

"Jessie, it's damn good to see you alive and well."

"Right back at you, old man. What's happening here? What did I miss?"

"The bombardment forced the rest of our people out of range, but now that the comms are working again, their artillery won't hold to the perimeter anymore."

"Do we have any plans for when they do come into firing range?"

"Well, we could always run the fuck away, but—"

Hammerhand marched to where they stood and the heavy steps of the Excalibur shook the earth beneath it. "We will make our stand here. I've promised this town and this world every ounce of goodness, sanity, and brotherhood I can give it. Keeping that promise is the hill I will die on."

Tinker turned to face the larger mech, and Jessica13 didn't have to see his face to know he was angry. Even in a mech, it was all about body language, and his body language screamed all kinds of pissed-off.

"What about us, Hammerhand? Have you thought about that? Will you have the rest of your Knights and the people of Auburn die on that hill of yours too?"

"My guess is that the hill is a metaphor and not a literal hill?" Jessica13 asked privately for only Mini to hear her.

"That is correct. It refers to the military strategy of finding high ground or an equally defensive position and being prepared to give it up only once you are dead."

"Understood."

"Every one of these men and women is willing to fight for what they know is right," Hammerhand continued.

"They fight for you and believe in you because they trust that you, as their commander, will make the right choice for their sake. And in this case, the right choice is to get the fuck out!"

The disagreement was cut off when the alarm was raised by those who acted as sentries to watch for their enemy's advance.

"We will talk about this later." Hammerhand was quick to

turn away and he marched toward the front lines, hefted his hammer, and rested it on his shoulder.

"Damn fucking right we will, and if we die, you can be sure that I'll hound your ghost for answers, you hulking shit-ton of useless fucking scrap metal!"

The other man either didn't hear Tinker still shouting at him or didn't deign to respond as both returned to the front of the combat lines.

The opposing squads had now begun a forward push and in the distance, the artillery mechs started to close as well when they realized the Knights had fortified their positions once more. Jessica13 had never thought it would be an easy fight, but at this point, surviving felt like a dream that seemed to slide farther and farther away from a very harsh reality.

The sense of impending doom strengthened when her gaze settled on something larger than the Guardians and Argonauts that moved closer. The flapping cape on the mech's shoulders and the spear in its hands told her that the most dangerous of their enemies now approached as if she had smelled blood in the water.

Athena strode forward and lightning crackled brightly from her spear as she advanced and motioned for the other mechs to follow her lead.

"Let's get this started," Jessica13 muttered, tightened her grasp on her rifle, and checked to make sure she had enough ammo for their last stand.

CHAPTER FIVE

Things hadn't exactly gone according to plan.

Not that anyone had expected them to, of course. They had fought against Lady Hoot and done better than anyone could have thought they would, given the circumstances, but the end was approaching and it was time for them to accept it.

This didn't mean that anyone had to accept living under the woman's boot any longer. But Auburn wasn't the only place for them to live, and as the fighting began to escalate inside the town, there was no place for women, children, the sick, or the elderly. They wouldn't be able to help in the fight either.

Even the mighty Hammerhand had agreed and those who were able to prepared for a final attack, which would hopefully prove enough of a distraction for the rest to make their escape.

It was the only kind of hope someone like Karina could dream of. Surviving an onslaught like this was likely not in her future, not if she stayed and fought. She had helped them set the traps up and even carried barrels of fertilizer to where they would be used to blow up the buildings that had been their homes and places of work only days before.

They had all been swept into this fight by the Knights Mechanica, but in this moment, it was best to simply call the end of their ability to help. The Knights and those capable and willing to fight would remain, and everyone else scrambled into what vehicles they had available and headed out on the other side of town. The enemy had bombarded the area but rather than hinder them, the smoke and fires would only help to cover their retreat better.

A handful of mechs were directed to help them, mostly selected from those that had been salvaged from among Lady Hoot's fallen. They were damaged and some were still stained with the blood from their previous pilots, but it was hopefully better than no escort.

No one could honestly say it was a pleasant situation but heading away from the shooting and explosions was something Karina appreciated, especially with the little one on the way.

The ATV continued to move over the bumpy roads that led away from Auburn. They moved quickly, but there was nothing that would make the vehicle comfortable. She and the other ten Auburn citizens were strapped into narrow, hard seats. The rest of the space was dedicated to giving the driver enough space to operate and the couple of assault mechs that rode with them enough room to fight should anyone be sent to pursue them.

All Karina could feel happy about was the fact that they were still moving. Every bump made her back ache and her shoulders tense as her eyes looked out the small round windows. She tried to keep herself calm and held her midsection, praying to something—anything—that would keep her little one safe from all this.

The fires were closer now. Hammerhand had assured them that the invaders wouldn't bomb any of the buildings inside the town. They had all believed him when the missiles soared overhead and beyond the town to start fires that would keep going thanks to the woodlands that had grown around the hamlet. The smoke climbed high and raised something like a curtain between Auburn and what lay beyond. Hopefully, it would be enough to keep them hidden as they made their escape.

All they had to do was get through the wall of fire. The ATVs slowed and the mechs disembarked and worked to clear a path through the blaze that would enable the wheeled vehicles to pass. They pushed in and tossed flame retardant grenades into the flames that gave them at least a few minutes of respite to drive their vehicles through.

Once they had created a path, the mechs pulled back, caught hold of the side of the vehicles, and climbed up but didn't bother to get inside as they surged forward. Karina could feel the heat from inside the vehicle and hugged herself a little closer.

She had nothing else to do but hum softly to herself to keep her nerves under control. The last thing the drivers and mechs needed was for her to panic while they tried to get her and the other refugees—which was what they were now—to safety.

Finally, the heat receded and the weight of leaving Auburn began to lift from her shoulders as she looked out the windows. There was still considerable smoke in the air, and the lack of any sunlight made it difficult to see anything. But they were past the fires, which meant that they were on their way to safety now.

"Shit!"

The driver yelled, and she leaned forward to look through the small partition between the back of the ATV to try to determine what had alarmed him.

The questions in her mind—and likely in those of the other the passengers—were answered when the entire vehicle shuddered and a flash of explosives flared outside, visible through the window. Her eyes were blinded for a second and additional explosions erupted around them and left her disoriented. The mechs leapt free and attempted to fight something, although she couldn't determine what.

Had they seen the people withdraw? Were they trying to fire over the blaze to kill those who tried to escape? That didn't seem right, but she could think of no other explanation.

She leaned forward and through the dust and smoke, was finally able to see the mechs that advanced on them. They were the same pristine white and gray ones that had attacked the town. Had they expected someone to flee and sent forces to block their escape, or had they planned to attack the town from behind and simply encountered the exodus by accident?

It didn't matter as the end result was the same. The lead ATV burned, in pieces where it had been shredded by whatever had hit it. A couple of the mechs were down too, and the others were already scrambling onto the two remaining vehicles and shouted at the drivers to get them the hell out of there.

Unfortunately, there was no way forward. All they could do was turn and return to Auburn. The mechs ahead of them held a solid line that might as well have been an impassable wall.

The journey was as fraught with tension as their earlier flight had been when rockets began to pound again. They destroyed a couple of their mechs but left the vehicles alone to continue the grim retreat into what offered little in the way of hope.

The faces of those around her mirrored her anxiety. Every one of them knew that they rumbled inexorably into the thick of the battle, with no way out.

A couple of hot tears ran down Karina's cheeks, but she didn't bother to wipe them away. All she could do was hold her hands on her belly while the heat of the fire receded again, which meant they were almost in Auburn and trapped in the nightmare they had tried so hard to escape.

It was like they were caught between the hammer and the anvil. She couldn't help but weep openly despite the gentle touch of the hands of the people around her who tried to comfort her. There was nothing they could do.

CHAPTER SIX

Davis5 watched the ATVs turn and head through the wall of flames and into the town they had tried to escape from.

He hadn't been happy to be assigned this detail. His platoon leader had selected the fighters to attack the town and rid them of the problems that had assailed them over the past few days. It was a shit job to simply huddle in the rear to make sure no one tried to bolt.

It was made even worse when high explosives and napalm-tipped missiles made sure no one could see them move into position behind Auburn. While it was tactically sound to give them cover to hide their movements, it was still a shit position to be in. Killing civilians wasn't a pleasant experience, even if they had fought tooth and nail against him and his.

The handful of second-hand mechs they'd brought for an escort hadn't even been enough to put up a proper fight, and it wasn't long before Davis5 raised his hand and closed it in a fist to indicate for his men to cease their barrage. The more experienced of his pilots already knew what was coming and had already held their fire. Those who weren't had the discipline drilled into them long enough that they didn't continue to shoot at those who retreated.

When he was asked why he didn't simply kill them all, Davis5 would say he didn't want to waste ammo. He'd also add that driving civilians into Auburn would force their enemies to fight from a more defensive position once they knew they had defenseless civilians in their ranks.

It made tactical sense, but the truth of it was that he didn't like the thought of killing civilians, even when they were armed and ready to fight back. The action didn't sit well with him, and while he knew better than to question orders—much less defy them outright—there were small technicalities that allowed the captain to find a loophole here or there.

He wasn't sure why he risked himself and his position in this. Was it an attack of conscience? Maybe, but the end would be the same and possibly worse for those who were sent into the town to die.

But it wouldn't be at his hand. He could say that much.

"What are we waiting for, Captain?" one of the men asked and opened a private comm line. "Shouldn't we finish them off?"

Davis5 lowered his rifle and checked the ammo to make sure he didn't need to reload. "They'll be finished off anyway. It makes no sense to charge after them into the fires. Let them head back."

The man knew better than to question his orders—better than Davis5 did himself, apparently. But the chances were, when it came time to submit reports on the operation, the man would probably raise questions in his report about sparing those who tried to escape the fighting.

It was a good thing he already had his story straight. There was no way his superiors would be able to question the decisions he made in the field. If they wanted to make problems, all it meant was that he would be taken off active duty while they investigated, and he would be back in combat when they didn't find anything.

Or, worst-case scenario, he would face a trial as a result of the incident and probably be demoted. Hopefully, they wouldn't give him the chair for something like this.

"Delta Company, withdraw to the defensive positions. We'll wait for word from inside if they need support, but we'll hold our positions for the moment."

He didn't need to hear them to know that they all groaned in frustration. The brief flurry of action they had seen wouldn't be enough to sate them, and he could understand because he felt the same way. All his men, like him, wanted to be a part of the force that was involved in the attack on the town.

None of them were happy and he could tell from the body language picked up by their mechs as they withdrew to the barriers that had been set up. These were mostly massive shields cut from steel and reinforced with inertia dampeners that would allow them to absorb impacts without warping.

In theory, anyway, but they weren't infallible. They were still shields, after all, and could be circled and flanked.

Fortunately, Davis5 didn't think that was something he needed to worry about too much.

The Quadrupeds and Raptors stationed behind the barriers settled in once again while their support mechs ran to the supply chain to replenish the rockets that had been used. Of the whole troop that held the rear of the town, they were the ones most likely to be ordered into the fight. Rapid movement would bring them into firing range, and while most of the artillery was on the other side of town, they could still deal a great deal of damage if it was needed.

But the higher-ups didn't think it would be needed. They wildly outnumbered the Knights and the Auburn rebels. Of course, that kind of underestimation had proven fatal for Epsilon Company as well as their Raiders, but it wasn't that big a loss.

"Davis5, sensors detect movement and sound coming in from behind you. Please advise."

One of his lieutenants brought up the signals that had been detected on his HUD. Sure enough, there was considerable movement approaching from behind them.

"What the fuck...antelope stampede?" He narrowed his eyes to try to understand what didn't seem to make sense at all.

"The seismic sensors detect that it's something considerably heavier," the lieutenant said.

"Elk?"

"Heavier."

"I have a feeling we'll run out of heavier animals that could stampede us from behind." There was no humor in his tone, and none of his men laughed, fortunately.

"Sensors do suggest that what is coming in from behind is not animal at all." The lieutenant sounded a little anxious, which mirrored his own misgivings.

"They can't be mechs. Our intel teams would know if the Knights had any troops in reserve," another pilot interjected.

"Intelligence could be wrong," the lieutenant pointed out. "Or they might not be reserves for the Knights at all. Perhaps FEMA has sent reinforcements in light of the failure of our first push?"

"That's actually possible," Davis5 responded. "The damn higher-ups don't consult us on how to properly deploy troops. They have to know that we outnumber them to the point where we don't even need to commit all our forces."

"You might want to communicate this to the incoming troops. Perhaps they are needed elsewhere on the front?"

He nodded, keyed his comm line, and tried to open a connection with the approaching troops.

"Let's see here…" he muttered and scanned the open lines for the closest troops to their position. "Alert, alert, Control. This is Captain Davis5, Control. Be advised, Delta Company does not need support in the Auburn Operation. Your support is not required at this time, over."

The reply required a little time but finally, the commander of the company keyed into the comm line. "Roger that, Captain Davis5, your message is received. Control has not received any orders to support the Auburn Operation and all forces hold their last known positions, over."

"Say again, Control. You have not ordered any troops to advance on our position from bearing five-six-eight-zero-niner, over?"

Another pause followed before he received a response. "That is correct, Delta Company, over."

"Shit," Davis5 snapped but remembered to cover his microphone for the brief profanity. "Disregard all previous messages, Control."

"Roger that, Delta Company. Out."

The captain quickly keyed into the commlinks that Delta company command used to coordinate their troops. "Delta Leader, this is Delta 5. Please respond, over."

The wait wasn't as long but still seemed to take forever

before someone keyed into his frequency. "Delta 5, this is Delta Leader, over."

"We have multiple signals advancing on our position from bearing five-six-eight-zero-niner. Possible hostiles. Please advise, over."

"Roger that, Delta 5. Maintain position. Report if signals are confirmed hostile, out."

Yeah, because he would have time to report if that many hostiles advanced on their position. Well, of course he would notify them, but they would also be too far out if they needed any help to repel a possible counter-attack.

The only piece of good news was that the Knights Mechanica could not possibly have held that many troops in reserve.

"Okay, everyone," Davis5 said to his men. "We have identified signals from behind us and they are advancing fast. In case they're heading here and are hostile, let's move some of the shields around. Raptors, make sure you can acquire targets from your current position. If not, alter your position to correct that. Let's move, people!"

They didn't need to have the command reinforced and it was somewhat gratifying to see them hasten to obey his orders as they picked the shields up and moved them to face the rear.

"So, wait," the lieutenant said, his tone a little anxious. "Those signals aren't reinforcements coming to support the attack on the town?"

"None of our troops are approaching from that bearing, no."

"Then who the fuck is it?"

"If we knew that I wouldn't wonder if they are hostile or not. Be ready for anything."

"Should we send flares up to get a better view of who they are?" one of the Raptor pilots asked as their support mechs returned to refill their rocket supplies.

Davis5 thought about it. "Negative. If they are hostiles, we don't want to give our position away prematurely."

"Roger that."

It was getting late—or early, in this case—and the sky had begun to fade from deep purple to dark-gray but grew brighter by the second. It wasn't something he intended to make into a problem, but the operation that should have taken only a few hours into the night had now lasted until dawn. The sounds of combat from the town began to get more and more volatile, so it could be assumed that a few more hours would pass before they had eliminated the threat in Auburn.

The light in the sky brightened with each moment, which made it difficult to keep their position a secret.

Davis5 narrowed his eyes when he heard something in the distance. It sounded vaguely like something was braying or like a vibrating piece of machinery had somehow gotten into his mech suit. He couldn't say it hadn't happened before, but he had programmed his mech to make sure nothing got in while he was out.

The noise continued, however, and the braying grew louder and deeper—like war horns being blown, he thought. In the increased light, he could detect movement in the distance but it mostly resembled clouds of dust raised by something approaching. Or a great many somethings, possibly, but nothing was clearly visible thanks to the small hill ahead of them.

Silence descended as every member of his team stared at the billows of dust that grew inexorably closer. Finally, forms crested the hilltops that obfuscated their position and the braying became much louder. Davis5 realized that his somewhat glib description was entirely appropriate. The source of the racket was revealed to be large and heavy horns that thrummed what could only be described as a battle cry by a great many blown at the same time. The cacophony didn't cease but became a continuous blare that rolled over the entire valley leading into Auburn.

"What the fuck?" He wasn't sure what he was looking at, but one thing was beyond debate. It was a shit-ton of mechs and they sure as hell weren't friendlies. "Delta Leader, this is Delta 5. You'll want to see this, over."

"What will I want to see, over?"

"A metric shit-ton of mechs. And they sure as fucking hell aren't ours, over."

It was fairly easy to confirm that statement. Even Athena's Raiders had a particular kind of decoration on their mechs, fashioned after hers with the banner and the owl ornamentation. These were different. A series of spikes ran over their pauldrons, over their spines, and down their legs. Some didn't even carry guns. And there were the horns, of course, and a number them held spears.

One of them stood out from the others. Most looked like the lighter kind of assault mechs and a few appeared to have been put together from three or four different mechs, although the armor did look solid. There were even small ATVs that had been fitted with weapons on the top and spikes up the sides. They were covered in what looked like camo tarps, and all were painted in pale brown and beige colors.

The only exceptions were three larger mechs—Argonauts, by the looks of them. Two carried banners that caught the early-morning sun. A hint of gold gleamed in the cloth and from the distance, it looked like desert dunes under a blue sky and a golden sun. As sigils went, it was fairly hard to miss as the flashing brilliance caught the light every time it flapped in the wind.

The two banner-carriers flanked a larger Argonaut, which looked considerably more modern than the other mechs. It could have even been a Guardian if not for what was very clearly an assault rifle that fired depleted uranium rounds. The plasma cannons had a different look to them.

The newcomers gathered at the top of the hill and revealed their numbers, at least in part, as they focused their attention on Delta Company.

"Who the actual fuck are these guys?" one of the Raptor pilots asked.

"Never you mind that," Davis5 told him sharply. "Get a targeting reticle on them, and prepare to fire if they're—"

His words were cut short when the leader lowered his rifle and aimed it at the Delta company mechs. Before he could react, the powerful gun fired.

One of the Raptors was the target, and the depleted uranium round cut easily through the joint of the knee, emerged from the other side, and struck one of the assault mechs that supported it.

The Raptor tilted and fell to the side as the war horns at the top of the hill grew louder. The other mech that was hit didn't get up.

The men at the top of the hill cheered loudly along with their ongoing horn blasts. As if the opening shot were a signal, they began to stream down the hill. The ATVs kicked dirt up as they careened beside the mechs in a massed advance toward Delta Company's position.

"Delta leader, we are under attack," Davis5 announced over

the comms and highlighted targets. "Get in position, you sons of bitches! Hold the line, and would someone please fucking fire?"

CHAPTER SEVEN

Jessica13 scowled, frustrated by the fact that she was out of ammunition.

Her bullets were long gone and she made do with the grappler to keep the enemies at a distance while she fought back. Fortunately, they didn't pay her too much attention at the moment and most only shot at her if she got between them and the other Knights.

The defenders held their ground for the time being. Athena's fighters didn't fling themselves forward to soak bullets in like they had before and now played the role of the attacker with far more care and caution. Even so, they assaulted a well-defended position and one that was difficult for their heavier artillery to reach.

That aside, she knew it was only a matter of time. The refugees who had been sent away in advance of the fighting had been forced to return. They'd told of troops who held the roads outside Auburn and made it clear there was no escaping this.

Hammerhand was still standing, as were Tinker, Windchime, and most of the Knights. None had died yet, but a handful had their mechs damaged to the point where they had to be dragged away from combat between waves of attacks. The same couldn't be said of the townsfolk. Even those who had mechs of their own weren't quite as disciplined or trained as the Knights and had a tendency to charge after Athena's men when they retreated, despite orders.

They could feel the heat of the fight and likely personally knew those who had been lost when the buildings were bombed. It explained their fervor, but it would also cause more deaths if they continued like this. Every time she saw one of them fall, unable to get up, something cold struck her in the chest. It was like the point was hammered in that they wouldn't get out of here alive.

Jessica13 had thought her reaction would have been different. She'd expected something a little closer to panic and the shaky rage she had felt when she'd faced the raiders who had pinned her down in the city. But that wasn't the case. She wasn't calm, by any means, but there was a certain serenity that came from knowing that she was on the right side of this, even if it meant they would pay the ultimate price for it.

And there was, of course, the fact that there wasn't much time to think about it. The fatigue in her body from moving to and from the Beast was evident but she pushed past it and largely ignored it. She was able to do that when she focused on her role to keep all the weapons loaded and ready to fire. When the opportunity presented itself, she assisted those she could and even joined the fray to distract and maybe drag a couple of Athena's fighters away with her grappler.

Mini had taken control of the mech when she needed him to, and with the nicks and dents in the armor, it was only a matter of time before something found her in the battle and that would be the end of it. Hopefully, it would be quick.

She steadied herself and studied the battlefield through the scope of her depleted rifle. Their attackers rushed the line much less than she'd expected, and the Guardians and Argonauts held their positions farther away from the Knights. If they had joined the assault with their other attacking mechs, it would have ended the battle long before. The only reason she could think of why they would have held back was their memory of what Hammerhand had done with those that had rushed in.

They didn't want to lose their heavy mechs—which was understandable, she supposed. Athena herself had held back from committing to the battle for the same reason, or so Jessica13 assumed. She gestured her men forward but she made no effort to join them herself. They seemed content to poke and prod at the defenses instead of committing their full might.

Even so, a few of the waves had ended with Hammerhand being forced to step into the fray. He swung his hammer to keep the enemy at a distance and blocked any further advance with his shield until his people had regained enough momentum to retaliate. There was nothing she could do except stand beside them and try to support them however she could. The Minato's magnetic clasp carried ammo and weapons from the Beast to the front lines and back again.

She had taken her shots where she could, but Windchime had been right in the end. The Minato wasn't designed to go head-to-head with mechs that had been designed to fight other mechs. Throwing herself into combat would get her killed, exactly like it had the Auburn residents who broke formation and ran out to continue the fight and were cut down in the process.

Not that anyone really expected to get out in one piece, of course. But there was still something to be said for fighting as hard as they could for as long as they could. They would last and make an impression on Athena and the rest of the area that she had held in an iron fist. This was a way to send a message of their own.

A ping on her comms snapped her out of her reverie. The alert told her that the enemy had initiated another assault and a handful of highlighted mechs needed more ammo. The townsfolk had been pulled back to mostly support roles to stop them from throwing themselves into the fray, although they were called in when the fighting grew intense. Their lack of tactical coordination was made up for by the need to have numbers to bolster their ranks.

Jessica13 put her rifle on the ground beside the Beast where she would be able to retrieve it later. Mini knew what that meant and immediately dropped the mech to all fours. They surged into a sprint and jumped and dodged as the Knights engaged the attackers. The AI made full use of the uneven terrain and raced around the other support mechs that moved in the same direction.

She chose two of her teammates who were in the most desperate need of ammo and highlighted them for Mini's benefit as well for the other support mechs that needed to know who needed a refill. A couple had their partners in the assault lines and were generally there to keep them alive, whether they needed someone to distract or to run and get them ammo. The coordination between those smaller teams felt akin to family. Their friendship always extended beyond the battlefield.

The idea was appealing. She wondered if she would ever have that kind of chemistry with someone to allow her to work together with them almost exclusively, but she still had to prove herself to the Knights.

With her teeth gritted, she braced herself as Mini brought them to a sudden halt beside one of the mechs that needed ammo the most. He was still firing and engaged three enemy mechs that took advantage of his rationed shooting and tried to drive their attack home.

Instinctively, she moved to pull the crate of ammo from her back but thought better of it.

"Thought?" Mini queried when she hesitated for a moment.

"Distract."

The AI remained in Bulletfoot mode and sprinted to the mechs that pinned her teammate down. She twisted, drew their fire, and jumped into the two-legged mode to barrel directly into the arms of the Lancer closest to her. Mini lowered the shoulders and impacted the midsection of the other mech to drive it back while remaining too close for it to be able to shoot at her with its assault rifle.

They managed to force him back a couple of steps, but the legs quickly locked and after a few more feet of dragging through the dirt, it finally managed to pull to a halt.

She was ready for that and already had the dart engaged to the grappler's gun. Quickly, she lowered it to the mech's left knee and pulled the trigger. The dart punched through the weaker armor and found the hydraulics inside, disabled the mech's leg, and reduced the pressure over the rest of it, which made it less effective overall. Mini pushed them forward again to bulldoze it into its fellows before he turned them to sprint to the Knight waiting for her.

"Nice fighting!"

"Thanks!" She didn't delay, pushed the crate into his hands, and made sure he was reloaded before she raced away to her next load-off. He was out of ammo and fell back as a couple of the townsfolk stepped into the breach that caused chaos in the rest of their line. She yanked the crate off her back and signaled the pilot before she tossed it to him. It landed a few meters away, which was better than hitting him with it, and the Knight moved to reload rapidly and return to the fight.

More alerts for ammo appeared and Mini dropped them onto all fours to rush to the Beast when a completely unidentifiable noise distracted them both.

Jessica13 had no idea what was, but something different now overshadowed the cacophony of war. The sun had begun to rise, although it was difficult to see through the clouds of dust and smoke that shrouded the town, but the odd sound was definitely not her imagination. It seemed to roll over them like a vibration that shook windows and buildings before it settled into the deep thrums of horns blown that grew louder with each passing moment.

She paused and squinted into the sky to see what was happening. It sounded like hundreds of horns blared and drew steadily closer. The blazes on the edge of the town had died down somewhat, and in the gap created in the greenery by the fire, it appeared that a battle of some kind was in progress.

Who could have started a fight out there? In the previous battle, they had managed to win with help gathered by Windchime, but that had been a last gasp kind of effort. Who else would come to help them this deep in Athena's territory?

They hurried to the Beast and she retrieved the rifle from where she'd dropped it and used the scope for a clearer view.

These were unfamiliar mechs and looked nothing like the raiders they'd encountered before. They had been put together using anything salvaged from wherever they could find the pieces, and spikes jutted from their armor.

"What the hell?"

She turned, almost unable to believe the evidence of her own eyes when more of the strange mechs pressed into the town and surged through the defensive lines that had been put up by Athena's fighters. They were all lightly armored and moved rapidly in a seemingly disjointed and yet coordinated formation to breach the defenses. Most used buzz tools and vibroblades to slice through armor and peel the pilots out of their mechs.

It wasn't long before they reached the artillery and swarmed over them, climbed up, and severed wiring and hydraulics to bring the heavy mechs down before they advanced on the others.

She wasn't sure how it was possible, but it appeared that someone was helping the Knights. A whole horde of some-ones, in fact, who were well-armed and well-trained, and even a group of heavy mechs now joined the fray as well. They delivered a concerted succession of shots that destroyed the defensive formations the enemy tried to put in place to counter the new assault.

Hammerhand realized that the tide was turning and immediately indicated for the mechs around him to press ahead to where Athena wielded her spear deftly to keep the attacking mechs at bay. Despite her obvious skill and the power of her suit, she was still forced back step by step.

The invaders attempted to stand their ground, but the Knights' leader decided he'd had enough of defending. Two Lancers tried to stand against him, but he swung his hammer into both of them and hurled them out of his way without missing a step. There was only one target on his mind —Athena.

The newcomers who had tried to harass the Excalibur quickly gave up. They didn't want to commit to a fight against a mech that large, especially with her being able to hold them out of range while she brandished a shield similar to Hammerhand's when they backed away.

Jessica13 didn't want to miss that fight. She noticed the moment when Athena realized that Hammerhand was advancing on her position and decided to do the same. Rather than show any hesitation or fear, she simply raised her shield and rushed to meet him.

They collided with a violent impact. The shields clashed with a crack of thunder and electricity sparked from the contact and forced both back. Neither seemed surprised by this reaction—which meant they had likely tried something like this in the past—and both dropped the shields as the mechanisms now smoked after the collision. Athena was quicker and thrust her spear toward the chest of Hammerhand's Excalibur. A subtle sidestep was enough to send the thrust wide and he clamped his arm over the weapon before she could pull it back.

The electricity that arced from her spear skittered over his mech, which showed that the improvements Tinker had put work into weren't only meant for absorbing a lightning bolt. No problems would be caused by the electricity that arced from the weapon.

On the other hand, the rocket on the back of the hammer activated and launched it around to power into her side. Athena was quick enough to drop her arm to block the blow, but some plate damage resulted even though the hammer was forced around. She leaned back, yanked her spear free of Hammerhand's trap, and took another step away as his weapon returned. The controlled swipe barely missed removing her owl-ornamented helmet.

More and more, it looked like Athena had no interest in remaining in the fight. The rest of her men had begun to pull back from the unerring onslaught of the newcomers and as Hammerhand tried to recover his balance from the swing, she retreated to where her men were gathering.

"Where the fuck are you all going?" she snapped and the speakers on her mech ensured that most of the town could hear her, even over the shooting and explosions. "Stand your fucking ground! Will you abandon the attack because of one setback?"

A handful of enemy mechs initiated an organized retreat. When Athena tried to stand between one of the Guardians and the rest of his troop, he circled her with no apparent fear.

"We don't take orders from raider scum," the man replied, careful to knock into her as he passed, and strode to where the rest of the troop began to withdraw from the battlefield.

A few stragglers remained, but not for long. The Knights realized that the impossible was happening and swept through Auburn once more. This time, they cleared the few pockets of resistance until not a single invader remained. Athena had melted away with the withdrawal of her troops and it seemed she had little stomach for a fight without her allies.

There were those who insisted on pressing their advantage against the retreating forces, but it was easy to see why it was a bad idea. The Raptors and Quadrupeds were still in position and launched flurry after flurry of rockets to cover the withdrawal of those who had managed to escape the town.

Once they were gone, the rockets ceased and all that remained was the carnage.

Jessica13 leaned back in her cockpit, breathed a little heavier, and smelled the sweat inside the confined space. Yet somehow, the sweat, grease, and hint of smoke didn't smell that bad.

She pulled the hatch open and stepped outside. All she could feel was the sting of cordite and smoke from the fires, but it was still the most beautiful sensation she had ever experienced.

Actually, when she thought about it, she recalled feeling something similar when she had escaped death at the hand of the raiders thanks to the Knights' intervention. She wouldn't complain, but after fighting for what felt like forever, there was little she could do other than sag against the leg of her Minato and rest for a few seconds.

Hammerhand's Excalibur marched through the clouds of smoke that were tinted with the glow of early sunlight. He dropped his hammer beside his mech as a trio of the foreign mechs approached him.

Most of the newcomers were light assault mechs and used spears and vibroblades, with some assault rifles or similar alternatives. The three larger ones appeared to be the only heavies among their number, which also included a few dune buggies and ATVs with heavy guns mounted on top or on the side with the same spikes as the mechs.

She wasn't sure if they were meant to be ornamental or defensive.

Either way, it wasn't relevant. The three larger mechs reached Hammerhand and held banners up that glistened in the sunlight and displayed desert dunes in gold and a blue sky.

"Who are they?" Jessica13 asked aloud although she was alone.

"I have a working theory," the AI replied.

"Which is?"

"I have no data to make any educated guesses and as such, would rather not reply until the data is provided."

The Knights' leader climbed out of his mech as the three stopped in front of him and seemed to stare at him for a long moment before the pilot in the center mech dismounted as well. Unlike Hammerhand, who was clean-shaven and looked lean and dangerous in his dark-blue flight suit, the man who emerged from the mech looked more like a prophet than a pilot. He had a thick beard and a mustache that curled upward, an odd contrast to his shaved head. His long, flowing robes were gold and blue like the banners.

He climbed down from the Argonaut he piloted and took the few steps to where Hammerhand stood.

"By the waters of Citta del Mar," the Prophet said in a foreign accent and extended his hand, "I am blessed to meet such a hero as yourself."

He grasped the man's hand and shook it firmly. "Your help arrives just in time. I thank you."

"When I see the bravery of you and yours, it is I who must thank you. I am the Voice in the Desert, known to some as the Prophet and to others, He Who Speaks the Word. You may call me friend, great warrior."

"I'm known as Hammerhand."

"You have earned this name, and so you will be called by the People of the Desert."

CHAPTER EIGHT

The smoke hadn't quite cleared yet.

The fires were mostly extinguished, although a couple of blazes had spread farther into the grasslands to die there. Jessica13 hadn't had much time to rest, and what sleep she had managed had been full of dreams of fighting at night while the fires blazed around her. In her nightmares, she felt the explosion when this time, she didn't manage to vault away in time and the rocket brought the building down while she still stood on it.

A few hours were necessary, though. All the Knights had fought through the better part of a full day and a half with little to no rest between them.

Still, it was a gorgeous sight to wake up to. The sun was rising again and painted the smoky sky red and pale yellow as it arced from the hills in the east and began its daily climb toward the west. After a little food, she trudged to where Mini had been parked for the night, plugged into the Beast's data-banks to give him something to do while she rested.

The AI could move the mech on his own and could have

already joined the work to help the town to recover from the battle it had faced. He hadn't protested when she had elected to let the Minato get some rest and maybe see if he couldn't put in a couple of repairs while they waited.

The hatch was already open, ready for her to climb inside, and she slipped into the comfortable and familiar cockpit she had spent more time in than out of.

"Good morning, Jessica13."

She scowled at the HUD, which displayed a smiley face and a flower from the AI. "I guess it is a good morning, isn't it?"

"Surviving an assault from enemies that have tried to kill you for the better part of almost a week does constitute as a beneficial element in the morning, yes. There could be detrimental elements as well."

"Is that your way of asking me how I slept?"

The AI paused for a few seconds. "How did you sleep?"

"Well, it was short and not very restful," she muttered. "I kept having the same fucking nightmare over and over again. I was back on that rooftop and I didn't react quickly enough to let you get us off before the rockets struck."

"I imagine that was a fairly traumatic experience for you but thankfully, we did manage to get clear of the rooftop in time. And you did your best to give the Knights as much time to recover as you could, which is fairly admirable. Humans might even describe it as brave."

"What would AIs describe it as?"

"Ill-advised."

Jessica13 nodded slowly. She could agree with that, at least. It had been a difficult fight, but they had managed to survive and in the end, they were on what looked like a long, long path of rebuilding. Many of the locals had returned to the work of tilling the fields that could still grow food, their focus on the long-term survival of Auburn. Those who had mechs and knew how to use them began to clear the rubble from the streets so they could begin to rebuild the town.

There was also the delicate and depressing task of clearing the dead from the area. Dozens had been buried in the buildings when they'd been bombed, and too many of them were left there because others had to look to their own survival. Who knew how many had not been killed by the initial impact and could have lived had help arrived to pull them out?

"Fuck, that's a depressing train of thought."

Mini appeared to know what she was referring to or at least had the good sense not to ask. "I suppose you might want to get some sleep in here while I get some work done?"

"Would you mind that? I have a little trouble keeping my eyes open."

"My databanks tell me that this is a common effect of physical and psychological exhaustion. You would do well to get what sleep you can and tell me whether you are capable of continuing to work later on in the day. If not, you might want to think about getting some proper rest."

"I can't go to sleep. Too many people are working to rebuild their lives out there for me to simply laze around."

"Assuming that you need the rest and it is required for your health, you might want to think that it is a priority. You will not be able to support or help anyone if you have some kind of infection that keeps you out of action for weeks. You would take up more supplies for less work if you don't take care of yourself."

The AI had a point. She couldn't remember the last time she had been sick, but the few folks who had been sick at

Sanctuary had always received side-glances from everyone else. People needed to cover for someone who didn't work, and that person needed to be cared for and so took up more resources than they did when they were healthy.

If there was something she didn't want to be, it was a burden. She had always prided herself on being able to carry her weight wherever she went, even with the Knights. She was learning from them but she was helping however she could too.

"You might want to hold off on the nap."

"Hmm?" Jessica13 straightened in the cockpit and realized she had already begun to drift off. She took a deep breath and looked at Tinker, who approached with an easy stride.

His head popped out of the mech and peeked at her. "Jessie, are you busy?"

"Not…not at the moment, no."

"Hammerhand wants to see you. Come on."

He dropped into the mech and she followed him through the town to where the newcomers had pitched their tents. They were literal tents made from tarps and sticks, and she wondered briefly if the spikes they had on their mech armor doubled as the poles to keep their shelters up.

Her companion led her onward until they reached the outer rings of the tents and moved toward the largest one, which was as big as one of the houses in Auburn. It was bigger than the Beast, without a doubt.

Tinker climbed out of the mech and indicated for her to do the same, and they entered the canvas dwelling. A dozen or so of the others from the desert were present, dressed in the same flowing robes although less colorful. All wore pale-blue and they carried weapons. They were the guards for the Prophet, the man who had come to their rescue.

She still didn't know how he had known to come or why. There appeared to be nothing to gain, but they had also remained after the battle. Of course, the threat of Athena and her people still hung over the town like a storm cloud, but they couldn't attack. They now lacked the numbers to launch an assault like they had before. Of course, the Knights couldn't either.

They were in the oddest kind of stalemate.

The Prophet was seated on a plush red velvet cushion on the ground, his legs crossed in front of him, and his fingers curled his mustache absently.

Hammerhand sat beside him and looked uncomfortable. He slouched on the cushion instead of sitting cross-legged and didn't look up as they stepped into the tent. Instead, his gaze was fixed in a glare at the man seated across from both of them, Mayor Jones. He also looked uncomfortable on the cushion, although he had adopted the cross-legged posture of his host. One more person was present who she wasn't familiar with.

The man was short and lean, although Jessica13 had never seen the likes of him before. He wore a uniform suit, although not a flight suit, and it was divided clearly into a jacket and pants of unmistakable quality. Beneath it, he wore a gray vest, and under that was a white shirt, which in turn had a small tie that tucked into the vest.

She recalled a few pictures of men and women dressed in similar fashion in the info archives at Sanctuary but thought the style had long since died out.

"Mr. Stone," the Prophet said and obviously continued a previous line of thought, "you have to understand that security must be established in this area. That is our only priority."

"Please, call me Levi," he replied with a polite smile as the

Prophet sipped from a tiny silver cup. "As Expedition Master for the New York Western Railway Company, I can't make that kind of a promise. You know that for security to be established in this area, the Citadel bunker must be defeated once and for all."

Jessica13 narrowed her eyes.

Tinker leaned closer to her. "The Citadel bunker is where those fuckers who attacked us came from."

"It's not actually a bunker, not in the way you think." The Prophet appeared to have heard what they had talked about and wanted to make sure everyone in the room was on the same page. "It is called FEMA City by those who reside within and it is a city, not a bunker. The population is larger than most, and that allows them to field more mechs in battle, as we are well aware."

"I thought all the cities were lost."

"This one was underground." The man seemed to enjoy having a captive audience and spoke with deep inflections that made it sound like he told a story. "It was founded by a long-lost civilization with the intention of being a fortress against the Invaders, one that would be able to field their culture once everything calmed, you understand? They invented the balloons that were used to attack you. They called them Zeppelins—those that can control the weather— and all the other technology to recreate the world from what it had become into something that allowed us to live on the surface again. This leads people to come and settle, like the founders of this town of Auburn."

She leaned forward and listened. The Prophet appeared to know a great deal about the world they lived in and seemed more than willing to share his knowledge with those who wanted to listen. "Is that why we need to defeat them once and for all?"

The man turned to look at her and smiled broadly. "Yes, child, and for many other reasons. They have technology from the Cities-That-Were gathered in their vaults. And they have gene vaults too, that maintain what was lost in the world—seeds from plants, trees, and crops that could be brought out into the world to feed everyone. Of course, they will not share this with the rest of us without a price. They are remnants of an extinct culture—one that is extinct for a reason. They would not tolerate the lives of those who live beyond. Those they accept must conform to the ways of their fossil society."

"Then why allow them to continue and remain so powerful?" Tinker asked and folded his arms in front of his chest. "These folks are right fucking pricks. Why haven't they been dealt with already?"

The Prophet stiffened a little, and Jessica13 could tell he wasn't used to being spoken to like that. Fortunately, he seemed willing to move past it. "You must understand, of course, that such a thing has been attempted—and failed miserably, as well. While none would say the lives of those who tried were lost in vain, they were unable to breach even the first line of defense of the city, and thus made it difficult to know what lies within."

"What kind of defenses are we looking at?" This time, it was Hammerhand who interjected.

"The kind that even I, with my eight companies of mechs and vehicles, wouldn't pose much of a threat to. You saw how they were able to assail the city with artillery. For the primary defense, they use the height advantage of the spire you can see from here. The aeries provide defense for sixteen heavy artillery mechs—heavier than anything I have ever seen in my years on this Earth. They can deliver enough power to obliterate any attacking army that advances. I have seen the effects of those mechs firing. If you approach the bunker yourself, the craters in the earth will be evidence enough for you as well."

The Knights' leader sighed and shook his head. "We do appear to be at an impasse, then. We cannot leave Auburn to the mercy of those who would attack once more, and we cannot take the offensive to them either."

"There is something to be noted here." Levi paused to accept one of the same small silver cups the Prophet was drinking from. "Auburn is important to them. It is why they have committed so many troops to attack it and why they chose not to raze the town to the ground as they have in the past. Perhaps its food is the reason for that. I cannot imagine that an underground city would be able to feed itself properly, and they must therefore exploit those around it to survive."

Hammerhand's eyebrow raised as he accepted one of the tiny silver cups. "Well, that's something at least. If nothing else, we could starve them out."

CHAPTER NINE

Jessica13 looked at each of the men in the room and tried to determine if they were serious or not. They talked about killing and attacking a large city that possessed the kinds of defenses she had only read about in the instructional texts on how land-based defenses were designed to ward off attacks from space.

Hell, the Katyushas the Prophet had made mention of had been designed to hit targets over the horizon. Of course, those mechs were made to be piloted by five or six people and could very well tear craters in the ground below.

And they talked about attacking it. The impossibility of surviving the assault on Auburn came to mind but comparing the two was like comparing apples to oranges that could destroy five or six mechs in a single shot.

She studied the group quietly and it seemed like they all came to the same realization as her. The sheer concept of trying to attack the Citadel bunker—or FEMA City, as he called it—was daunting. Even thinking about it sent a small chill into the pit of her stomach.

The Prophet continued after he'd given all present enough time to digest his words. "It is said that FEMA City was built with making starships in mind—the kind that rose into the skies to combat the Invaders. A dry dock, one might say, but with the sea above instead of below."

Everyone else in the room nodded, understanding the metaphor. She had no idea what a dry dock was, but she nodded as well because she didn't want to seem ignorant to the people present.

"That makes sense," Tinker added. "They wouldn't have put those Katyushas simply anywhere but would have positioned them mostly in strategic locations, places that would need to be maintained in case of a battle. The sheer amount of energy needed to launch their projectiles... I can't even calculate how much power could go into that."

"One megajoule per every kilogram being launched," Jessica13 interjected when she recalled the texts she had been able to read. "The Katyushas were designed with a complex magnetic system to launch their projectiles, which usually weighed around five kilograms each. They heated them in the barrel without compromising the barrel itself, which allowed them to fire faster than if they were fired through explosives or fuel. The single downside was that the rounds needed to be loaded and locked into place by hand, with the calculations run by the main control of the mech. A skilled crew could load maybe five rounds a minute. Each Katyusha has two barrels to fire from, with three separate crews of two—two crews reload the barrels and one makes the calculations that would allow it to fire accurately."

She looked up and realized that the entire group had gone quiet and most eyes were on her. All but Levi, who looked away and took a sip from his tiny silver cup.

The Prophet grinned openly and nodded. "Yes, yes. Very good, child. How did you come by this knowledge?"

She looked at Tinker, who shrugged.

"They had them in instructional texts in the bunker where I grew up."

"They didn't teach me any of that stuff," the mechanic muttered.

"No one taught it to me either. I was digging around to find schematics on the Minato and they had the texts mixed in at Sanctuary's hard drives."

The Prophet still looked rather pleased that she had gotten the right idea from what had been shared. "Excellent. Excellent. The knowledge of the weapons is very good, indeed. Anyway, as we now know the power in the weapons that we would face, you should know what those defend. And of course, what they do not."

He dragged a handful of larger maps across the floor between them and a couple of his attendants helped to spread one out. It was large enough that they could all see it.

She recognized the area around Auburn immediately and noted the town itself, surrounded by greenery as it had once been. Much of the vegetation had been burned in the attack but there was some left, at least.

Her gaze moved to a town farther to the north, the one Athena had burned and tried to attack the Knights from. It wasn't as long a distance between the two towns as it had felt and yet somehow, the spire looked much farther away from Auburn than it seemed. It had since stopped sparking with electricity, and she assumed it was because it took too much energy to run it constantly. Even so, it appeared to be about a two- or three-days' march to reach the location that had been cleared by the Katyusha cannons.

And from there, it was almost a full day's march to the final destination. It was like they said—no army would be able to march through a full day of being bombarded like that.

The Prophet, however, directed their attention to a section that was a little to the east and well-removed from the range of the cannons.

"If you will turn your eyes to this mesa here, you will note that the city extends underground a great many kilometers. Whether this was intentional or not, this section is beyond where the Katyushas can fire. This, it has been observed, is where the balloons are launched. I believe you interacted with them, and they are a part of the system to remake the world. As I think you are aware, they have found out how to weaponize these effectively."

Jessica13 scowled at the map and tried to understand the logistics of it. There was a small legend on the side, but it would require more study before she understood it all. For the moment, it was best to let the others continue their planning.

Hammerhand leaned closer. "I assume you don't mean that we should simply take the area for their balloons. As effective as they may be, they are also easy pickings for the cannons should they approach."

"True enough, my brave friend, and it is for this reason that I guide your attention toward this area—a lake made by a crater. It is assumed that they store their gene bank under the crater lake, as my spies have noted large heat exchanger towers rising during the drier months of the year."

The landmark was about a hundred kilometers from the spire and an equal distance from the mesa, much like the numbers on a clock face. She couldn't see how they could be connected to the Spire or FEMA City or whatever it was called unless it spanned hundreds of kilometers from the center all around. It would certainly make it bigger than Sanctuary.

"Both would have settlements underground," the Prophet continued. "They would also be connected to the larger structure of FEMA City, possibly through tunnels branching from the main cavern under the spire."

Hammerhand nodded when he saw where the man was going and the point he tried to make. "You think that if we threaten their food supply here in Auburn, take their balloons, and seize their gene bank, we would be able to sue for peace?"

"A just peace would be found, yes, and it would prevent imbalance from occurring in the future as it has up until this point."

"And our only other option would be to simply wait them out and hope we can last longer than they can," Tinker observed grimly.

"That is correct as well."

Levi finished his drink and let one of the nearby attendants take it. "If the Knights and the Prophet's troops were able to coordinate this kind of peace, the New York Western Railroad Company would be in place to make sure that it is maintained. We could enforce it, if you will, with the troops we would be able to provide."

Hammerhand nodded but hesitated for a moment to wait for Tinker to add his input as well, but all the older man could offer was another nod.

"It is a good plan," the Knights' leader stated firmly. "And a good step toward solidifying peace in the area. We are in agreement."

The Prophet clapped briskly. "Most wonderful. Most wonderful indeed! We should like to begin planning this immediately. You cannot wait for the rain to fall on the desert but must bring the water yourself, as they say."

Jessica13 didn't know who had said that, but it did make some sense to not wait for the rain to fall but rather to dig for another source.

Of course, in this particular case, they appeared to know where the water was. It would merely be difficult to dig.

She wasn't sure how the metaphor held up from that point forward.

The whole group stood from where they were settled on the red velvet cushions. Hammerhand stretched, clearly not used to sitting in that position. The Prophet and Levi both appeared more comfortable and shook hands with each other.

Once Hammerhand was finished, he turned to Tinker and the two quickly began to discuss logistics, almost as if they'd forgotten that Jessica13 was there with them. It wasn't like she had really contributed to the battle plan, anyway.

The word had already spread by the time they reached the other Knights. News that they had found a way to go on the offensive—which was what they had hoped for from the beginning—generated a sense of renewed purpose. The Beast needed to be prepared for the battles ahead, and Jessica13 joined her teammates as they worked to get everything ready. Most of their equipment had been pulled out for easy access during the battle. A great deal of it had been used, as well, and had to be replenished from what could be recovered from the battlefield.

She knew they would probably head into the toughest fight of their lives, which included the two they'd fought over the fate of Auburn. But she had to be honest, sticking around after a battle to clean up and help rebuild did not appeal to her at all. It felt too much like looking the consequences of what had happened in the eye—like they stared at the death and destruction they had faced and even caused and somehow tried to find a way to make it all better.

At least when they were moving again, she could put this all behind her. Unlike the people of Auburn, she would not be able to enjoy the fruits of their labor once everything was rebuilt.

"Jessie, a word?"

A little surprised, she turned quickly to where Hammerhand stood behind her mech. His Excalibur had been left where Tinker and some of the others now fussed over it, and the man seemed a little reduced without it. Of course, an Excalibur was something to see in action, and it was easy to forget that the man inside was, in fact, a man. He was lean, tall, and shaved to his skin to prevent any gunk from getting in the processors, but still a man.

"Sure," she replied and climbed out of her Minato to face him. He was still taller than she was to the point where she had to crane her neck to look at him.

"We discussed the logistics of the attacks that will be required and considered the nature of the fight ahead to determine if all the Knights would be able to hold their own or if some should remain here."

His low tone of voice and the slow, deliberate way in which he spoke said all that needed to be said. Jessica13 couldn't help a small scowl at the man but quickly removed the resentment and irritation from her expression. She might not like it, but he was the leader of the Knights. He could have simply ordered her to stay behind. At least he had taken the time to explain the decision to her, although it appeared as though he wished he didn't need to.

She steeled herself, straightened her back, and tried not to let the disappointment she felt show. "You've decided that I'll stay behind."

Hammerhand clenched his jaw. "The Minato is a fantastic mech, to be sure, but we face combat situations where the style of hit and run we are accustomed to might not play out as well as it usually does. Tighter confines underground and in the bunkers mean that you will not be able to move out of hostile situations as quickly as you might out in the open. Not only that, you do not have either the experience or the weapons to protect yourself."

That made sense. It still didn't help the sting, though, but once again, she tried to keep any of that from playing on her face.

"In the meantime," he continued, "your time in Auburn should not be seen as having no value. It will mean a great deal to me that you will remain in Auburn and continue with the mission of rebuilding their homes and their lives."

She had nothing else to say, and it seemed he didn't either. Neither appeared to be any good at this kind of tense situation and after a few seconds during which he simply stood silently in front of her, Hammerhand spun away and returned to his mech.

He'd done his best, at least. She breathed in and released it slowly in an effort to settle the rampant urge to scream before she climbed into the Minato again.

"I'm sorry," Mini said, having heard everything.

"There's nothing to be sorry about."

A few seconds ticked past while Jessica13 got herself situated.

"He did make a good point. The Minato is best equipped for a battle out in the open where its mobility will give it an edge. That advantage is removed when in the tight confines of tunnels and bunkers."

"I know. I know he's right." She looked at the HUD and ran a couple of system diagnostics before she put them in motion to join one of the work parties and begin her task in Auburn. "It still sucks, though, especially since I'm the only one."

"Indeed it does."

CHAPTER TEN

"It's not that I like being out there in the action," Jessica13 said. "I'm not a violent person when it comes down to it, and I'm not the kind to get into altercations on my own. You know that, right?"

Mini added a thumbs-up to the HUD.

"It's only... I want to feel like I'm contributing and pulling my weight with the Knights. It's not that I wanted to be a fighter or a champion like Hammerhand is. I only wanted to head out and be free here in the Outside."

"On that we have to disagree."

She paused in her work of clearing rubble from the road. "What are you talking about? You know me better than anyone else and you have to know that all I really wanted was the freedom the Outside provided."

"I will not deny that freedom to do as you will plays a large part in who you are. But, if you will recall, one of your first actions once outside the confines of Sanctuary was to go and help people who were in need. And when they needed more help, you went out of your way to provide it. That included putting yourself in danger to find Hammerhand and bring him to aid those you couldn't help yourself."

Almost absently, she noted that the AI core ran a little hotter than usual, which was what usually happened when Mini considered human behavior.

Or her behavior, in this particular case.

"Well…I couldn't leave them out there without any help. They had lost their home and there were children who would have died if I didn't help. How could I not at least do my best to help them rebuild? Kind of like what we're doing here."

"Calculations picked up from the database tell me that the average response to seeing the bunker smoking as it was would have been to turn and walk away. The second most likely action would have been to loot whatever you could and kill those who stopped you. Helping people would have come in as a very distant third."

Jessica13 scowled. Was it too much to ask that people stop making excellent points when all she wanted to do was sulk at not being called in to help the Knights in something that felt more relevant than putting Auburn together again?

Maybe it was. Mini only wanted to help, not unlike she did, and to the AI, that meant pointing out that she liked to help people.

A small alarm emitted inside the cockpit to cut her sulk off and she looked around.

"What the fuck was that?"

"An alert."

"No shit. What kind of alert?"

"The kind that advises us that there are life signs buried under that pile of rubble."

They turned the mech toward the section where the explosives had collapsed buildings on top of the invading forces. Or maybe that was the section that had been demolished when FEMA's artillery shelled the town. If she had been outside the Minato, it would have been fairly easy to distinguish.

The fertilizer that had been used for the explosives left the smell of manure hanging over the area.

But, reluctant to expose herself to the possible stench or any falling debris, she was relieved that she was still in the Minato and intended to remain in the mech. They clambered over the rubble and wreckage around them while Mini called up a couple of programs that would help them clear it and hopefully not injure the person beneath. The delicate nature of the operation forced them to move a little slower than they had before.

As they inched deeper into the fallen building, it became more and more apparent that the structure had been brought down by the fertilizer bombs. The presence of the pale white and grey mechs was telling of exactly who they might find still alive under there.

"How could someone survive having a building dropped on them?" Jessica13 asked, more wondering aloud than actually asking Mini to tell her.

But she also liked it when he went through the process of educating her. "The chances are infinitesimal, although they depend on a number of variables, but they are there. Besides, someone in a mech does stand a better chance than someone without."

It wasn't necessarily comforting to hear, and as they dragged one of the mechs away, the auditory receptors on the Minato picked up a human voice.

Another couple of layers of rocks needed to be removed before they located the source. A man covered in dirt, grime, and soot, coughed when her actions raised a cloud of dust.

He had already managed to climb out of his ruined mech and begun the process of digging himself out. The movement had likely been what had triggered the sensors on her mech.

"It would seem the survivor is one of Athena's men." Mini had a knack for pointing out the obvious. "Or, should I say, attackers from FEMA City?"

"So it would appear, yes."

She honestly didn't know what to do. A small, angry part of her insisted that she simply leave the man to his fate. The chances were that no one would be around this part of town for a while, and his injuries would make sure he didn't last very long.

The solution was enticingly simple. She didn't even need to do anything herself except turn and walk away from him.

The man looked at her, his demeanor tense and frustrated like he was ready for her to simply trample him. He held a rifle in his hand and struggled to pull it up to aim at her. It was made to be carried by a mech and he would have had difficulty lifting it even if he were in perfect health.

He was afraid, that much was obvious. Now that the cloud of dust had dissipated, she registered that he wasn't much older than she was or maybe had one of those younger-looking faces.

"Not a step closer," he shouted, coughed, and dragged one hand across his mouth. "Not another step or I'll blast you in half."

Jessica13 sighed and shook her head. "I will regret this, I know I will."

"You're going to help him, aren't you?"

She didn't reply, not in so many words anyway. Mini did

know her rather well, there was no denying that. And she wouldn't cold-bloodedly kill a wounded man. She retrieved the first aid kit from her cockpit and opened the hatch, climbed out of the mech, and approached the man.

"Stay…stay back. I mean it!"

"It's only the two of us here." She snorted and tried not to laugh. "You don't need to pretend you could even lift that cannon, much less reach the trigger in your condition."

He looked at her and tugged resolutely at the rifle a few more times before he gave up. "Why are you…. What are you doing?"

In response, she merely snorted again as she removed a few chunks of rubble before she dragged him clear of the fallen mech.

"The battle's over. What's your name?"

He said nothing as she propped him up against one of the mechs and inspected his injuries. She wasn't a doctor, of course, but he didn't appear to have any internal bleeding. Bruises and cuts were visible almost everywhere, but nothing appeared to be life-threatening.

At least, not immediately.

She took padding from the pouch, together with the cleaning agent, and set to work on the cuts on his shoulders.

"Robert7."

She looked up. "Hmm?"

"My name. It's Robert7."

It seemed like an odd time to tell her what his name was, but at least it meant he'd moved past the need to threaten to blast her in half.

"Nice to meet you, Robert7. I'm Jessica13, by the way."

"You're…not one of the town people."

"What gave it away?"

"Well, they don't use our name-numbering system, for instance. How old are you?"

"Not that much younger than you are." She finished with the cleaning and applied the bandages. While she had attended a few classes on how to help people who had been injured, it certainly hadn't been her strong suit. Still, cleaning and bandaging were fairly instinctive. She paused in her efforts to remove a few small pieces of rock and gravel from one of the wounds and Robert7 gritted his teeth while his breathing became a little heavier.

"Well, still, it seems like a battlefield isn't the place for you," he said once she resumed her ministrations.

"It seems like even less of a place for you, Robert7. Besides, the battle is over and people are talking about a lasting peace in this area, which means you have no reason to threaten me with that rifle you can't even lift. Now please, stop squirming and stay still while I bandage you."

"I'm sorry, but it hurts."

"It'll hurt more if any of the injuries get infected," she snapped in response and covered the last of the cuts she could see.

"I…I don't understand. I mean…okay, the fighting is over, but why would you help me? Not that long ago, we were fighting each other. How…how long ago was it?"

"A couple of days now. Some folks from the desert came in and pushed your FEMA asses out of town. I think they didn't want to risk losing more troops here, even if they won. I merely assumed that you don't know how the battle ended and are curious as to why it's me and not one of your comrades coming to rescue you."

He nodded slowly. "Well, I guessed that when no one came looking for me after a day buried under that building."

"Speaking of that, I do remember there being lung complications from inhaling so much dust. Aside from the other injuries."

"Which means I'm still confused as to why you're spending resources to help me."

Jessica13 sighed and shrugged noncommittally. "I don't know. There's something I was told about, and I think that carries over. Like I've promised this world every ounce of goodness, sanity, and brotherhood I can give it. Not that it's much, but if it means treating someone in need, I guess that's how it works."

He studied her as she double-checked to make sure she hadn't missed anything. "I guess that means I surrender to you now."

"Not that you had a choice. Now, let's see if someone can make sure you won't die sometime today due to internal bleeding or something. Let's get you out of here."

Mini moved the Minato to where Robert7 lay and slowly pulled him up to support the man while they scrambled out.

She wasn't sure if they would find a doctor there but hopefully, they would find someone better equipped and trained than her to handle a person who was wounded.

CHAPTER ELEVEN

Robert7 wasn't one of the most talkative characters in the world, although Jessica13 didn't think she would have been that talkative while she was marched into the town she had failed to capture.

Of course, she wouldn't have said anything at all and FEMA's fighters probably wouldn't have bothered to take her in either.

"Where are we heading?" her captive-patient asked. He was perched on the Minato's back and used a couple of smaller, empty crates to give him a position to relax on as they moved through the town. It probably wasn't that comfortable but it was certainly better than being trapped as he had been with little option but to wait for help.

The people of Auburn certainly put the hours in to rebuild their home. It wasn't the kind of place she could think of as home for herself. There were too many confining walls, which she now realized had been one of the things she had left Sanctuary to avoid. Of course, it wasn't something she had thought of at the time, but after months spent in the open, she doubted that she could spend too much time in that kind of environment again.

But it was still their home. People needed something established, a haven where they could protect their children and loved ones, and she could understand that. They willingly expended the effort it required. Those who still had mechs continued to help to clear the rubble, although a couple of the ruined mechs had been repurposed and taken out into the fields, where crops were being sown to raise food to sustain the rebuilding process. Not much reconstruction would happen on empty stomachs, after all.

Others had worked to set up temporary living situations in the town center for those who had lost their homes. A few buildings still remained standing, of course, but those were already filled to capacity.

Jessica13 remembered asking why people didn't reclaim the buildings that hadn't been demolished, and one of the builders still in the town had explained that the attacks had weakened the structures and many were currently on the cusp of total collapse.

They didn't appear to know of any way to effectively repair them. All they could think of was to tear those down and build something else. No one seemed overly distressed about it.

Maybe it was simply preferable to living in a building that could collapse on top of them at any time of the day or night.

They continued the journey through the town, where a few of the makeshift shelters were open and long tables were set up. Kitchens worked to stir huge pots of steaming liquid, and clay ovens had already been stoked to bake bread that was kneaded in large amounts by a group that had been designated to prepare the food for the rest of the residents.

They were all brought in and organized to work together to supply the other elements that would enable them to accomplish the enormous task ahead. While they could have thrown everyone at the physical and material demands this involved, Mayor Jones had proven to be an effective leader. People knew something was being done to repair Auburn and were willing to make sacrifices as long as it meant that everyone worked toward the same goal.

Maybe the man didn't have the same raw charisma Hammerhand did when he strode around in his Excalibur, but she had to say he knew how to keep people motivated.

"You lot sure do seem determined to cover any signs of the attack," Robert7 noted from the back of the Minato.

"They have nowhere else to go," Jessica13 replied. "Leaving this place in disrepair would simply mean they were exposed to the elements. To avoid that, they'll work together and ultimately rebuild the whole town again."

"Why do you refer to them like that?"

"Like what?"

"Them, they, their—you talk about it like you're not in the same fight as they are."

"I'm not from the town of Auburn. This isn't my home, and the moment they no longer need us here, we'll head out again. The Knights Mechanica have much more to do than settle down."

"Your group is the Knights Mechanica?"

She turned her head, even though she wouldn't be able to see him. Hopefully, he would see the motion and interpret the surprise. "Of course we are. Who the hell did you think it was who put up that much of a fight?"

"Our commanders only told us that the town was in rebellion. We assumed they had bought combat mechs and used them at an opportune time and maybe hired a couple of mercs to add to their numbers or to train their folk on how to fight. But I didn't think the Knights Mechanica had actually come all this way to fight us. I thought they...well, you only fought for those who needed help."

Jessica13 scowled. "And when we saw people herded into a church and burned alive, we realized that the people of Auburn were among those who needed our help."

"None of our people ever did that."

"I saw Athena do it personally. Her and her men in Cinder mechs."

"Athena?"

"You know—the woman in an Excalibur who likes to fight with a spear."

"Oh, Lady Hoot. Well, she's not really one of ours. I'm not sure what kind of arrangement was worked out with her and her raiders, but the general idea is that they are the muscle we would have hired to maintain order in the area."

"Well, they've done a fantastic job." She didn't bother to hide the sarcasm in her tone. "You did see that they burned a whole damn town, right? They set it all on fire and then hid in it and waited for us to arrive to catch us off-guard while we tried to find survivors."

"I don't... I'm sure the commanders at FEMA didn't realize she would go that far—"

"Do you really believe that?"

Robert7 didn't reply and his silence was telling enough. They had to know what Athena was doing, especially if these towns were the source of food for the underground city. Maybe she had done it without their permission, but without their knowledge?

Impossible.

As they moved away from the center of town, what looked like a militia had begun to assemble. The group of men and women were armed with a selection of improvised weapons. They didn't include any of the Knights in their number and they didn't appear to join any of the work that was in progress throughout Auburn.

It wasn't something Jessica13 thought to question. These people had been through enough and if they wanted to find ways to protect themselves, they had that right.

They turned to look at the Minato as it moved across their line of sight. It took her a few seconds to realize that what had caught their attention wasn't actually her but the man on the back of her mech.

"What are they staring at?" she whispered. "It's not like it's the first time someone's used a mech to carry anyone before."

"Well, I suppose not, but I think what has their attention is the fact that your prisoner is in a FEMA City pilot sleeve."

Mini once again had a point, and she came to a halt when a smaller group of the militia began to approach. She looked at them a little more closely and realized that only some were members of the militia. Those with weapons in their hands and who stood at the edges of the group were, while the others wore the black pilot sleeves she had begun to associate as being worn by FEMA City's fighters.

Robert7 attempted to straighten on her back and had seen that at least a dozen of his comrades had survived the battle, although they looked a little battered and bruised. Some had cuts that showed fresh blood. Maybe they had all recently been rescued from under rubble?

One of the militia noticed her prisoner and raised his hand to bring the group to a halt.

"Don't you mind him…"

"Jessica13."

"Jessica13, right. You can turn him over to us and we'll take care of him for you."

The man gestured for her to approach, but there was something off about his manner and maybe the way he carried himself. He seemed a little too aggressive and it gave her pause.

"Don't worry about that," she replied. "This man is injured and needs medical attention. I'll find someone who can help him and then get back to work."

"Why would we waste any medical attention on this bastard?" one of the women asked loudly, and a few of her comrades nodded in agreement.

The apparent commander made no response to this, either for or against, but fixed his gaze on Jessica13. "Hand him over and go about your business. We'll make sure he's tended to."

"Jessica13," Mini said and drew her attention to him rather than the man in front of her. "I thought you might want to know that the injuries the prisoners sustained are fairly fresh and appear to have been caused by the weapons carried by the Auburn Militia."

She narrowed her eyes. The claim sounded ridiculous but Mini wasn't the type of AI to spin lies out of nowhere. Sure enough, when he highlighted and enhanced the weapons in question, she could see fresh blood which left her in no doubt that they were the cause of the marks on the bodies of the prisoners.

"I think I'll keep an eye on him myself if you don't mind."

She took a step back when the man approached her and sensed the focused gazes of all the militia around her. None of them were in mechs, of course, so she didn't feel she was in any real danger, but Robert7 had no armor between him and any bullets that might be fired, either deliberately or accidentally.

And with him injured on her back, there was no way they could move to all fours and race away. It would force him from her back, which defeated the entire purpose of their escape.

"Don't make this any more difficult than it needs to be," the man said and scowled at her, while some of the militia grasped their weapons a little tighter and tensed as if to ready themselves for action.

Some who guarded the improvised stockade began to move behind her, likely intending to drag the man off her back before she could protest.

"What's happening here?"

They all turned as Mayor Jones walked down the street toward them. His clothes looked a little grubby and ragged and were stained with gray dust, likely from having helped to clear rubble. His beard, face, and hands were similarly affected by the work, yet he still looked fresh and a small, friendly smile played across his handsome features.

"We were merely trying to take this prisoner off Jessica13's hands, sir," the commander stated. He made an effort to wipe the scowl from his face to present a cool, calm exterior. "I'm sure someone with a mech has better things to do than to ferry prisoners to and from the stockade. Considerable work is required to get Auburn up and running again like you said."

"Indeed, I did, and indeed there is." Mayor Jones patted the man heartily on the shoulder and turned to look at her. "Why can't you hand your prisoner to them?"

Jessica13 didn't want to seem like she was avoiding the work since, as the man said, there was a daunting amount to do. "This prisoner is severely injured and needs immediate medical attention. I wanted to find someone who could provide it."

"That attention would as easily be provided while he's in the stockade with the other prisoners."

"But not as quickly, I don't think."

The mayor nodded. "Well, suit yourself. Far be it from me to order any of the Knights Mechanica around, and I'm sure you have put a great deal of thought into your reasoning. Carry on, men, and let Jessica13 go about her business."

The commander turned and glared incredulously at him. "But sir—"

"There's nothing to add, Shem. Go about your work and let her go about hers. There's nothing more to it than that."

Shem looked like he intended to say something more and perhaps question Mayor Jones' judgment, but his mouth snapped shut and gestured for the militia and prisoners to move down the road.

Jones strolled over to where she still stood. "I think you might find doctors out to the west section. That's where most of our skilled hands have helped the injured. Likely as not they won't be able to help someone who's desperately wounded, but they shall certainly try."

"I hope so." Jessica13 wasn't sure what to say to that.

He nodded and patted the side of her mech briskly. "I'll join the militiamen and women to make sure they tend to their duties as well as possible. Carry on."

The man swung on his heel, proceeded down the road toward the prisoners, and increased his pace to reach the commander. Jessica13, Mini, and Robert7 moved in the opposite direction and toward the area where Jones had directed them.

"Why…"

Jessica13 craned her head to hear what her passenger was saying. "Why what?"

"Well…why didn't you turn me over to the others?"

She shrugged but realized he couldn't see her do it. "Like I said, you need immediate attention and that's not likely to happen while in the stockade…"

Her voice trailed off when gunfire cracked loudly behind them. She turned but tried not to move too quickly with Robert7 on her back.

"Is the town under attack again?"

Mini showed a few audio repeats of the gunfire. "Those were small arms, not the kind carried by mechs. Unless FEMA has sent unarmored troops to attack us, I don't think so."

Something cold sank into her stomach and she strode back the way they'd come. The shooting had originated from where the militia had guided the prisoners. At the edge of the town, she located their tracks heading out into a couple of the unsown fields. The farmers probably hadn't managed to get to the area yet.

Even so, with the obvious trail leading into the open and out of the town, she couldn't see anyone—no militia and no prisoners. And it wasn't like they had vanished in the minutes between the gunfire and her arrival.

Her chest tightened when the tracks led to where a large hole had been dug, with the mounds of dirt still piled beside it.

"I would suggest you don't look closer."

Jessica13 ignored the AI's warning and stepped forward. Shells ejected from the weapons the militia had carried still lay in the dirt, possibly to be collected later by those who were supposed to come and refill the hole that had been left.

Unfortunately, she couldn't ignore the bodies that were in the pit.

There were more than the dozen or so she had seen herded by the militia, and if she hadn't heard the gunshots, she would have assumed they had died in the fighting and were being buried outside the town.

But the wounds were fresh and it looked like more than only the group she had seen had been guided to the hole and executed.

Even a dozen was too many.

Something hot and angry roiled in her stomach and she gagged and fought the need to throw up. There was nothing worse than having to clean that from her cockpit.

"Oh...fuck..." she whispered.

CHAPTER TWELVE

The Excalibur was good for a number of things.

The size advantage made sure of that. Virtually nothing could stop the hammer it wielded when it was in full swing, and the shield he could set up was certainly a tactical advantage whatever the combat situation might be. It was a useful mech, which was why he had chosen to use it, even though it had come to mean more than merely a bigger mech that could push the smaller ones around. It was a symbol among the Knights Mechanica.

There was, however, one thing that it was no good at —scouting.

Hammerhand liked to leave that kind of work to those who piloted mechs better suited to the job.

It wasn't that he didn't know how to pilot a mech designed to excel at scouting. He, like most pilots, had started out using support and light assault mechs.

But after years of using the larger Excalibur in combat, it didn't feel right to be in something smaller and more mobile.

And yet, when the Prophet called on him to join him in

scouting ahead of their main force, he couldn't turn him down. He was something of a mystery, and his knowledge of Citta del Mar was certainly something to be tapped. But there was no way to force something like this.

The two larger mechs inched forward and away from the main force of joined Knights and Desert Warriors. They moved through the dense grasslands and managed to get a better view of the path ahead of them without giving their current position away.

"I thought it would be best to move immediately." The Prophet paused and glanced at their assembled forces before he moved into step with Hammerhand. "Given the kind of loss we inflicted on FEMA City's forces, I assumed it would only be a matter of time before they increased the numbers of their patrols around their perimeter sections, but the losses in men and mechs would mean they cannot do it immediately. It would be to our advantage to catch them unawares and unexpectant, as they will assume we are also struggling with reduced numbers."

Hammerhand grunted his agreement but didn't offer anything further. The Knights had held their own well enough against the attack, but the losses to their numbers had been hard to swallow. There weren't that many of them, to begin with.

Tinker had been right to question their engaging in pitched battles like this, where skill took less precedence over blind luck and years of training and experience would be lost thanks to the effects of a stray bullet.

Of course, his mechanic and friend was right about many things. There was a reason why the man was his most trusted confidant. And while Tinker hadn't openly stated any protest against their current objective, it was only a matter of time.

He knew the best time to engage Hammerhand in a dressing down was when outsiders weren't around to listen in.

"You are quiet today, my friend. Why is that?"

The Knights' leader scowled at the Argonaut. It wasn't like he was the most talkative character, to begin with.

No, that wasn't quite right. Tinker had often noted that he had a tendency to go on sometimes, but that was only when he felt the inspiration to do so.

"I'm making sure we won't be followed. We've left a wide trail, should someone come behind us. If a scouting mech caught sight of our advance and reported it to the city, any chance of a surprise attack would be lost."

"True, and yet we can trust in what has guided us thus far."

"Blind luck?"

"Destiny."

Hammerhand shrugged and settled firmly into his cockpit to guide the Excalibur through the higher routes that would give them a better view of the surrounding landscape. He could already see the vague shapes of the mesa ahead of them, almost three klicks away as the crow flew. Of course, the uneven landscape that gave their troops the cover they needed to advance without being seen would extend the distance a little.

"Ex, check the surrounding landscape for any foreign mechs that might be following us once you have a clear view."

Commencing scans now, the AI displayed in text across his HUD, and the sensors expanded their parameters into the surrounding area in an attempt to pick up anything that might indicate that they were being followed. The AI even scanned for encrypted comm lines that could reveal if there was communication about the troop's movements.

No signs of foreign mechs in the area, Hammerhand. Would you like me to continue periodic scans? the AI said in the scrolling text across his screen.

"Yes."

He was always tempted to complain about the fact that a mech as complex as the Excalibur was fitted with a simple interactive AI, but a quick look into the AI core would discourage that notion. The interactive software was fairly basic but that was only because most of the processing power was used to keep the mech itself functioning, and that was no easy feat.

When they reached the top of the hill, the two avoided sky-lining themselves using rudimentary cloaking devices and kept themselves positioned lower in case someone ran visual scans from the mesa.

The sun hung over the west of the base, already on its way toward sunset, which meant it wouldn't set behind them and give the Knights and Desert warriors an easier opportunity to move through the uneven terrain without being identified. They likely wouldn't stop until late in the night and would use the darkness for cover as well, but it was still best to know where they were going beforehand. Ex would be able to plot a course for them once they had it all visualized from the top.

The top area was used as a defensive position, and it already began to look impenetrable. Hammerhand knew from experience that it would only get worse the closer they got. Steps led to the base from the valley and circled the mesa, but they were large and likely designed to be scaled by mechs. Progress up these would be slow and open to attack from the men above every step of the way. There was no cover available unless they brought it themselves.

The Prophet sidled closer to him. "What think you?"

Hammerhand studied the scans for a few more seconds before he bit his bottom lip. Tinker said he always did that when he thought but it didn't stir the need to try to stop it. The thought was more important than the accompanying action, after all. "I have scans coming in that show mechs patrolling the area around it. The approach is defended, and even if we could break through the ground defenses, every step up would be hampered by people firing down at us. It's not the best situation to attack, although certainly better than the one we would face if we assaulted the main entrance."

"Agreed," the Prophet replied, likely having noticed the same movements he had. "I would say attacking at night would give us some advantage. To be able to scale the walls without being seen would likely be the best tactical decision for us to choose."

He shook his head quickly. "It's possibly the best tactical decision in the long term, but not the short."

"What do you mean?"

"A night attack would likely give us an advantage in the short-term but in the long-term, it would be seen as a foreign invasion by a foreign enemy—Knights Mechanica and Desert Warriors attacking their base. There's nothing like a foreign threat to raise defensive morale and make them fight harder."

"So, your tactical suggestion would be to attack in broad daylight in hopes that it will not be seen as invading forces?"

"They'll know who is attacking and the word will spread faster. That way, they will know it is the people of Auburn and their defenders fighting to regain their land. Otherwise, it will allow their leaders to twist the narrative and make it seem like an invading force."

"I suppose this is true enough. However, we would not be able to break into that mesa using force of numbers alone.

There would need to be tactical alterations to this, those that would allow some advantage if not surprise."

"It is likely that surprise will still be on our side, but there will be an element of trickery to it. The Knights and our Auburn allies could present as the first line of attack, make a show of assaulting the stronghold, and when it fails, fall back quickly. When we retreat, they would be forced to pursue and leave an opening for the rest of the force to slip in behind them and attack the mesa."

The Prophet didn't respond for almost a full minute, possibly while exploring the likelihood of an attack like that working. "Very well. It shows ingenuity and planning that would make our enemies think twice about how they conduct their operations. I like this. Let us make it so and discuss the details of how it shall be done."

CHAPTER THIRTEEN

There were a great many details involved in launching an attack on a well-defended position, and Hammerhand had to admit it wasn't his strength. It was like Tinker had told him—their strength lay in being able to strike at mostly unprotected locations quickly, hit them hard, and move on before any retaliation could be mounted.

It was what kept the Knights alive and prospering while in the areas infested by raiders, who had no sense of how to defend themselves properly and knew only how to attack from numerical superiority.

He did know a thing or two about mounting defenses and even a proper attack, which was how they had surmounted a few middling defenses they had come up against. But something like this that had been set up to be defended in the long-term? He was out of his depth. Tinker had a better mind for it, however, and talked to the Prophet and the other commanders of their troop to determine how it should be conducted.

"All right. All teams, listen up!" Tinker called and opened a comm line with the whole group. He brought the march to an almost instant halt. "We will assault the mesa ahead of us in the next few hours and coordination will be important. You'll all need to know your positions and your roles. The details and your places in them will be sent to every mech individually. From this point forward, there will be complete radio silence since the closer we get to them, the more likely it will be that they will be able to intercept our comms or even realize that encrypted comm lines are deployed close to them. That will be enough for alarms to be raised."

The Prophet said a few words over the comms as well, likely repeating what he had been said in a language some of the others could understand. Most spoke the same language they did, but some had difficulties with terminology and others spoke another language altogether, with running translation required for solid communication to be possible.

Hammerhand didn't mind. They were a cohesive group that appeared to want the same thing. He did harbor a few doubts, but those were kept close to his chest for the moment. They still needed the Prophet and his troops and offending them for no reason would be the very definition of self-sabotage.

The messages were sent and from the battle plan that had been drawn up, he would lead the first charge, which would inevitably be a feint. It made sense, he acknowledged, given that an Excalibur charging their front lines would catch their attention to the point where any thought that it could be a trap was forgotten. The chances were, if they didn't respond to the assault as expected, the Knights could thin the lines of their enemies before they called for a retreat, thus forcing more troops from the top of the mesa to descend to support the counterattack.

Obviously, it was rare that such plans worked out exactly

the way they had been devised. There was no telling what might go wrong in the middle of the fight and what kind of alterations would need to be made.

Until then, they would have to plan for failure while hoping for success. Besides, there was nothing to say that they couldn't bring comms up again when the battle started. The surprise would already be gone and they could coordinate better.

Hammerhand noted Tinker walk toward him, and the smaller mech moved smoothly through the ranks that prepared for combat.

"What's on your mind, my friend?"

The mechanic huffed over the comms. "Don't 'my friend' me. And how did you know I was angry? Or that there was something on my mind?"

"Well, the fact that you came all the way to me with a full head of steam says you're angry and that you plan to give me a piece of your mind, which means you have something on it. Do enlighten me."

"Well, I think the plan is, for lack of a better word, shit. It's a shit plan, Hammerhand, and from what the Prophet told me, it was your idea. Oh, and we need a better name for the man than 'The Prophet.' I'm tired of calling him that. There must be a real name we can use if we're not a part of his...one of his followers."

"I agree with that, but it doesn't seem wise to ask the man for his name rather than his title when that's what all the others call him. At least for the moment. It could cause offense."

"Well, as long as we're not trying to offend the man."

"Do you think it would be wise to sabotage our alliance

with the only fighters in the area who have the numbers to help us in this endeavor?"

Tinker didn't reply, which was all he needed to hear.

"For the moment, let's not do anything that could put that relationship at risk. With that in mind, what was it about the plan that you thought was absolute shit?"

"I didn't say absolute. I only said shit."

"Carry on, then."

Tinker paused for a few seconds to collect his thoughts. "Well, the plan itself is decent enough. I would have called for a night assault myself since success would be more important than how that attack was seen by those we attacked. Even so, I understand the thinking behind it."

"I assume there is more to it than that?"

"I don't like the fact that our Knights and the Auburnites will be at the front lines and take most of the risk and responsibility on ourselves. I don't like it."

"How do you mean?"

"I mean that we're the only ones taking a risk. If the Prophet decides he doesn't want to risk his men in the attack, we'll be left with most of the losses at the end of it and holding the bag besides. I don't trust them enough."

"In a fight like this, especially with the coordination required, trust is a necessity. In everything we intend to do to fight against FEMA City, we will need to trust each other. Establishing that is fundamental, and in knowing they'll have our backs and them knowing we'll have theirs, all future attacks will be the better for it."

Tinker continued to stare at him and glared through the faceplate of his mech. There was something about the man's anger that drove Hammerhand to continue. He didn't want to disappoint his friend.

"However, should there be something that goes wrong in the attack—should we not be able to hold their counterattack off, or should...our allies not come through in the way we need them to—there is already a retreat plan in place that we'll institute when the time comes. This will be a test of whether our new allies can be trusted or not as well."

The silence continued from the mechanic's side for a few more seconds. "So you...made plans in case the worst should happen?"

"Of course. I wouldn't risk the lives of the Knights Mechanica or those loyal to us without having a plan for their protection in place."

"Well, that's all I needed to know."

"Are we clear on this? Is there anything else you need?"

"No, I don't think so."

"Then let's get ready for a fight."

CHAPTER FOURTEEN

She made her mind up not to leave him alone.

Not after what they had seen in the pit outside of town. It had probably been covered by now, but the memories of it remained rather vividly in her mind. She could think about nothing else for the rest of the day.

Something about winning a battle had left her feeling elated. She'd been exhausted immediately after, of course, but still filled with elation that she had fought on the right side of the battle and walked away with the victory. While timely help had been needed for that to happen, it had still happened, and she had been absolutely sure that she had been on the right side of it.

And while that was still how she felt, her confidence was shattered. Would the people in the right elect to summarily execute the prisoners they had captured during the battle?

If she were in the position Mayor Jones was in, would she have made the same decision? Hundreds of different scenarios rushed through her mind as she thought about it. Maybe it had been a decision made with resources in mind.

Feeding and treating prisoners might have been seen as a waste, while they couldn't simply release them.

But why didn't they use the captives who were in good enough shape to help with the workload? Jones constantly went on about how much work there was to do, so why not spread the labor to those who could help and make up for their role as the aggressors in the battle?

No matter how she looked at it, there was no justification for what had been done, and the more she thought about it, the more it appeared that she was in the wrong. Or, at least, those she had fought with were in the wrong and she had thrown in with that, which made her culpable by extension.

Not a word had been shared between her, Mini, or Robert7 as they made their way to where the mayor had told her someone with medical expertise could treat him. And as much as she wanted to help and make sure he was safe and recovering, the images of the pit constantly returned. Thankfully, they located the medics, who removed the man from her back and took him into one of the makeshift canvas structures.

The stark and vivid images were the kind that made her lean over and throw up the remains of her last meal, thankfully into the mud outside the medical tents and not her cockpit. She worried that someone might try to hurt Robert7 while she was away, but her fears proved groundless. They fitted a splint to his injured leg and applied better bandaging to the cuts and scrapes.

The nervous and sometimes downright hostile looks the man received from the other people in the tent made her remove him as soon as the medical team completed their treatment. While she couldn't expect them to see Robert7 in a friendly light, she had to remind herself that not all of them would react by marching him to a pit and shooting him.

They left the tents and paused for a moment. Jessica13 had no idea where she could possibly take him and know he would be safe. Mini didn't have any suggestions either, and her prisoner seemed lost and confused. All she knew was that she wouldn't turn him over to be shot and thrown in a ditch like the others. She couldn't stand even the thought of that.

Eventually, though, she needed to ask the question she had dreaded from the moment when they had left the medical post.

"Where to now?"

Robert7 looked around, unsure of how to answer.

Mini appeared to have a couple of ideas, at least from the sudden spike in his core temperature. "Do you think you could return to work and keep Robert7 employed at your side to help clear debris from the town?"

"With an injured leg? How the hell is he supposed to recover?"

"His recovery time could be hampered far worse should he be killed."

"Now? You think now is the time to be facetious?"

"I think the term is 'accurate.'"

"Maybe we should have a chat to Mayor Jones about it."

"That might be unwise, given that those militia members likely acted under his orders. Remember how he went to lead them?"

"Even so, we could talk to him to confirm that we have all the facts and make sure he was involved. If that is the case, maybe we can convince him that killing all the prisoners is a bad idea. We could point out that they could help us with the work, make up for their actions and, in the end, earn the goodwill of the people they injured. Something like that."

"Do you really believe it is possible?"

"I have to…"

Her voice trailed off. An odd sound issued from the center of town, where most of the living areas had been set up. It sounded very much like what came from a machine that was overworked and under-oiled—the kind of roar she had learned to dread.

Mini initiated a quick scan. "In case you are wondering—"

"I am."

"The sounds are human in origin. A great many humans, their voices raised in what I have learned to interpret as anger and violence."

That brought no encouragement or assurance. Jessica13 shook her head as she strode deeper into the town and kept Robert7 close to her. He was in better shape and was able to maintain his perch on the magnetic clamp on her back as they hurried forward.

"What the…fuck?"

His voice hauled her to an immediate halt. The signs around them indicated that the shouting had at least started in the area they were in. It was a small square between the residential buildings that had been partially damaged in the battle. At this point, it looked mostly abandoned, but the state of destruction was recent. Where small stalls and selling points for vendors once stood, piles of sticks and tarp were all that remained. The structures had been demolished, torn apart, and set on fire, although the flames hadn't lasted for very long.

"A mob," Robert7 muttered.

"What was that?"

"It would appear that a mob was formed," Mini explained. "They destroyed the stalls in this square and attacked the vendors themselves."

"What happened to the people?"

Mini didn't answer, and she thought about it for a few moments before she realized that his silence probably meant the answer was obvious. She fought her growing reluctance and forced herself to look at the partially damaged buildings around them. While part of her expected the worst, she still wasn't fully prepared for the reality

Four bodies hung from ropes around their necks. Like macabre necklaces, wooden plaques with rough words carved into them were strung around their necks to rest on their chests.

Her hand trembled as she zoomed in a little to see what was written on them as the dead vendors were almost twenty feet off the ground.

One of them read *informer*. Two others had *traitor* carved deeply into the wood, and the last looked like they spelled out *collaborator*.

It wasn't surprising that the stalls had been emptied of all the supplies the vendors had been selling. A couple of people still sifted through the remains of the structures, trying to find something useful. They didn't look even vaguely bothered by the bodies that were suspended over the square.

In fact, Jessica13 walking around in her Minato caught their attention more than the dead did—either her or the man on her back. The looks were a little more hostile than they had been at the medical tents. A couple of them muttered something she couldn't hear, although she could guess that it wasn't good.

None of them was armed, however, and no one appeared

to have anything that might be used as a weapon. While they didn't appear to be in the mood to challenge one of the Knights Mechanica in a mech, they weren't happy to see the man there. If she left him alone for so much as a second, they would happily tear him to pieces and string him up like the apparent traitors, informers, and collaborators.

That wouldn't happen, though, and not only because she had no intention to leave him. The looters seemed to lose interest and began to move away from the square, drawn by an unmistakable roar that confirmed the presence of the mob close by. More people were likely being strung up for helping the FEMA invaders, or maybe for helping Athena or her cretins, and it didn't sound like the townsfolk went about it pleasantly.

Jessica13 didn't want to get involved, but if she had a propensity for gambling, she would have to guess that Mayor Jones was somewhere in or near the mob.

If he wasn't leading them in their frenzy, she reminded herself. That was always possible.

She could ask Mini to run the numbers for her, but that would merely delay the inevitable. If she wanted to put a stop to all this or at least get an idea of what they tried to accomplish, she needed to chat to the mayor before things escalated and became more serious than they already were.

"I suppose I should ask you why we are moving closer to the noise," Mini commented as she strode forward.

"We need to talk to Mayor Jones, and that's likely where he'll be."

"You do know that they will not take you protecting Robert7 lightly? The chances are, with the numbers that remain, they would be able to overwhelm you—and that's assuming they don't have a handful of mechs with them."

"If they do become violent, we could always run away. Robert7 is able to hold on better, so we would at least be able to get away quickly enough."

"I do hope you are right."

"It's not like an AI to hope for anything. Aren't you supposed to give me all the numbers that support the fact that this is a terrible idea?"

"I could, but would that change your mind?"

"No."

"And would it gain us anything?"

"Probably not."

"And we do need to speak to the mayor, as you said. Which means that all the numbers I could provide in an attempt dissuade you would merely be a waste of my core processing power when all it should do is find us ways to escape a potentially lethal situation."

He wasn't wrong and she wasn't about to question it as they continued to approach the growing din that represented the mob of Auburnites who gathered in the center of town.

The militia was present, and they appeared to escort another group toward the stockade. The prisoners mostly included surviving FEMA pilots and raiders, but what looked like a few townsfolk were swept along with the others.

Six men and women were dragged along by their guards and seemed to have taken a beating before they were captured by the militia. Those people who followed yelled insults and as Jessica13 drew closer, she realized that similar plaques hung around the prisoners' necks. These once again denoted traitors, informers, collaborators, or other ways in which they had apparently helped Athena's men while they were still in control of the town.

She could understand the Auburnites' need to vent their

frustration. They were in a shitty situation and it was easy to pick it up and blame it all on someone, but this was taking it too far.

Someone in the mob found one of the kitchen's refuse bins —the kind usually saved to be added to the fields as fertilizer —and distributed the contents among the others. Before long, the crowd hurled the garbage at the prisoners. When that ran out, one of them picked up a rock.

Jessica13 couldn't help but wince when the rock struck one of the men in the stomach. He shouted in pain and doubled over. A second caught him in the head and he fell, bleeding from where it had opened a gash in his scalp.

The militia didn't bother to try to help him to his feet. They stepped around him, and the mob snatched him up, slipped a noose around his neck, and hauled the unconscious or dead man into the branches of a nearby tree.

His plaque read *collaborator*.

"What's happening?" she asked in a strangled tone. She'd never seen anything like this. The people of Auburn, who had seemed so peaceful and hard-working a few hours before, were in a frenzy that made her feel unsafe, even inside her mech. She could only imagine how Robert7 felt with no protection and nothing between him and the crowd.

They finally noticed her arrival, and while none wanted to engage the mech piloted by one of the now-famed Knights Mechanica, there was no shortage of hateful looks directed at the man on her back. She didn't know what to say or do, having seen what they were more than willing to do to one of their own.

No more rocks were thrown and there wasn't any more refuse to fling either, but the full attention of the people began to settle on her, especially when the prisoners were herded into the quickly filling stockade.

Mayor Jones was nowhere to be seen.

"Why are they locked up and not this one?"

Jessica13 couldn't see who said that, but the crowd seemed generally in agreement. Some held ropes up and demanded to have Robert7 strung up like the rest, and the militia was quick to approach. It seemed pathetically ironic that Jessica13 and Robert7 were essentially back where they'd started. She couldn't recognize any of those she had encountered earlier and who had executed their prisoners, but that wasn't saying much. It seemed reasonable to assume that this group would behave no differently.

At a guess, she would have said that any one of them was responsible for the executions.

"Get him down and let him be tried like the fucking rest!"

The mob persisted with the demand, and more began to take up the chant. It seemed most of them wanted to kill the man, although none appeared to have the courage to advance on Jessica13 yet. No mechs were present, and no one wanted to try their hand against one of the Knights Mechanica.

Except for the militia, possibly, and even they appeared a little hesitant to approach her. The man at the front shoved a couple of the townsfolk aside and snatched a rope from the hands of another before he turned to her.

"You have to surrender him to us," he shouted in an attempt to be heard over the yells of the crowd behind him. "He must be locked up like the rest or he will be torn to pieces."

Maybe the militia didn't approve of the way that the mob handled their own version of justice, although she couldn't banish the memory of how they'd stepped over an unconscious man. Not only that, but they'd also left him to be strung up by the Auburnites and made no effort to intervene.

She studied them and realized that they looked tired and even exhausted. Certainly, they weren't in the mood to have to deal with her and the other people at the same time.

"I can't," Jessica13 said and took a step back.

She regretted it instantly. Maybe they saw it as a sign of weakness or merely didn't like her to defend one of the FEMA pilots, but the crowd surged forward.

Mini had already disengaged the grappler gun from its dart, ready to repulse anyone who tried to attack them.

"This man needs to be held with the others," the militia leader yelled and tried to gain control of the situation once more.

Even so, Jessica13 couldn't agree to simply hand Robert7 over. The chances were that he would be executed like the others. She trusted the Minato to protect him more than a stockade.

She was about to say as much when she noticed that the weight on the magnetic clamp on her back had disappeared. Robert7 didn't move quickly but with the help of a makeshift crutch, he managed to climb off her back and moved out in front of her.

"What are you doing?" she demanded and took a step forward. Her first instinct was to protect him as some of the folk behind the militia began to gather rocks again.

He looked at her and her gut twisted. His nostrils flared and his wide eyes told her that he was terrified but still, he stood his ground.

"I can't let you or Mini put yourselves into any more danger on my account," he said, his voice soft. It quivered like he tried to convince himself that he was doing the right thing.

She didn't think the FEMA pilots qualified as the best people, all in all, but they certainly didn't have cowards in their ranks. Robert7 wasn't one, at least. He was scared, that much was plain, and she wondered if he regretted his actions when the militia grasped him by the arms.

"Thank you for keeping me safe!" he called to her and his voice trembled a little as he was dragged away. The militia pushed at the townsfolk to clear a path for him through the mob.

No rocks were thrown, although a few spat on him as he passed. Finally, he was shoved inside the stockade and the makeshift gate closed behind him.

The crowd's yells turned to mumbles. Maybe their thirst for murder and vengeance had abated, or maybe they understood that there would be another time and another place.

Their reasons seemed irrelevant and they drifted away to their improvised homes or perhaps to work. A few threw dirty looks at her and shouted something she couldn't quite pick up, but the rest appeared more than willing to simply leave.

Jessica13 vehemently agreed. Nausea churned in her stomach again, and when she released the controls of the mech, Mini immediately picked them up and eased them into a steady pace.

"What should I do?" she whimpered, put her hands over her face, and felt hot tears streaming down her cheeks.

He didn't answer immediately but pulled the Minato to a halt once they were a safe distance from the scene.

"Maybe you can introduce a little goodness, sanity, and brotherhood to the mix."

CHAPTER FIFTEEN

Night began to fall and cast long shadows across the sweep of grassland around them. The uneven terrain was enough to cover their movements, for the most part, but that would change when they approached the mesa.

Still, this was close enough. Hammerhand didn't like to step into the open like this. Charging into battle while shouting for attention seemed pointless, like empty bravado that would get people killed unnecessarily.

In this case, however, they needed to capture the attention of the men defending the stronghold and make them come down for a fight It was imperative to draw as many of them as they could away from their defensive positions.

As much as he disliked the idea, the first order of business was to attack those same defensive positions while they shouted for attention.

"I will fucking regret this."

No comms were allowed, at least not until the fighting started, but he could only imagine Tinker commenting as to why Hammerhand should already regret their decision.

The Knights were positioned behind him together with a group of the Auburn pilots who had volunteered for the mission. So many of them had done so that there weren't enough working mechs available to outfit them all.

While the numbers had surprised him, it was understandable, of course. They wanted to avenge themselves on those who had oppressed them for years. Possibly even decades, he reminded himself, given how long the FEMA city had been in place and had taken advantage of the people living in the surrounding areas.

The sky above was painted by a bright red streak of dying sunlight that stretched beyond the tall grass. The hillocks and even slight rises lengthened their shadows as the flow faded and bled into the first hint of twilight.

Sunset. It was time.

And about fucking time too.

Hammerhand welcomed the familiar sensation of adrenaline spiking in his body as he took the controls of the mech and guided it slowly out of a ravine. The defile had been carefully chosen because it was the last one between them and the mesa. This would be the point they would have to fall back to if things went wrong, which was why a handful of Sherlocks would remain there with their rifles at the ready to hold the position.

All the others would make the charge and do so as loudly as they could.

The cooling vents popped out of the Excalibur as he began the ascent. Climbing wasn't the massive mech's strongest point so cooling it was necessary, but it also made it look like a cloud rose from their position that would draw the focus of those watching from above and provide quite a show as they emerged in numbers, ready for a fight.

He reached the top and took a moment to steady the mech before he continued. A couple of assault mechs flanked him, and Tinker moved in behind, ready to support them if it was needed.

Cora, who piloted their Raptor, advanced as well but remained to the rear. She would provide cover fire if things got messy during the retreat.

The remainder of his group had already begun to surge forward when Hammerhand raised his weapon and brought it down slowly to point at the defensive positions held at the base of the mesa.

"And it came to pass, at the end of their days, that the hammer of the Lord smote them from their peak and cast them asunder to be scattered by the winds so that none would stand before them!"

The massive speakers vibrated the entire mech and carried his voice well across the open plains toward the concrete barriers that had been set up to stop any attacking mechs. As his hammer pointed toward it, the first volley of rockets from Cora's Raptor streaked away and left plumes of white smoke in their wake.

Alarms were immediately raised at the top of the mesa. Sightlines were established and mechs moved toward the edge. That was all they needed.

The defensive barriers were struck by the rockets, exploded, and were effectively shredded in three different sections of the perimeter, which gave the Knights three clear routes of attack while Cora prepared to set the Raptor up in position.

She knew what to do from that point forward. Coordinating the inevitable retreat would be their only chance to survive this.

Hammerhand pushed the Excalibur to increase speed with

every step. Something as massive as his mech couldn't really run in the strictest sense, but the long strides were enough to make it move faster than most of those around him.

A couple of his group fell as the incoming rounds and rockets from the defense at the top of the mesa impacted them. The alarm continued to sound and more enemy mechs appeared to join the defensive formation at the top, and their firepower increased. They realized that the Knights had cleared paths through the barriers and focused their attack on those three entrances.

The sheer volume of fire was difficult to contend with. More mechs took damage and used the comms to call the support mechs for on-the-go repairs as they continued to press forward toward the mesa.

They hadn't expected it to be an easy fight, but Hammerhand had at least hoped they could reach the base without taking casualties. The defenders were quick to respond to the threat, annoyingly enough.

The air was thick with bullets and he raised his shield to give his people as much cover as he could while still allowing them to advance. Not all the Knights and townsfolk could crowd behind the thick blue layer of film, but the brilliance of it drew fire from all angles.

His HUD alerted him that the generator for it had begun to heat faster than usual and spiked well above the acceptable parameters.

Of course, those parameters had been tested in pristine conditions and usually only took fire from one source.

Still, it would be best to not burn it out. He stopped when he reached one of the sections of obstacles that hadn't been destroyed and dropped his shield. In that moment, the mechs behind him opened fire in a solid volley and tried to reach the mechs above them as they continued their advance. They didn't appear to do much damage but it was enough to make the defenders back away from the edge, which gave them a small reprieve from the barrage.

It was a start. Hammerhand led a group through the central path and waited for the enemy to resume their fire again before he raised his shield. He held it above him now to deflect a rain of bullets and explosives as they advanced toward the steps.

The cutoff from the top of the mesa was sharp, which meant they would have some cover from the fire when they were close to the base. As long as they hugged the towering rock, things would be easier. Not much, obviously, but every little help counted.

The Knights were organized enough to know this and sure enough, as they moved in closer, the shooting diminished. Hammerhand moved first and held his shield up to block any rounds that might be fired at them.

A few of the defending Raptors aimed their launchers over the edge and began to fire straight down, but they did so almost completely blindly.

"Keep moving!" he roared at his men and guided them successfully to the first step.

When they reached the second, he looked up and scowled when he realized that not all the defenses were at the top of the mesa. Scaffolds were visible at the edge, where a group of Quadrupeds held position. They lacked the height advantage of those above but their heavy armor would make up for that.

And unlike the higher defenders, these had a clear firing line on the advancing Knights.

"Shit," he muttered. "Hold the fucking advance!"

Either some hadn't heard him or the townsfolk wouldn't

be dissuaded from their charge, even though the artillery rounds pounded into the ground around them. A few found their targets with direct strikes, and all that was left were smoking craters with scattered chunks of metal.

The shield came up and blocked a handful of the shots, which immediately triggered alarms in the Excalibur and he was forced to take a step back for balance.

It had been fun while it lasted.

He opened a comm channel to the other Knights and rebels in his group. "Pull back! Fall back, you motherfuckers!"

They had all waited for the order, and although they seemed as reluctant to follow it as he was, they obeyed without delay. It was a wise decision with literal hell now unleashed on them in a lethal barrage.

Hammerhand was the last to drop from the step and gave the FEMA pilots something to shoot at. The armor took a beating in a handful of non-vital areas but he'd been lucky thus far. There was no telling when they would hit something critical, however, and he brought the shield up as soon as the heating vents stopped screaming bloody murder at him.

Overall, they had made it farther than he had thought they would but not as far in as he'd hoped. As futile as the entire assault was, he hadn't held out much hope that they would manage to reach the top. Still, the closer they got, the more likely it would have been that those above would elect to abandon the high ground to attack.

The cost, of course, was almost too heavy. He counted two of his Knights being dragged out of the fight by support mechs and another whose mech was being opened to help the pilot get clear. Six of the Auburn pilots had gone down as well, and three had to be helped to the ravine.

"Cora, tell me you have some targets."

"They're still too high."

Hammerhand turned and shifted his shield to deflect the continuous fusillade that followed their retreat. The mech continued to move backward and still at a good enough speed to keep pace with his men. The sensors would tell him if they would be tripped by anything.

The shadows had grown longer and the last traces of daylight had almost completely disappeared from the sky. The smoke had already begun to fill the area and made it even more difficult to see anything.

Tinker opened a commlink with him.

"Hammerhand, what's the situation at the front?"

His gaze turned toward the mesa, where weapons continued to flare as they maintained their fire from their secure position at the top.

"I wish I could say there was good news."

"Shit. If they don't come down from the fucking top there, all this crap will have been for nothing."

"And exactly what the fuck do you want me to do about it?"

"Something! Anything! We need them out of position."

"Fuck!"

Hammerhand held his shield for as long as he could manage it but already felt the heat from the generator begin to tell on the rest of the Excalibur's mechanisms.

They wouldn't go back and attack the mesa because they simply didn't have the numbers for it. But the initial attack hadn't drawn anyone down and Tinker was right. It all had been for naught.

He stared balefully at the stronghold while he maintained his backward motion and still tried to give his men cover. The enemy showed no inclination to halt or even slow their ongoing barrage.

"Fuck!" he said again, turned the Excalibur, and allowed it to increase speed to keep up with the other Knights as they retreated.

CHAPTER SIXTEEN

Hammerhand ran a quick scan of the area surrounding them. He ran across the open ground and without being able to use his shield, it left him feeling vulnerable. Still, he reminded himself, he needed to show that they were vulnerable in their rout, which would entice their enemies to abandon the high ground and give chase.

It didn't look good. He needed to think of something quickly or accept that the whole feint had been run for nothing.

Tinker organized the troops and kept them together and in an organized fake retreat. Hammerhand connected to Cora. They had never really trained to look like a disorganized mess while still acting in a coordinated and disciplined fashion, but he didn't know how they could do it any better.

"Cora, please tell me you have good news!" he shouted into the comms.

The pilot of their Raptor didn't respond immediately, which was all the response he needed. When she did, her words were not what he wanted to hear.

"I could move closer and into range—"

"Negative! You'll be in their range long before they're in yours. Hold your position."

And pray, he almost felt like adding. If there was ever a time to call on help from on high, this was it.

Suddenly, the scans displayed movement from behind them. Not on the steps, it seemed, but something that appeared to be airborne.

He turned, not sure what he was looking at in the growing darkness and smoke that now obscured most of the open area. His gaze drifted from the sky to the mesa itself and while he couldn't reconcile what his scans had shown with what he now saw, there wasn't much in the world that moved quite like the Quadruped mechs. They slowly descended the steps from where they had been positioned on the scaffold.

It was a start, at least. There were five of them and they were already difficult to coordinate, but they made good time given their size, range of movement, and what they had to negotiate. When they reached the third step from the ground, a handful of mechs that had been on the back of the Quadruped at the front caught his attention.

The design was more than familiar. Balthazars were hard to miss with those rockets on their backs, but they lacked the customizations that many of the raider mechs had. He wasn't surprised by that, of course, but it was still odd to see.

The rockets flared, and after a few seconds to stabilize, they became airborne and careened away from the mesa toward the knights. They also increased speed.

"I have targets!" Cora announced and sounded excited to finally have something to shoot at.

"Hold your fire. Wait until those Quadrupeds enter your range and fire on them."

"Roger that."

Her disappointment was palpable, but there wasn't much to be done about that. They needed to make it still look like they were running away.

The Balthazars moved quickly and illuminated the area around them while Hammerhand continued to run. They were almost three-quarters of the way toward him when he finally turned again.

His initial reaction to activate his shield proved pointless when he saw they carried melee weapons. He turned it off immediately as a couple landed in front of him while the others pursued the retreating knights.

The two in front of him backed away when he activated his hammer, but he adjusted his weapon and tried to catch one of those that soared over him. It wasn't a clean strike, but it catapulted away from its flight pattern and landed solidly.

"Targets in range," Cora shouted.

"Fire when ready," Hammerhand replied and waited while she acquired her targets among the Quadrupeds as they reached the bottom step.

The Raptor fired a volley that trailed plumes of white smoke behind and impacted precisely with the points she'd defined. The mechs themselves weren't the target, of course, but the limbs. When the first two had all their limbs blown at the knee, the others were forced into a halt.

They were unable to move in either direction and instantly became sitting targets for additional attacks.

The people at the top realized this too and immediately poured from the top of the mesa.

Hammerhand's hint of elation that their feint had worked, if somewhat delayed, was cut short when the Balthazars that had chosen to face him began to press their assault. They were quicker than his Excalibur, and the vibroswords they carried were more than enough to cut into vital functions on his mech.

More importantly, their airborne comrades rapidly closed on the Knights.

"Knights, cease the retreat and regroup! We have a fight on our hands."

They did as they were told. The Balthazars were no surprise, but two of their group narrowly avoided being cut down almost immediately when the flying mechs drove into their line.

Windchime would show them a proper greeting.

"Tinker, get them formed up!" Hammerhand called over the comms, brought his Hammer about, and activated the rocket.

He caught one of the Balthazars and clipped it in the side with enough force to crush most of the armor and damage the fuel tanks. The other backed away quickly as the fuel caught fire, which surged into the tank.

The explosion was so powerful that he could feel it in his bones, and he backed away slowly as well. Beyond the blaze, his gaze settled on the full numbers of those who had been at the top of the mesa and now raced to join the attack.

Most of the FEMA troops had already reached the ground and pressed hard to try to reach the combat area. It was about time the Prophet appeared as well. What the hell was he waiting for?

"Fucking shit."

With things as they were, Hammerhand had to trust that Windchime would be able to hold the Balthazars away from their front line long enough for the Prophet to get his shit together. While they waited, he would have to help the front line to slow the newcomers as best he could.

"I've prayed for a day in which there would be no end of enemies to fight!" he roared at them and raised his shield once the approaching defenders opened fire.

Tinker moved beside him, plugged in, and ran a rapid check to make sure no on-the-spot repairs were needed before he withdrew again. Hammerhand turned and brandished his shield.

The defenders would think they had the Knights bogged down in combat and that soon, the superior numbers would bring the victory. If the Prophet held his charge for too much longer, they would be right.

The Knights' leader couldn't help a twinge of pride in his team. Tactical plans made far from the field of battle tended to go out the cockpit in the moment when the fighting started. It was to be expected, but that didn't mean the troop didn't have the coordination to continue to fight when they needed to and to cover each other and give their enemies hell at the same time.

He couldn't have coordinated it better himself, and because he was able to trust his men, he was able to focus on the part of the battle that required his attention.

His shield began to overheat and he put up the notification on the HUD of the mechs that took cover behind it so they'd know the moment when they would have targets to shoot at.

In the second when the shield fell, the volley decimated the front lines, which mostly consisted of Cinders trying to sneak in to where they would have the advantage. They had expected it to drop eventually, but they were too far out of their preferred range and he watched a number of them erupt in flames when their napalm tanks were pierced and ignited.

"Where the fuck are they?"

He took care not to air his doubts on the comms, but as every second ticked past, he began to suspect more and more that they were on their own.

They would have to call a full retreat. It would mean guiding those who would follow into the ravine and he'd have to break through the Balthazars at their backs, but a retreat at this point would save more lives than it cost.

Assuming, of course, that nothing went to shit when they withdrew.

He growled with annoyance before he keyed the comms. "Tinker, bring us—"

His words were cut off by the loud horns that broke through the evening air and rose well above the noise of furious combat.

Hammerhand knew the sound and a wave of relief washed over him when the Prophet's Desert Warriors began to rush in from the flanks and circled to try to strike at the rear of the defending mechs' line.

"And it's about fucking time," he muttered, his comms inactive for a moment.

Tinker pinged him and brought him online again. "What were you going to say before?"

"Never mind that. Get us moving forward again!"

CHAPTER SEVENTEEN

There was no logical way to explain the delay. The FEMA mechs had been out in the open for a while before the Prophet decided to bring his mechs into the fight.

But now was not the time to determine who was to blame or why the delays had happened. The FEMA mechs attempted to pull back, not quite sure what was happening but very sure that something had gone wrong.

The Knights had drawn them out and they'd thrown their full contingent of assault and support mechs into an assault designed like a pincer around the Knights and rebels, but all that had gone wrong. They were now flanked and their Quadrupeds and artillery mechs were exposed and under attack by the new force that had come seemingly out of nowhere.

In all their efforts to repulse the potential invaders, they had neglected the possibility that they might be drawn into a trap themselves. They now attempted to withdraw and connect with their rearguard to protect them, but it soon became clear that it wasn't enough. The Prophet's mechs and vehicles already swarmed onto the Guardians that attempted to drive them back and their combined onslaught of both bullets and blades cut the mechs down as quickly as possible.

Hammerhand raised his weapon and gestured forward with it, a clear sign to drive the Knights and rebels forward to take advantage of the moment of desperation and confusion of their enemies. They did not intend to wait or rest on their laurels.

The Knights wanted to engage the enemy again, especially now that they were in a situation to win.

The desert fighters made quick work of the artillery and rocket mechs that desperately tried to pull back to the steps of the mesa. There was no cover for the defenders as their assault mechs faced a powerful attack from the Knights, a second prong that was spearheaded by Hammerhand. His shield was up to allow him to close the distance between the two groups, but once he was in close, they wouldn't be let off so easily.

He rushed into their lines and used the shield to push them back. Heat flared from the generator and alarms warned him urgently that it was close to overheating from the pressure of the five or six mechs he shoved against.

In that moment, he let it drop. They fell forward when the wall they had pushed against disappeared, and the hammer swung. The crunch when the mechs were crushed by the rocket-powered weapon was more satisfying than Hammerhand would ever openly admit.

The battle had finally swung their way. It would have been more difficult if they had tried to fight while scaling the steps or even if they had tried to sneak to the top under the cover of night, but it had been an enormous risk. Their chosen tactic had involved complete reliance on the defensive mechs to break their position and try to pursue.

It had been a gamble and one they had almost lost, but it had ultimately paid off. Hammerhand didn't intend to deny that, but he also acknowledged that the situation might have cost them a little too much.

Not only that but the fact that the price had been paid by the lives of rebels from Auburn and damage inflicted on his men rather than shared with the Prophet's Desert Warriors stung considerably. He recognized the cold anger within and directed it to fuel his efforts to annihilate the rest of the mechs who continued to resist them.

Those who remained saw that they were caught between a literal hammer and a metaphorical anvil. The desert fighters finished dealing with the Quadrupeds and artillery mechs and began to circle to finish the others.

The defensive troops didn't like the idea of fighting from that position and one by one, they stepped away from the fighting and began to drop their weapons and hold their hands up in the universal sign that they had given up and now surrendered.

A few still fell as Knights, rebels, and desert fighters alike were a little slow to react to their surrender or maybe too high on the adrenaline of the battle to call it. Hammerhand immediately pinged those he could on the comms and allowed his voice to be carried into the field over the din of battle.

"Lay your weapons down and you will be spared. Continue to fight and you will be destroyed. Make your choice now and be prepared to live with it!"

It was meant for his allies as well as the defeated defenders, and all groups were quick to respond. The FEMA company survivors who hadn't dropped their weapons did so almost immediately, while the Knights, rebels, and desert fighters alike responded by restraining their assault for the moment.

There was something almost unnatural about holding back like this. He'd dealt with raiders for years and that had culminated in the engagement with Athena's zealots, and his instincts were honed to finish the fight himself in violent fashion. There had been times when a few of their enemies had promised surrender before, but it had almost inevitably ended with their attempt to stab him in the back. As a result, he'd reached the point where he learned to not provide them with the opportunity to do so.

But in this case, they fought not only for the victories on the battlefield but those off it as well, and that would be earned by showing that they weren't the bloodthirsty raiders who had likely had been a problem in this area for so many years. They were different, looked for a peaceful solution, and were there to help to achieve that.

Hammerhand lowered his weapon and let the head rest near his feet while Tinker ran a hasty headcount. It had been a victory but at one hell of a cost. He wasn't sure he was willing to commit to these kinds of losses in the future. Aside from the high regard in which he held every member of his team, this kind of combat would mean the end of the Knights Mechanica as a whole. Only their skill, determination, and experience had saved them from fatalities, but it had come horrifyingly close to a massacre.

For now, however, they were committed. They had a plan and damned if he would be the one to pull away from it. Even so, he intended to demand that the Prophet provide some answers while they collected themselves. It was an easy climb to the mesa using the steps provided. There might be a couple of mechs waiting for them as a last line of defense, but the bulk of the fighting was finished for the night.

For now, anyway.

CHAPTER EIGHTEEN

Regrouping after the battle proved more challenging than Hammerhand had anticipated. Over the past few days, he had found that they were increasingly involved in the complicated kind of battle and with every moment, it became more difficult to decide what the right move was.

In this case, there was prolonged discussion over what should be done with the defenders who had surrendered. There was no way they could simply kill their prisoners outright but leaving them in their mechs was also not an option. Even without weapons, they were too much of a threat.

Leaving the mechs behind was clearly not the way to go either since virtually anyone could stroll in and take them for themselves. While that might not be a problem if such strangers proved to have integrity and could be prevailed upon to support them, but the chances of that were nothing short of miraculous. The most likely scenario was the type of dissolute raiders the Knights spent most of their time eliminating.

It was eventually decided that some of the Prophet's men would remain on the ground. These were mostly the dune buggies and smaller mechs that would have trouble climbing the mesa anyway, and it made sense to leave them to guard their rear and secure the prisoners as well.

Hammerhand moved to the front of their line and climbed the first few steps of the stairway slowly. A moment later, he was joined by the Prophet, who piloted his altered Argonaut.

"It would seem that your plan was the right one, my friend," the man stated. "I cannot say I am surprised, of course, as I expected that your acumen when it comes to battle strategies is not to be underestimated. I am glad to have been able to fight alongside you."

He didn't quite know how to respond to that. Of course, it had been a decent enough tactical call, but it hadn't only been made by him and it sure as hell would have been much better if his counterpart hadn't held his people back for as long as he had. It made no difference that those who had died weren't Knights. They were allies and their losses couldn't be easily replaced.

But the Prophet wasn't finished speaking and had merely paused as they began to scale the next step.

"Of course, I will note that your losses were harsher than expected. Indeed, they were tragic, and I would not wish a repeat of them. Your Knights and the townsfolk fought valiantly but were forced into a less than desirable position, I think, by the need to draw their numbers out fully."

"It would have been an improvement if your men had been able to move into position on time," Hammerhand replied. His mood was still a little foul over the result of the battle, despite the victory. "We were forced to engage them out in the open when outnumbered while we waited for your men to sweep in to deliver the final assault."

"Indeed, and I am aware of the delay. However, the necessity to cut them off completely from the mesa was paramount and I could not engage my forces until then. Of course, your men's bravery was something for mine to envy and we would prefer to be at the front lines and take the most dangerous positions like yours did when the time comes for us to engage our enemies again. I feel as though this will happen soon, so they will have a chance to prove themselves as your men did."

Once again, he was unsure how he should correctly reply to that. Bravery wasn't something he considered enviable. It was more of a requirement that came with being a member of the Knights Mechanica, but it was meant to be tempered with wisdom. From his perspective, it was wise to not force themselves into positions where their bravery would end with their unnecessary deaths.

But maybe the people from the desert didn't see things in quite the same way. Their culture was different and so were their ideals. Maybe sacrificing themselves for a good cause and being seen as brave when their sacrifice was witnessed was something that was considered desirable.

Before Hammerhand could speak, he saw Tinker push his mech a little faster to be able to catch up with the two leaders. If he knew the man at all, he knew he was all kinds of pissed and they would both hear an earful.

Hammerhand steeled himself for what he could only call an assault.

"Oy, the both of you—slow the fuck down, because I have something to say and by every single god out there, even those who aren't paying attention, you will hear my words."

Oh yes. Tinker was pissed and he wouldn't be restrained

from venting on the men he considered responsible for his ire.

"Tinker—"

"I'll fucking get to you in a minute, Hammerhand. You, Prophet. I don't know what your real name is, but the title has some connotations about seeing the goddamn future, so how the hell was it that your group ended up coming into the fight about ten minutes late? You're a clever bloke, so I suppose you would know how to fucking count?"

"I understand your anger, my friend, and I commiserate with it. Your losses will not be forgotten and neither will the bravery of the fallen."

"Bollocks to that. You were supposed to attack the moment their heavy mechs were out in the open. You held back on that and it cost way too many lives. Explain that."

"I regret your losses. Truly I do. Yet from my vantage point, had we joined battle sooner, we would not have been able to flank them and we would, even as I speak, still be fighting. And for a far higher price."

Tinker looked like he had no clue what to say to that either. He was still angry, though, and mumbled something under his breath like it was building into a crescendo. Hammerhand knew he needed to intercede before the man blew a gasket.

"Tinker, take a deep breath."

He was grateful that the glare he knew was on the older man's face wasn't visible.

"Shit to that," Tinker said finally.

The Prophet moved between the two men. "I would not wish to interrupt your conversation, but I have already assured Hammerhand that the next time there is a more dangerous position that cannot be avoided in the battle, my men would be more than happy to equal the valor and bravery of your Knights and allies. They would feel insulted and their courage diminished otherwise."

"Yeah, I'll take what you have to say with a large fucking pinch of salt there, mate."

"Pinch of...salt? I do not understand this."

"It means I'll believe it when I fucking see it!"

"Tinker! That's enough."

The Prophet was again quick to interrupt. "Please, he is right to raise his concerns, and it is a poor leader who does not listen to them."

Tinker seemed to feel it was enough as well, though. Either that or he'd said all he had to say on the matter. Whatever the mechanic's feelings, Hammerhand didn't want to risk potentially alienating their ally due to his anger, even if it was well-placed and well-meaning. The man felt a great deal of responsibility toward the Knights and those who fought with them and would always react to their lives being lost with anger he directed toward an attempt to make sure something like that never happened again.

Still, the Knights' leader couldn't help but feel that the Prophet had suggested he was somehow a lesser leader for wanting to have this kind of conversation in private. It was how he tended to accomplish things with Tinker anyway— away from outsiders like the Prophet.

Maybe he realized that or maybe he didn't. Either way, their new ally continued to move forward and guided the troop to the top of the mesa.

The structure of it was unlike anything Hammerhand had seen before, in person at least. He'd visited enough of the bunkers out there to know how they were generally built and set up, but this one appeared to be far more fortified. It went with the idea that they had constructed it to sustain anything up to and including an orbital bombardment, and this certainly didn't disappoint.

The entrance into the bunker was built into the structure of the mesa itself and thus managed to retain the defensive qualities of being underground while having the visual advantage over the terrain around it provided by an elevated structure. It was fairly ingenious, and Hammerhand had to wonder if they had set the groundwork up for those elements to be used or if the mesa had already been in place and they had merely taken advantage of it.

It was difficult to see into the minds of the people who had lived on their planet that long before. The culture was too different for him to be able to even try.

He did like the way it was built into the mesa, which enabled the earth to carry the first line of defense, but as they moved into the bunker building itself, it looked more like a hangar. A huge chamber greeted them, large enough for the Excalibur to stand in it with room to spare, which meant it could house the few medium-sized orbital defense ships he had seen the schematics to back in the day.

Although, he decided, it was unlikely that any production happened there. As large as it was, it was still too small to be a manufacturer of the ships it could house. It was more likely that the hangar bay had been designed for transportation purposes.

Again, he couldn't possibly assume that he knew much about what they had thought back then.

The hangar was reinforced with steel plates, which were in turn held in place by steel-reinforced concrete. He could see the plates only because the concrete had begun to erode and reveal what was beneath. It didn't seem safe, especially as the floor they walked on was covered in a light coat of the concrete dust that had fallen. If he didn't know better, he would have said the place had been abandoned for years.

Of course, he did know better. More importantly, tracks in the dust revealed where the mechs they had recently fought had strolled through not long before. In addition, the massive steel door at the back of the bay—which appeared newer than the rest of the structure—still showed the gleam of clean steel.

A quick scan revealed that the metal was almost a full meter thick and the supports around it were even more secure. It wasn't only steel either, he noted, but the scanner couldn't detect what alloy had been used to forge it.

They would definitely not be able to cut through it, though, that much was clear. Even Windchime's swords would likely dull themselves and break if they tried.

"I suppose we should have anticipated something like this," Hammerhand said, moved closer, and placed his hand on the steel door. "I'm reasonably sure that the number of explosives needed to break through a door like this would turn this whole mesa into a fucking crater."

"We could speak to my men at the bottom," the Prophet suggested. "They would have a steel-cutting lance that would find a way through. It would take considerable time, but—"

He stopped talking when something moved suddenly behind the door—or perhaps it was the door itself. Low yet unmistakable clunking issued from inside the steel and something ground to indicate motion.

Seconds ticked past as it continued while they simply stood and stared.

"Do you suppose they're reinforcing their position in there?" Tinker asked finally when no one else seemed inclined to speak.

They didn't have to wonder long. After five full minutes had passed, a loud creaking filled the hangar bay and the door swung open.

It moved outward, which forced Hammerhand to take a couple of steps back to keep it from knocking the Excalibur over. Movement was slow and it inched wider until there was enough space for a small mech to pass through.

Instead of a mech, however, an unarmored woman stepped out in a white coat and with her brown hair secured in a braid.

"My name is Erica8," she said as loudly as she could. "Welcome to the Hall of the Ecologists."

CHAPTER NINETEEN

Hammerhand reminded himself that he had seen his share of bunkers during his life. In fact, he had seen more than a few people's fair share of bunkers over his time traveling the Outside to help those who needed it so he could make a way for as many as possible to live in the peace he wanted for all.

It seemed necessary to remind himself of what was necessary and familiar—what he considered normal—because he had never seen anything quite like this.

Of course, it wasn't exactly a bunker, at least not in the traditional sense. Erica8 invited him and the Prophet down the hallway that led to a staircase and guided them past row after row of what looked like giant freezers. Within, men and women worked wrapped in thermal suits.

Eventually, they reached what looked like a mess hall but once again, it was unlike any he had ever seen. The walls were decorated with dozens of paintings of nature scenes from before the Invasion. These included waterfalls and forests, for the most part, as well as depictions of great scientists of times past, complete with small plaques with their names and contributions.

The food was similar to that of the other bunkers, although the thick green stew was a little more fragrant and the protein patties were spicier than he was used to.

"I have to admit, Erica8," the Prophet stated and examined the food closely before he took a mouthful, "of all the receptions we expected from people inside, a warm one with food and a show of fantastic artwork was not highly anticipated. Although it is, of course, appreciated."

"We're ecologists here, for the most part," she explained, brushed the hair from her face, and pushed her glasses up the bridge of her nose. "There are biologists and an assortment of other specialists, but there is one thing we share within these walls. We're all pacifists and believe that war and fighting should be a thing of the past if humanity is to reach the elevated position it once held. You know, of course, that our view is not shared by the residents of FEMA City, who would rather enforce their own ambitions on all they meet, by force if necessary. When they asked us to use our terraforming processes—including the weather blimps—for combat purposes, we refused."

"I will assume that answer was not acceptable," Hammer-hand interjected.

"Indeed, and they took it all by force despite our protests and placed us under what can only be described as a military occupation. We didn't have the weapons to resist and seeing them turn the efforts of decades of work over to barbarians like that Lady Hoot character… Well, it was sickening. Therefore, to see people from the neighboring towns fight back with the help of the famed Knights Mechanica was gratifying, even if we did see you destroy one of the blimps."

Hammerhand nodded. "I'm sorry, but it was necessary. The lightning—"

"Is why they wanted to use it as a weapon in the first place. Believe me, I understand. All we want to do is return to the work of rebuilding this world without pointless dick-measuring by means of mechs and guns."

The Prophet leaned forward. "I'm sorry, but how would one measure genitals while wearing a mech?"

She stared at him for a few seconds as if to decide whether he was joking or not. "Metaphorical dick-measuring."

"Ah."

Hammerhand stepped in to keep the conversation from deviating from the point. "We have every intention to allow your people to continue your work unimpeded, but we also aim to make sure that FEMA City will not be allowed to take control of this area again, so we must ask for your help."

Erica8 pursed her lips pensively. "Our stance on non-violence does remain, you understand?"

"Of course, and we would not ask you to step into combat at all. We merely need your help to contact the people in the gene bank west from here. Since attacking the city itself would be impossible, we wish to force them into a position where they have to negotiate for peace instead."

The woman once again flicked her short brown hair from where it had begun to creep over her eyes and pushed her glasses up the bridge of her freckled nose almost by reflex.

"We've had some contact with the Gene Bankers prior to the coup. From what we were able to understand, they held themselves as neutral while FEMA consolidated their power in the region. A few militants were granted asylum by them against the orders of the junta, though. Like us, they are their own society and would much rather be allowed to work in peace than have political ambitions get in the way of rebuilding this world. I guess you could say they are their own mandate, in a way, and they will follow it regardless of who might be in charge at one moment or another."

Hammerhand took a moment to enjoy the food again. It wasn't odd that it tasted different—most bunkers used different ingredients for their food, after all—but it wasn't common to find any that were more palatable than the others. "So, do you think they would help us to convince the city to sue for peace?"

"I doubt they would help anyone at this point, but that doesn't mean they would try to impede you. They had fewer technologies that could be weaponized, which would explain why there was no military occupation of their area, but they would want independence from the city as much as we do."

The Prophet grunted. "And here we always assumed you were all connected to the city. Satellite bunkers, as it were."

"I'm sure that is what those in charge at FEMA would want people to think. Regardless, you might want to discuss negotiating passage with them. That, at least, would be a place to start in the negotiations. Now, if you will excuse me, I have issues to tend to and scientists to calm. The show must go on, as they say."

Hammerhand wasn't sure who said that but could only nod as she stood from the table and made her way to where a small group in white coats waited for her.

"Do you trust these people?" the Prophet asked once she was out of earshot.

"Do you?"

The man paused to think for a moment. "I do not. How could I? Their pacifism will be applied equally to us, of course."

Hammerhand could only shrug in response. "In the same way that we needed to trust you, I feel you and I must trust them. There is no way the world will heal if we're not willing to put faith in those around us."

The Prophet did not look convinced. "If you insist, I can only agree, but my reservations remain."

CHAPTER TWENTY

Jessica13 took a deep breath. "I can't shake the feeling that this is a really bad idea."

"And yet you are proceeding with it," Mini pointed out.

"Well, yes, it's not like we have any other options. The only chance we have to return Auburn to some semblance of order is in the hands of Mayor Jones. The Knights have gone with Hammerhand and the Prophet, which leaves me with precious few people who would actually listen to me, especially after I tried to keep Robert7 alive."

"The data corroborates that assumption. And in appealing to the highest power in Auburn, you will address the law on how people are punished and how they are treated despite their status."

"In a town hell-bent on exacting vengeance on those who wronged them, finding a way to give people justice instead feels like the best path."

"And yet you have reservations?"

"Well, obviously. I don't know if Mayor Jones was involved in the lynching, but he certainly did nothing to stop them. It means he was either a participant or he doesn't have the power to stop them himself."

Mini paused and the processors' usage spiked for a second. "I now understand your reservations."

But it was like he said. They didn't have a choice in the matter. What could a girl in a mech do against a whole fucking town?

She opened the hatch, climbed out, and took a deep breath to calm her nerves before she walked into the small tent Jones had used as an office. He did spend most of his time out and about the town, but it was good to have a location where people could talk to him and discuss the various issues that confronted him.

Which was what she needed to find him for.

When she entered, she immediately realized that the man was in the middle of a conversation with the leader of the militia, a tall, powerfully built man with a bushy red beard and long hair.

Both stopped talking immediately when they saw her. In the silence, she could hear construction happening behind the tent. Or maybe it was behind the nearby building since she hadn't seen anything like that on the other side of the small shelter.

"Jessica13." The mayor stood from his stool as the other man pushed away from the beam he had been leaning on. "How pleasant to see you again."

The militiaman looked considerably less pleased. "Should I…"

"Why don't you check on the progress outside? I have the feeling Jessica13 wants to speak to me in private."

The militiaman made no further comment but walked out of the tent and glared at her the whole way.

Once the flap dropped again, the mayor settled onto his stool.

"Would you like to sit?"

"I think I'll stand, thanks."

"Suit yourself. How may I help you?"

Jessica13 steeled herself and gritted her teeth. She wasn't used to these kinds of conversations and certainly not while outside her mech. "I don't suppose you knew about what was happening out there with people being lynched for presumed crimes."

"I do know now. That's what Wilbur had come to report on, actually. I could not be more ashamed by the actions of my fellow Auburnites. In the rush to rebuild after we deposed our oppressors, we have failed to institute a justice system that would properly address the crimes committed during their oppression. I will admit some responsibility. My inaction was based on the hope that the townsfolk would be willing to wait. They were not and now, extreme measures must be taken for that."

She sighed. "I think that trials should be instituted—a process that would prevent people from being strung up with no way to defend themselves. And you should probably find a way to punish the guilty that doesn't involve simply killing them. As you continually tell us, there's considerable work to do. Having them work to make up for their crimes does seem more productive than outright killing them."

"That is true, but for the moment, the people of Auburn need to see a more solid form of justice in action to calm their nerves and help them settle into their work. That means examples need to be made, and those examples need to be large, loud, and to the point. Here, allow me to show you."

He stood again and gestured for her to follow him as he

moved out of the tent and circled toward the back of the building behind it. She had heard the sound of construction but had assumed it was merely people working on the buildings and the temporary living locations that were so desperately needed. They all faced an enormous challenge in order to have everyone under a roof before the weather turned foul.

Although without the balloons, there was no telling how long it would be until it rained.

When they reached the other side, Jessica13 realized how wrong her assumption had been. They weren't focused on housing at all.

The structures were elevated above the ground by a solid meter and a half, although the tallest parts extended well above that. Most of it was merely a scaffold propped on six wooden beams. Rising above it by about two and a half meters, two parallel beams supported a crossbeam over which five ropes had been slung with nooses tied at the ends.

Across from the gallows, an open area had been created to make space for a large table and three chairs.

Mayor Jones seemed proud of what he looked at. "Of course, as Auburn is still in a state of war, it precludes the use of juries. There will instead be a tribunal, which will enable crimes to be detailed and justice taken swiftly. I will sit as one of the members of the justice tribunal, together with a member of Auburn's populace and Wilbur, the head of our militia. As such, we will be able to listen to all sides of the argument, including those who are on trial, before we determine their guilt. We are not barbarians, not like Lady Hoot's raiders. We will have justice."

Jessica13 swallowed against the bile that rose in the back of her throat. She felt nauseous, not only from watching the workers putting the finishing touches on the gallows but also from hearing the pride Jones appeared to take in their work and the system he had created.

Mini had walked the Minato around with them, and she retreated slowly to the comforting confines of the mech.

"Are you all right, Jessica13?" he asked as she slipped inside.

She shook her head. "Nope. I don't think so."

CHAPTER TWENTY-ONE

A tall woman dressed in a drab, gray robe that emphasized what Hammerhand assumed was a frail frame narrowed her eyes, which were made that much bigger by the glasses she wore.

"If you'll allow me, let me see if I understand this correctly. You intend to overthrow FEMA City, as well as to depose and throw out those owl-faced jackals?"

Hammerhand inspected their surroundings. He had never been the best at diplomacy and usually helped those in need, pounded his hammer into those who required it, and moved on. Those who had the skill handled the complexities of maintaining the peace he had so carefully arranged.

As such, he wasn't sure if the woman was incredulous, sarcastic, or legitimately asking a question.

They were at the edge of a massive lake made from a crater, which measured almost ten kilometers across. A small island in the center provided the access point to the bunker below. The water was mostly still and only the surface was buffeted by the powerful winds. Every few minutes, a heat exchange tower would emerge from the clear blue surface, remain visible for a minute, and vanish into the water again, only for another to appear at a different point in the lake.

It was an incredible view and one he would have enjoyed a little more if they weren't surrounded by a group of mechs while he had elected to leave his Excalibur a few hundred meters behind them with the other Knights and the Desert Warriors who supported them. Only a handful of each group had come as a guard. The Prophet stood at his side, though, and they were surrounded by a troop of mechs painted blue, silver, and yellow.

Thankfully, only five of them stood close, while others appeared to patrol the edge of the crater lake. Even so, five would be more than enough even if they were in the dismount position.

They were called the Gene Guard, at least according to the woman they were in discussion with, who went by the name of Archivist General Nina2. It was difficult to guess what she was thinking as her face was mostly expressionless and also hidden by the large, thick round glasses. Her voice was always a monotone, so that provided no insight either.

But with them all seated at a small table sheltered by a small tent that was erected beside banners showing truce colors, it was clear that she at least intended to parlay with the Knights and Desert Warriors.

Levi Stone had made the trip to meet once word had gotten back to them that the Gene Bankers had been willing to talk. He'd insisted that he was probably in a position to make concessions in exchange for their help. There was far more to it than that but Hammerhand hadn't followed most of what he'd said.

In all honesty, there was something about the man that irked him. Maybe it was the clothes or the fact that he was somehow so clean all the time. There was no sign of grease on his hands and not even a hint of a callus. In a world where people needed to work to survive, how did he manage to have soft hands?

It wasn't something Hammerhand would ever address openly, of course, but he'd learned long before to trust his instincts, and those told him unequivocally to keep a watchful eye on Levi.

They had been joined by the commander of the Gene Guard as well, Lord Captain Gustav15. A tall, burly fellow, he had all the familiar looks of a man who spent most of his time inside a mech, including the blue, grey, and yellow flight suit and not even a hint of hair on his skin.

"Overthrow might be a little harsh a term," Levi stated and folded his hands on the table. "Attacking them outright would end poorly, so we aim to force them into an agreement by removing their ability to be maintained by the surrounding area. We are, in the end, looking for an end to their oppression of this region with as little bloodshed as possible."

"But there will be bloodshed, yes?" the lord captain rumbled while he scratched his chin idly.

"We can't rule out the possibility that FEMA City will try to break us," Hammerhand interjected before Levi could speak. "But our goal is peace and certainly not a protracted war."

"If that is the case, we have no reason to support either side in the conflict. Combat would drain our resources and all things considered, if the fighting makes it to our lakes, we are more than capable of defending ourselves. We have all we need and so, it seems, you have nothing to offer us in exchange."

"True enough, in the short-term." Levi was quick to speak and glared at Hammerhand in an unspoken warning. "But you know the numbers the city commands and the weapons. Should they suddenly decide to remove you, they will be able to do so. With great losses, true, but your losses will be far more significant. You know what they did to the Hall of Ecologists. What is to stop them from offering you similar treatment?"

Gustav15 clearly didn't like being spoken to in such a manner, and his hands clenched on the table. "The Gene Guard would withstand—"

"Enough." Nina2 interrupted him and raised a hand toward the lord captain. It was clear that he held a great deal of respect for the older woman as he immediately fell silent. "As you say, Mr. Stone, we stand to profit greatly from each other in the long-term. However, for that to come to pass, certain guarantees must be in place for the Gene Bank's security."

"Of course."

"Firstly, and above all else, all parties present will recognize and guarantee the Gene Bank's independence from FEMA City. This will include the Knights Mechanica, the Prophet and his Desert Warriors, as well as the New York Western Railroad Company."

Hammerhand couldn't help the feeling that the last was the most important.

"I am in a position to make such a guarantee," Levi replied.

"Secondly, that all ecological matters within the southwest region of what was once known as the United States of

America will be ceded to the Gene Bank and its administration for all time."

The man's lips twitched downward. It was something he had hoped not to hear, but he nodded. "On that I can place a guarantee as well."

Hammerhand nodded his agreement, but the Prophet looked more dubious.

"If you will forgive my curiosity..." He let his voice trail off until Nina2 nodded to encourage him to speak. "Thank you. I would only ask why the Gene Bank administration would consider supporting us at all. Even with these parameters in place, it would seem you and your guard would be capable of putting up your own defenses and making your own guarantees without our help."

Nina2 looked down for a moment, then at him again. "I have reasons—two of them. One is practical. Allowing you passage is not a passive act that FEMA City would forgive. To grant you passage is to cast our lot in with you. If you march at all, it must be with us. As Mr. Stone has stated, a siege would be to our disadvantage and could lead to the death of the people in my charge. This I will not tolerate."

She took a deep breath before she continued and spoke quickly in her monotone. "The second reason is more personal. I have seen what Lady Hoot and her owl-faced cretins have done while given free rein in this area. She is monstrous and dangerous, a condition that compels one to put her down as one would a rabid dog. I would add, furthermore, that whoever knew this woman before she became the animal we now know and before she was equipped with such a unique weapon has failed the world in a terrible way."

Hammerhand couldn't tell if the woman was speaking to him. Her voice and lack of any expression made it difficult to pinpoint if she knew that he and Athena had once been partners or not. The fact that she didn't look at him once while she spoke indicated that wasn't the case.

Even so, she wasn't wrong, and he couldn't help shifting uncomfortably in his seat.

CHAPTER TWENTY-TWO

Hammerhand had never been the best at waiting for people to talk their way into some sense. True, that was the aim—for people to talk instead of fight—but he wouldn't pretend it was his strength.

And he could tell that the lord captain was more of a fighter than a talker as well. The man looked as bored as he felt and yawned and stretched his arms over his head while Levi and Nina2 did most of the negotiating. Levi had brought a map they marked to show which points the Gene Guard administration would have control over. He intended to make sure there was no room for erroneous or creative interpretation in the guarantees he would give on behalf of the New York Western Railroad Company.

All in all, it seemed that Levi was only a middleman and would transfer all the information to his employers at the company. He said on more than one occasion that he had been sent and granted the power to accede to certain demands as long as they did not contrast too harshly with the ideals of his employers. From that point forward, there was little else to say other than semantics.

According to Tinker, this was how people did business back in the day. The Cities-That-Were had once used paper to enact certain deals and contracts and the like, which created all kinds of issues not only with its manufacture but also with ways to store the documents. Hammerhand could only be happy that this was a small taste of that particular way of life.

After a few hours of discussion, Levi finally stood, shook Nina2's hand, and gestured for the others to do the same. That somehow led to everyone shaking hands and Levi plastered on a greasy smile that wouldn't go away before they began the routine journey to their mechs. The Gene Guard now appeared to be a little more relaxed, and even Gustav15 seemed a good deal less incensed than when the debate had started.

Nina2 still looked her regular, immovable self and chatted to the lord captain while the other three men made their way to where their mechs waited for them.

"I would have a word with you in private if you don't mind," the Prophet said suddenly once they were out of earshot of the Gene Bankers.

Hammerhand turned, expecting the man to have spoken to Levi, but realized he had, in fact, addressed him. He indicated for the NYWRC man to walk on toward his transport, which was a dune buggy similar to what some of the Desert Warriors used but without the spikes and other accouterments.

"What do you have in mind?" he asked and raised an eyebrow at the man who strolled slowly beside him.

"How do you feel about our new allies, the Gene Bankers?"

"Let me guess, you don't trust them either?"

The Prophet shrugged but kept his hands clasped behind his back. His long black hair whipped in the winds that gusted around them. "I cannot say that I do. They are fiercely independent, yes, but I think they would likely make an alliance with the City as readily as they did with us if they achieved that which they desire."

"Why would they agree to treat with us, if that was the case?"

"Well, they hold a higher position. Should we move our troops through their territory, their two companies could find our troops quite vulnerable during that stretch of the march. They know their tunnels and are quite well-armed. Should they choose to support the FEMA City instead of us, they could prove the fatal thorn in our side. I feel the chance that they could double-cross us cannot be ignored given the consequences of what would happen should they make that choice."

Hammerhand couldn't help a deep scowl from touching his face as he thought about the Prophet's words.

"What is your mind on the matter?" his companion pressed.

"I feel like we need to trust them. And should, in this case, show that we are willing to give them the benefit of the doubt, which would go a long way toward making them trust us. They are rightfully wary of outsiders, and it is thus important for us to take that first step."

"And yet, should they prove untrustworthy—"

"When one looks for suspicion and double-dealing in others, one most often finds it. I've learned that the world is much more livable when I look for the good and honest in others instead. Of course, I would be disappointed and that can't be helped, but I'll be rewarded for that expectation as well."

The Prophet smirked. "I fear it is a dangerous path that you walk—like along the top of a sand dune. One misstep, possibly not even by you, would end in a very long fall."

Hammerhand nodded. "I know, but it's a path I've chosen to take. Honestly, if it is the wrong path to follow, I'm not sure there are any other paths out there for me. If I find there is no trust to be found in my fellow man, this isn't a world I want to live in. Truly, I would rather die than live in it, even if my end comes by my own hand."

"I understand and applaud your courage. I do pray that your faith is rewarded in this instance."

"Yeah…me too."

CHAPTER TWENTY-THREE

Jessica13 had expected the trials to get underway immediately once the gallows were in place, but it appeared that Mayor Jones preferred to take his time. Perhaps he wanted the population of Auburn to calm after the day that had preceded it.

She found a place to hunker for the night and despite feeling exhausted, sleep didn't come. All she could think about was Robert7 being called, someone putting the noose around his neck, and making him hang from it.

Maybe meeting and talking to the people she was supposed to be killing was a bad idea. It had been somewhat easier when she had simply fired at those who were hidden by mechs and they returned the shots and tried to kill her in return.

But as morning dawned, there was little she could do aside from push herself out of the improvised cot that had been set up for her. It wasn't specifically for her, of course. There were a few dozen of them set up in the tent. She was the first one up of the group and made her way to where Mini had been parked.

Even so, a hubbub issued from the center of town despite the early hour. Apparently, the trial had already started and she had to be there to study the proceedings herself.

"Damn."

"Did you get any sleep at all?" Mini asked as she climbed inside the mech.

"I tossed and turned mostly. Does that count?"

"It does not."

"Well, it doesn't look like I'll get any more, so why don't we hurry to the gallows where they want to start those trials Mayor Jones talked about?

The people grew louder as they moved closer and the crowd grew by the second. Even though their numbers increased, they showed no signs of the apparent rampage they had been on the day before. It was like they had accepted the fact that there was now a system in place to punish the people who had wronged them, although Jessica13 wasn't sure how long that would last.

What if the tribunal delivered a sentence they didn't approve of? Maybe if Jones had told the truth and they intended to give them fair trials, those few who would walk free might find themselves in less forgiving company among the other townsfolk.

After what she had seen the day before, nothing would surprise her, at this point, and she could only hope her negativity was misplaced.

Jessica13 climbed out of the mech, and while she could hear Mini take control of the Minato and follow close behind her, it was easier to slip through the crowd that had begun to form on her own. She was still smaller than most of the people gathered there, which gave her some advantage as she wriggled closer to where she could see the tribunal already seated and waiting for their first prisoner.

Cautiously, she looked around and her gaze settled on the huddle of townsfolk she recognized as having been incarcerated with the enemy pilots. The five of them weren't bound but they stood under the watchful eye of one of the militia and all seemed numb and dispirited. From what she could tell, they had been forced to watch the proceedings from as close as possible—a position that also placed them in full view of the crowd.

The previous signs around their necks had been replaced with new ones that said, *I Betrayed My Neighbors For Money.* The length of the wording made them larger than the others and also heavier, and they fumbled with them constantly as if to ease the drag around their necks.

It surprised her that they had been separated from the others, but before she could consider this further, a group of prisoners was led to the scaffold and she identified Robert7 climbing the steps. He was at the front of the line of five, while the others were put under guard and held behind the gallows, where they would await their sentencing.

She could only assume that seeing their comrades hung would be an added terror element to the trial and one that had not been accidental.

Mayor Jones was seated in the middle of the table, and to his left was Wilbur, the leader of the militia. If she had to guess, he was the one whose idea it had been to put the prisoners below the gallows.

A woman was also seated at the table and looked middle-aged, but there was something desperate about the way she looked at the prisoners that made Jessica13 a little nervous. She thought she recalled her name—Claire Jennings—and vaguely remembered being told that her children and grandchildren had been murdered by raiders. The angry, twisted expression seemed to confirm this, and her attitude engendered no encouragement. The woman was clearly bitter, and her inclusion in the tribunal could not be good for those on trial.

The city's leader finally stood and beat a wooden cup on the table in front of him to silence the crowd. "By the authority vested in me by the good people of Auburn, I bring this tribunal to order. We will begin immediately. Prisoner Robert7, please step forward."

The man did as he was told, nudged by one of the militiamen who stood behind him.

"Are there any present who would represent this man?" Wilbur asked. He looked hastily around the crowd and made no attempt to listen for any who might have agreed. "None have stepped forward to represent the prisoner, so he will represent himself."

It wasn't like anyone would have stepped forward anyway.

Mayor Jones looked at the papers in front of him. "In the case of prisoner Robert7, who is accused of the crime of conspiring to and participating in the attack on the town of Auburn, how does the prisoner plead?"

Robert7 looked around, unsure of what he had been asked.

"Innocent," he said finally to the jeers and boos of the crowd.

"Then we shall proceed. We have found evidence that you were among the invaders and you have been recognized as one of the pilots of the mechs that participated in the attack. Witnesses have stated that you are not a citizen of the town of Auburn and you were among those that participated. Do you deny any of these facts as they have been presented?"

Robert7 looked panicked and more people jeered at him. They were all anticipating and likely hoping for a quick execution.

"I... Well, I was in the attack, but—"

"The prisoner admits his guilt and part in the attack," Wilbur interrupted, unable to keep a smile from his face.

Jessica13 tasted the bile in her mouth again but this time, there was no need to get away from the scene as quickly as possible. She wanted to act and she wouldn't simply wait for the sham trial to continue. Instead, she shoved through the last line of people who were held back from the scaffold.

"What are you doing?" Mini asked from behind her.

She ignored the AI and pushed forward, shrugged off the hands of the militiaman who tried to stop her approach, and sprinted into the open area between the gallows and the tribunal table.

"When you asked whether the prisoner would be represented by anyone in the crowd, you did not wait for a reply," she shouted as loudly as her lungs would allow. "I will represent the prisoner."

The militiaman tried to catch her but stopped when Jones motioned him away.

"The selection of representation has passed," Wilbur noted with the hint of a sneer. "You will have to wait for another prisoner to be tried and represent him."

"You didn't allow time for someone to step forward," Jessica13 snapped in response, unsure of where all this bravery had come from. She wasn't about to question it now, however, as she had more important things to focus on.

Before Wilbur could say another word, Jones patted him on the shoulder. "As presiding judge over this trial, I will allow Jessica13 to represent Robert7. Do I hear a second?"

The woman beside him stared daggers at her but nodded slowly.

"Seconded," Jones said softly. "And passed. You may take your place next to the prisoner."

A few of the jeers and boos were directed at her now.

"The bunker types always stick together."

"Sympathizer!"

"Go fuck Lady Hoot if that's what you want."

She ignored them and climbed the steps to where Robert7 stood. He stared at her and looked confused.

"What are you doing?" he whispered.

"I'll let you know when I find out." Her voice was also in a whisper but gained volume when she addressed the three seated below. "If there is anything I learned from my time fighting alongside the Knights Mechanica, it is this. Any man or woman can find a way to redeem their past actions. The crime of following orders and being a soldier in the army that attacked Auburn is determined. But I have to ask, what do we gain from executing him? What does the town of Auburn stand to gain from killing him when he can instead atone for his actions and help us better than he would be able to do by hanging from a rope?"

The shouting, jeering, and booing stopped for a moment, and she wondered if her point had actually come across.

Wilbur snorted and shook his head in disbelief. Mayor Jones revealed no emotion on his features, which was contrasted sharply by the woman seated beside him. Claire had turned a deep shade of purple and she bolted out of her seat.

"I say based on those of our loved ones who suffered under the oppression of Lady Hoot and those who died deposing her. In their name, we would benefit from seeing the man hang. Fuck whatever help he claims he could offer us. He'll say anything to avoid the rope."

The crowd rumbled in agreement, and Jessica13 was surprised when Robert7 stepped forward. Maybe seeing someone stand up for him was enough to give him the courage to defend himself.

"I can help!" he shouted. "I know you're trying to fight against FEMA City, and if you want to have any chance to attack them, you will need to find a way in that bypasses the defenses. I know of a secret way inside and I will share it with you if you free me and the other FEMA City soldiers."

"What about the raiders?" Jessica13 asked in a whisper.

"What about them?" he retorted.

CHAPTER TWENTY-FOUR

All three of the judges conferred for a moment, and the people around them did not sound happy. They didn't want any conversation that didn't confirm that the prisoner would hang.

Mayor Jones stood from his seat and banged his improvised gavel on the table to silence the crowd. "I have to ask, Robert7, why would you offer us such a deal, especially as it would be considered a betrayal of your own people? Why should we trust that your information would be accurate?"

Robert7 was silent for a moment and looked like he was working up the courage to continue to speak, especially since the jeering continued from the people around the gallows. "I was not born in FEMA City. My people are from the Hall of Ecologists, a separate bunker system. FEMA City's military government put us under martial law and forcibly conscripted us to fight for them."

Wilbur was already shaking his head. Jessica13 knew that if Hammerhand had been present for this, he would have been at least willing to hear the man out. But from the look of the other two judges, she could tell they would not be moved by what he said. She clenched her jaw as Mayor Jones took his seat again and folded his arms.

"The prisoner cannot be trusted," he said and used his curt voice to silence the people who had begun to get loud again. "This could be a trick. People might stand in your position and say anything we might want to hear to avoid the rope."

"We have to give him a chance!" Jessica13 protested.

"You are too close to this," Jones retorted caustically and looked annoyed by her persistence. "You are a young woman, and he is a young man. Besides, how can we possibly trust him? He is willing to betray his own people by what he says that he will give us, and so what would keep him from betraying us when the time is right?"

Heat blossomed in her cheeks and intensified, and not only from the rising sun beating down on them. The way the people reacted to seeing Robert7 in front of them seemed to light a furnace of indignation in her. They demanded more violence despite the fact that they had been through a fight for their lives. It was as if they wanted to find a way to somehow keep the wave of violence in motion since it had ended in their favor.

She wondered how they would feel if the positions had been reversed and they were on trial for following orders in a military they didn't want to be a part of.

The heat grew steadily, and Jessica13 clenched her fists. "This is bullshit and you know it!"

Miraculously, the people quieted and ceased their renewed demands that he be hanged immediately. They looked at her, startled by her very obvious anger.

"The fighting isn't over," she continued and forced herself

to look away from Jones, Wilbur, and Claire. It seemed that even looking at them was enough to make her pissed again.

She dragged in a deep breath and glared at the crowd. "The Knights Mechanica, our desert-based allies, and fighters who hail from this very town are out there, fighting a war to keep this town free right fucking now. Do you think they would turn their noses up at an advantage that would allow them to win that fight? Or do you think they would allow their blood-lust to get in the way of victory? And do you really believe they would prefer to see every person here hang? And for what reason? Why does this man need to die? And if he dies, how many of our people will die fighting because you refuse any help he offers?"

Her gaze swept across all present, genuinely searching for an answer they might have for her. Maybe they understood the situation better than she did. Perhaps they simply knew better than to trust someone like Robert7 and so wouldn't listen to her.

But if they had a reason to refuse his help, they had better explain it. She let the question hang expectantly and from the look of shame she could see in the eyes of the people around her, she knew there was no answer. They wanted him to die—wanted all of the City's fighters to die—but they had no real reason for it aside from a desire for revenge for the death and destruction of their town.

The silence in the square was deafening and the crowd around them appeared to be subdued, but the three judges looked unaffected. Wilbur smirked, and when she looked at him, she could see him clapping sarcastically. The woman at Jones' side still looked furious, while the mayor himself showed no emotion whatsoever.

Finally, he stood and took a deep breath before he spoke.

"Justice must be served, and even if what Robert7 said is true, we still cannot let his willingness to turn against his own people stand in the way of the justice he deserves." She opened her mouth to speak again, but he held his hand up to silence her. "The moment for deliberation has approached, and the tribunal will confer and deliver our sentence in due time."

Jessica13 wanted to say more and even to stamp her feet and insist that they answer her, but she stopped herself. She couldn't ask for there to be a system of law in place only to become angry and insolent when it delivered in a way she didn't like.

Robert7 placed a hand on her shoulder. "Thank you. For everything."

She tried to smile but failed utterly and made it look more like a grimace. "I'm so sorry."

Once she'd climbed down from the scaffold, she didn't feel comfortable enough to rejoin the crowd. Even though they were subdued, there was no telling what they would attempt if she was there with them. Mini had moved the Minato to the front of the group, likely in case she needed to make a quick getaway if the crowd turned on her.

But there wasn't a single man, woman, or child among them who was willing to look her in the eye. At least that much of an impact had been made.

The decision was a quick one, and Jones banged his cup on the table again to get their attention.

"We have agreed that there will be no clemency given for information," he said, and his voice carried easily through the quiet courtyard. "Robert7, for the crimes you have committed against the city and people of Auburn, you will hang by the neck until dead."

The crowd cheered. Jessica13 wondered if it was as loudly as they could have had she not tried to fight for Robert7's life, but it didn't matter. The end result would be the same.

CHAPTER TWENTY-FIVE

"Go, go, go!"

Hammerhand gestured for the last group to enter the elevator. It was one of the older models, the kind that most bunkers had already upgraded from. The knowledge told him that these tunnels to the City hadn't been used for a generation, maybe longer.

He stepped into it once everyone else was inside. There was barely enough room for the Excalibur. It wasn't the most practical of mechs to use in the close confines of the tunnels if there was any need to fight in them. The size of the mech would be a disadvantage, and he hoped that the only combat they would see was when they were already in the town.

Still, the shield would be there to block any shooting from ahead of them, which would allow them to push forward and deliver significant damage every time he needed to drop it to cool off.

It wasn't the worst position to be in, especially since they would catch the FEMA forces on the back foot.

The elevator thudded to a halt and Hammerhand was the

first to step out. He hefted his weapon in one hand and raised the other down the fork of the tunnel they would not move down.

The Prophet wouldn't be able to see his gesture, but it was more for his own peace of mind.

"Good luck, my friend," his ally said over the comms. "I wanted to say before we go out of range in these damn tunnels that I trust you. I may not feel the same about our new allies, but my trust in you will never waver."

"You have earned my respect and my trust as well, Prophet. Now, let's finish this fight once and for all. I'll meet you on the other side."

"On the other side, my friend."

He pulled away from the fork without wasting another moment and his link with the Prophet soon garbled into static. The interference meant he wouldn't be able to stay in contact with the man who would coordinate the second prong of their assault, as Hammerhand would lead his Knights and the Auburnite rebels from the Gene Bank. The Prophet and his desert warriors would advance from the tunnels that started at the Hall of Ecologists.

Hopefully, he reminded himself but without anxiety. As anyone involved in any kind of combat could express, all plans went through the shitter when the battle started.

All he could hope for was that they could get out into the open where the Knights and the Desert Warriors would be able to fight in a position that was most beneficial to them.

Once again, the adrenaline pumped through his veins as he marched through the passages to where the rest of the Knights awaited him. It wasn't only his group, however.

"We were naive to think that peace could be sued for." Gustav15 connected through a private comm line.

"I never really believed they would go for something like that, but it was the hope that they would understand that their time of controlling this area is finished. This way, we can drive the point home and keep the bloodshed to a minimum."

"The fact that your aim is to keep the fighting to a minimum is the only reason that Nina2 is willing to work with you."

Hammerhand couldn't help a smile as the man in a blue, silver, and yellow-painted mech fell into step beside him. The other Gene Guards were waiting, already in formation and ready to march, and the Knights greeted them courteously.

His people weren't waiting for a speech. They had been in the fight with him for long enough to know what the stakes were and reminding them of it would only seem like him lording something over them. There was no point in it anymore.

He rested his weapon against his shoulder and motioned for them to move. They complied with no cheers, no excited shouts, and no war chants. They were already on the battlefield.

As they began the march, a familiar pit formed in his stomach like his body was preparing to be in combat once more. He steadied himself and made sure there were no jitters in his fingers or muscles, nothing twitching, and nothing unsettled.

He was ready for the fight.

They continued to move through the labyrinth and the temperature dropped steadily with every step. His flight suit would protect him from the cold that seeped in through the mech, and it meant that there would be no need to vent the coolant systems until they arrived somewhere warmer.

"I guess this is where they keep everything cold?" Hammerhand asked aloud and not to anyone in particular.

"The Gene Bank extends for kilometers beyond the bunker itself," Gustav15 explained. He was a little surprised that the commlink had been kept open but chose not to question the lord captain. "The amount of energy needed to keep it all cool was impossible based on the tech of the time, and we couldn't have put it all through once the battles in the skies were finished. But they found a way to pull power in from the hot water lakes hundreds of kilometers deep and generated enough energy to keep the City and the bunkers powered without needing to use nuclear reactors, although they used those too. It was considered folly back in the day, but in the end, they had found an untapped energy source that would last them until the literal end of the world. I wonder whose idea it was, in the end."

Hammerhand couldn't fathom the sheer amount of time and energy that would have gone into building something as massive as this, and especially during a time of war. Most people would have pushed for all resources to go into readiness for the war against the Invaders, with only a few having the presence of mind to start preparing for what would come after.

He grasped his weapon a little tighter as they left the cooler sections and entered a larger tunnel. Rail lines ran to massive steel doors that were so cold the fog drifted away from it in small rivulets. It was all well-lit and gave them far more room to move through.

Pillars were carved out of the rock to support the roof of the cavernous tunnels, struts designed to look like statues, although the original designs were impossible to make out. A hand and a foot could be seen here or there but aside from that, most of the pre-war architecture had turned into a vague and distant memory.

Hammerhand couldn't help but feel a little sad to see what had once been a display of the ingenuity of the great minds of the world slowly began to disappear. They were now little more than the last remnants of what had been.

"This tunnel leads directly into FEMA City," Gustav15 explained and gestured ahead with his rifle. "I doubt they'd even guard it. It hasn't been used in decades."

"We should remain on our guard anyway," Hammerhand muttered. "There's no need to make things too easy for them, after all."

He cut the comm line and motioned for the group—who had taken a moment to appreciate the architecture of the subterranean corridor—to keep moving. They couldn't lag too far behind lest the Prophet's troops be forced to take the brunt of the defenses.

Hammerhand moved toward the front of the lines but held himself in check and tried not to act on the violent impulses that rose from the pit of his stomach. They told him to rush them forward into battle, but he knew this wasn't the time for that kind of tactic.

Windchime organized the troops into squads and made sure that at least one of the Knights was in every troop of the Auburn rebels, hopefully to keep them organized and in control. It was important to prevent them from being too exposed.

Tinker, finished with his part of the planning, jogged his lighter mech to where Hammerhand led the advance through the tunnels.

"How do you plan to swing that big fucking hammer of yours in these tunnels, laddie?"

He could only shake his head. "There's not much room to do that with any effectiveness. No, I'll use the shield to push the rest of the line forward and let you dumbasses time your shooting for when I have to drop it. Until we get our asses out to somewhere a little more open, anyway."

"Do you think you want me to fit you with something that can shoot in these tighter corridors?"

"If we had time, I would ask. But as of right now, we need to strike fast and hard. With that in mind, the shield will have to do and you assholes will have to watch my back."

"I've always got your back, laddie. You've always earned it."

"I hope that doesn't change now."

"Don't be like that. We have something going here. We can all feel it. There's victory in the air, and we'll taste it. All the lads can feel it. Well, except those Gene Guard fuckers. You can't tell a damn thing about them."

"Never mind them. Keep moving the teams forward and we'll get it done. Nothing's won yet."

"That's the fucking spirit."

CHAPTER TWENTY-SIX

He had learned many things since he had arrived in this place. The desert was a brutal environment, the kind that didn't forgive or forget.

People in the grasslands were less harsh, which was reflected in their environment. The land always made the culture. That was what he had been taught back in the day.

They called him the Prophet because they believed he saw into the truth of things more than others did. And maybe he did, but in the end, they followed him because they thought he had answers.

And while he did have some, they were for the desert. Maybe not for these grasslands, though. Hammerhand had been cut from an altogether different cloth, of course, and so had most of his Knights. They were all fighters to the core, but a different kind than those who followed him into battle. For one thing, they were more forgiving and more helpful instead of feeling that their actions were ordained.

It wasn't that he envied the Knights' leader's position, of course, and the man's morals made it difficult to live in a harsh world. But there were some who were able to come to terms with morals like his and stand by them.

And having an Excalibur mech didn't hurt matters either.

His teams advanced through the tunnels at a decent enough pace, and the Prophet steadied his nerves as the darkness began to close in around them. Spending most of his time out in the desert meant his days were lived in the open with the sun shining on his face and a breeze touching his skin.

Being confined in tunnels like this had to be one of his least favorite feelings, especially as it felt like they grew darker with every passing step. He didn't like it but damned if he would let any of his men see his hesitation. They believed in him and his ability to lead them through anything, which included a long dark tunnel. It wouldn't do to have that confidence shaken in any way.

If he wanted to lead them forward, he would need to be the first one to step into the darkness.

As they continued to move, the lights they carried—helpfully provided by the ecologists they had been in contact with—revealed that the chambers they walked through were a great deal less tight and confined than his imagination had painted them. He had no idea who had put this much work into building them, but he had to admire their determination and their skill. There wasn't much opportunity to create something out in the Sands, and all that could be created was carried on their mechs.

Out here, where there was stone to work with, they could create.

And the evidence confirmed that they did, even though these creations were old, derelict, and falling to pieces. It was still their creation and still beautiful.

"What the...fuck!" He snarled when red alarms flashed across his HUD to tell him there were a few crossed wires in his hydraulics systems. They were being isolated from the rest of the system, which made sure there was still pressure in them to prevent the whole Argonaut from crumpling.

But there were still problems. They were closed off and situated in his right thigh, but issues of this kind tended to cascade when more pressure was put on the rest of the system. The Prophet couldn't afford to have his mech come apart at the seams in the middle of the battle. But he also couldn't afford to be the last man into the fray, if only because the Argonaut, a heavy mech, would always be an advantage in a battle. This was especially the case in the closer ranges he would commit to in these tunnels.

He had always advocated for speed over heavy armor, but there wouldn't be room for any speed and maneuvering, no matter how wide the passages were around them. They would need to keep moving, of course, with the lighter mechs able to hit and pull back before engaging too tightly.

But only if Hammerhand's mechs were in there to draw most of the fire and attention.

He could see another Argonaut approach him. Calina, his second-in-command and one of his standard-bearers, had noticed him fall back and came back to check on him. She contacted one of the support mechs to help with the repairs.

"Keep them moving," the Prophet ordered. "We can't leave Hammerhand and his Knights to take all the glory in this fight. I only need to put in some repairs and I'll join you presently."

"As you wish, my Prophet."

Her response was curt and to the point, not that he expected anything warmer from her. He trusted Calina above almost any other member of his army, and that included with his life.

Not that he didn't trust any of the others. It was her judgment he valued the most.

The Prophet left the support mech to conduct the repairs, climbed out, and helped to perform them himself when he felt the man wasn't moving quickly enough.

Finally, the red lights stopped flashing in his HUD and he entered the cockpit again and sent the support mech to continue the march with the others. They were almost all past him and only a few stragglers brought up the rear behind him.

He grasped the controls and began to move the mech forward once everything was certified as working. Satisfied, he drove the mech forward at a steady march and much faster than he had before. He wanted to catch up with the front of the line and to be involved in the fighting himself.

Another red light flashed across his HUD and the Prophet growled.

"Fucking… Not again…"

He stopped immediately. There was no sign of anything wrong with the mech itself. It was the sensors that had gone crazy as he continued to move forward. The seismic sensors told him that something was wrong but not with the mech. The problem lay with the ground below him.

Or rather, he realized—although he was still bewildered—the ground above him. He couldn't feel anything at first, but he could see that the others had the same readings and they had begun to get anxious with every step down the tunnel.

It was only when a low rumble in the earth around them added an edge of tangible danger that the Prophet called the troop to a halt.

"Get back!" he shouted and put his voice into all the

commlinks he could access as well as the external speakers of the mech. "Get back! All of you pull back. Right fucking now!"

They didn't question his orders and in a few seconds, they had no reason to. The rumble happened again. By the third time, there was no break between the waves, only more and more noise as rocks and dust plunged from the tunnel roof.

"Back! All of you get the fuck bac—"

He was cut off. Something struck him hard in the back, the force sufficient to knock him off his feet. He actually felt it through the mech's heavy armor.

The pressure on his chest grew with every passing second and all he could hear was the rumbling that had become loud enough to make his ears hurt. It was broken only by blaring alarms in the mech before everything suddenly stopped. The lights no longer blinked red and everything turned black instead.

CHAPTER TWENTY-SEVEN

The Knights made good progress down the tunnels. If the maps Nina2 had provided them with were accurate, they needed to proceed for another kilometer and a half to reach the areas that were still patrolled by the city.

From that point on, it would be tough going, which was exactly what they needed it to be. Otherwise, they wouldn't achieve their purpose to draw attention away from the secondary entrance. Unless they managed that, the Prophet would be embroiled in heavy fighting for which his light desert mechs were ill-equipped.

Hammerhand steeled himself while the adrenaline fought to assume control within.

"Heads up, laddie," Tinker called over the commlink. "The sensors pick movement up down the corridor. That's some five hundred meters closer than they should be."

"Do you think they could be non-military?"

"I very much doubt it unless non-military folks are allowed to run around these tunnels in mechs."

It was possible, he reminded himself, although highly

improbable. These tunnels would most certainly be dangerous for non-military personnel and there was no logical reason for civilians to be there. That aside, he wouldn't simply assume that anyone they might encounter were combatants, exactly like he wouldn't assume that everyone in the City was guilty of the same crimes their soldiers had committed.

The tunnel plunged into darkness when the bulbs shorted out for no apparent reason. Even before the first reactionary curses were heard, the area suddenly illuminated. Flares were fired on the other side of the tunnel, where he could see a series of shadows move toward him.

Their appearance and the circumstances ended any debate over their identity. These were definitely not civilians.

"Weapons ready!" Hammerhand announced, strode five steps ahead of his group, and focused on the mechs that moved forward to meet them. Even from five hundred meters away, it was obvious that they were preparing weapons. They marched in formation with the kind of precision and steady rhythm that made it clear they were ready for a fight.

It seemed they had advance knowledge that the Knights had initiated an attack. Whether they had tripped a sensor or someone had informed FEMA City about their plans didn't matter. At this point, they were committed.

The tunnels blazed brightly when massive rifles began to fire. A couple of the enemy Cinders tried to secure cover for themselves and clearly wanted to push in where their close-range weapons would be able to do the most damage.

That was a real concern. Hammerhand highlighted their presence on his HUD for the team to see.

"Form up behind me!"

The opposition was still too far away for their volleys to be accurate, but a few rounds struck closer to home than others, and he turned his shield on. The reduced setting would mean it would take longer to heat up. The additional time would be needed given the sheer amount of firepower he hoped it would absorb.

He steadied himself and increased the pace of his march. The heat began to rise with every round that impacted with the shield. He would keep it up as long as possible but could not risk having it overheat, which would inevitably exclude him from the fight entirely.

Unfortunately, they wouldn't survive an all-out assault without the shield, which left them in a precarious position either way.

The heat began to redline and the focused fire of the mechs ranged against them revealed the numbers the Knights faced, which also increased steadily.

This was unsurprising, of course. FEMA City had taken losses but they still greatly outnumbered any other group in the area. It was how they had managed to hold control for so long.

An alarm blinked in his HUD and displayed how long it would be until his shield overheated, and Hammerhand alerted the Knights behind him. They had kept their distance and waited for the order he issued in the same moment that the blue film dropped out of sight. Even without its light, he could still see a fair amount from the muzzle flashes of the barrage around him.

Fifteen alerts showed where his mech's armor had been hit, and he settled in place, steeled himself, and moved forward. A couple of Cinders rushed toward him, hoping to catch his team off-guard and knock the Excalibur out of the fight. All Hammerhand could do was push the hammer forward.

There was no room for him to swing it, although activating the rocket on the end might do some damage.

The closest Cinder was caught in the chest by the top of the hammer—which was almost twice the size of its cockpit—and it was driven back with enough force to make it stumble and topple heavily. He activated the rocket as the other two tried to advance and the kick of it twisted his mech uncomfortably but it did the job. One of the attackers was caught and hurled against the wall with enough power to leave it crushed into the stonework, and another was struck by the rocket blast. After a few seconds of flailing, the fuel in its tanks ignited and exploded in a powerful and brilliant blast.

The other Cinders were caught out in the open and the Knights leveled a second salvo into them. More fire resulted as they stumbled into their own lines.

The FEMA mechs had no mercy and no intention to let even their own pose a threat and simply annihilated them.

It was something to keep in mind. They hadn't shown that kind of cold-bloodedness during the battle for Auburn. Maybe they had to be less merciful, even to their own people, when they defended their city.

Hammerhand raised the shield again and made a note of the damage that had been done to his mech before he continued the advance. Pushing forward would give them room to fight back, and in the tighter area of the tunnels, the Knights would hold the advantage. Windchime's swords whined, ready to slice into anything that stood in his way.

A smile touched the Knights' leader's face as they pushed closer. He kept his shield up and once again, gave the men behind him the alert to fire the moment it dropped.

The FEMA mechs began to fall back when they realized they were suddenly at a disadvantage. Orders were issued as the shield came down and a fusillade immediately erupted from the Knights.

More alarms blared and Hammerhand almost ignored them until they revealed damage to the back of his mech. Something had attacked him from behind, although he couldn't see how that was possible.

"Tinker, what the fuck is going on back there?"

"Hold on, just—hold the fuck on!"

There was no further explanation for a second and Hammerhand tried not to turn around to see what was happening. The hammer pushed forward again and drove the front line of enemy mechs back. He activated the rocket and scorched a Lancer into falling back, which opened enough room for Windchime to charge into the fray. His enhanced mech moved at a speed that made it almost impossible to track if not for the muzzle flashes from his assault rifle and the sprays of sparks from his blades cutting into the enemy. A couple of others who piloted Lancers and Predator mechs rushed into the fight to support him.

"Tinker! Report."

"We're under fire from behind!"

Hammerhand startled and pulled back but the reaction was cautious as he didn't want to accidentally crush one of his own mechs. "What the fuck are you talking about?"

Tinker didn't reply for a second and focused his energy on lobbing smoke grenades into the area behind them. There was no shield back there and it was enormously frustrating that he couldn't see who was shooting at them from the rear. He had sustained damage from behind, and it wouldn't be long before something vital was struck.

"Who the hell is shooting at us? Did they set something up in the Gene Bank or something?"

"Fuck! No! The Gene Guard are the ones shooting at us."

Hammerhand could think of nothing to say in response to that. He knew better than to question it since the man wouldn't shout it like that if he wasn't absolutely sure of the facts.

The next question, obviously enough, was why they were shooting. The Gene Bank were soldiers and would not fire accidentally into their own allies. Even a first-year pilot would know to keep their lines of sight clear.

Which left only one alternative. The Gene Guard attack was deliberate.

"Son of a whore." Hammerhand growled with anger-tinged frustration and raised his shield once more. "Tinker! Casualties?"

"We have a large number of disabled mechs. I have light mechs getting the survivors out and into cover and others creating smoke screens."

It seemed like the man was in his element and if anyone could effectively manage that kind of calamity, he could. The Knights' leader hefted his hammer and drove it into the line of mechs that now tried to circle Windchime and his team. The man still moved like a whirlwind to slice and hack into anything his weapons could connect with. Along with the work of his assault rifles and the others in his team, he inflicted an impressive dent in the City's pilot numbers.

Unfortunately, that wouldn't last. Any losses the City took at this point would have almost no meaning compared to the damage the Knights had suffered until this point.

Hammerhand brought his shield up and shoved forward.

"Windchime, pull the fuck back and bring your team with you. Now, damn it—now!"

The Knight didn't question his orders and the rest of his people withdrew as well. Before they could rejoin the ranks, two Cinders moved out from behind pillars where they had been effectively hidden. Their shotguns flashed and one of the Lancers lost its leg and pitched over. The second took a round through the cockpit with enough force to knock the entire mech forward before it simply fell with the Auburn pilot already dead.

"Shit!" Windchime shouted as Hammerhand lowered the shield to let him and his two remaining men through. The smoke had begun to fill the tunnels, which made any kind of real visibility all but impossible. Despite the visual challenges, a concerted barrage cut through the tunnel to damage his mech and those around him. Of course, the Knights were confined in a limited area so it didn't require much to deliver an effective assault.

He squinted to focus on Tinker, who stood at the center of the subterranean passage with an assault rifle in an improvised strap on his arm. The man returned fire at the Guard and attempted to hold their ground while the other support mechs drew their comrades away from the fight and into cover behind the pillars.

With his attention on the condition of his troops in the rear, it took a while for him to realize that the air had begun to fill with more than only the smoke from Tinker's canisters. From what he could tell, the ongoing and concentrated exchange of gunfire chipped away at the pillars that supported the tunnel. Before long, they would all be buried inside.

Assuming, of course, that they survived that long.

There was only one way that any of them would get out of this alive. The chances were, if the Guard had betrayed them, the desert warriors would face similar difficulties. Perhaps his decision would help them as well, although he didn't know what they intended to do.

"Hold your fire!" Hammerhand ordered over the comms and made sure his voice carried through the speakers on his mech. In case it was unclear as to who he had addressed, he dropped his shield, let the hammer fall from his hand, and raised a white flag from the mech.

"What the fuck are you doing?" Tinker snapped and spun to face him.

"Hold your fire and drop your weapons. That's a fucking order!" he commanded the man with as much authority as he could muster.

"I won't give up, laddie, so you'd better pick that fucking hammer up again."

"I'm not telling you again—"

"Good, so I won't have to smack some sense into your brains again."

"Tinker, I won't let any more die on this hill of mine. Understood?"

It had been difficult to make the decision and Hammerhand couldn't ignore the irony. He now commanded that they stop fighting, and Tinker insisted that they continue.

The other Knights and rebels had already ceased their efforts and put their weapons down.

Their enemies, thankfully, had chosen to hold their fire and appeared to be willing to accept their surrender.

"Fucking...hell." Tinker hissed in disgust, yanked the strap off the assault rifle on his arm, and let it clatter on the stone floor.

CHAPTER TWENTY-EIGHT

Surrender was a bitter pill to swallow. It was also one that Hammerhand had once sworn he would never take because he preferred death over kneeling before an enemy.

There had been a mention of an old poem at the time. He couldn't remember the exact line or the name of the poet in question, but the words, "Bloodied but Unbowed," had stuck in his head.

He remembered it mostly because Athena had told him about it. She'd shared it over a campfire after they'd both gone through about three bottles of something alcoholic that had been brewed in his old mech. Once she had recited the whole poem to him, they'd vowed that they would never surrender and would die first.

In this case, he knew they didn't have a choice. They had been tricked, trapped, and drawn into the tunnels where they had no way to escape or fight back. Every inch of him wanted to make sure they would all pay for the lives that had been taken, but he pushed the instinct aside and focused on what he had to do.

Hammerhand climbed willingly out of his mech, and the Knights followed. The rebels needed a little more convincing, but they wouldn't be able to continue the fight on their own, especially with many of their mechs already too damaged to ignore.

The FEMA City pilots and a few of the Gene Guard exited their mechs. They worked together to surround the survivors, push them to their knees, and tie their hands behind their backs.

The wounded received no treatment and were merely secured and bound like the others.

"They need medical attention," Hammerhand stated and fought to hide the anger that bubbled under the surface. "We surrendered to you and by the rules of war, you need to tend to the wounded."

"And do you think we give a shit about what you people need?" one of the FEMA City pilots shouted. He swaggered to where the Knights' leader knelt and regarded him with a sneer. "If you wanted medical attention, you should have thought twice about attacking the great FEMA City."

He returned his captor's stare and once again, struggled to keep his anger at bay. "They need help. Do you intend to simply let them die?"

"I might do. Or I might not. Ask me again when I feel like being talked to by some shit raider."

Hammerhand had no response to that and the pilot clearly didn't expect one. He laughed as he turned and strolled down the line of prisoners.

"Oy! Laddie! I think you didn't hear what the man said about those in need of medical attention."

There was no mistaking Tinker's voice and there was no telling what purpose he had in mind that involved shouting like that. The FEMA pilot walked to where the old man was on his knees.

"Maybe I heard him, old fuck, and simply don't care what he had to say about our enemies dying a little quicker."

"Well, I think you should listen to him anyway."

"And why the fuck is that?" The man loomed over the mechanic, who returned his stare as if entirely unfazed that he was on his knees and didn't stand eye to eye with his enemy. "I think you need to shut the fuck up, or you'll find yourself—"

He didn't manage to finish whatever he intended to threaten Tinker with. There wasn't much in the world that could put the old man down when he was sufficiently riled, but even Hammerhand was surprised when he drove up from his knees and his head pounded into the man's gut to cut him off in mid-sentence. The air rushed from the FEMA city pilot's lungs in a whoosh and the prisoner found his feet.

The mechanic leaned back a few centimeters before he jerked his head forward. A few people winced when the other man's nose broke with a distinctive crunch. The young pilot fell, clutched his face, and groaned in pain.

Tinker, apparently, hadn't finished his lesson in manners and the rules of war.

"Fucking prick!" he shouted and kicked the moaning pilot in the gut and the ribs. "Learn some fucking respect, or you'll—"

The tunnels echoed with the sound of a single gunshot that left ears ringing. Tinker stiffened, a look of shock on his face as he fell forward to his hands and knees.

A man wearing a pilot suit walked from the shadows and into clear light. Gustav15 stood over the mechanic with a small sidearm in his hand.

He stared at him for a moment, raised the weapon again,

and pulled the trigger. All life vanished from the old man's body and he sagged on the tunnel floor while blood, bone, and other viscera sprayed over the stone.

"No!" Hammerhand roared. He couldn't believe the indisputable evidence of his own eyes. This couldn't be the truth. It simply couldn't be. He surged to his feet and expected the killer to turn his weapon on him but honestly didn't care. The lord captain would manage perhaps two shots before he closed the distance between them, and there was no way those would be enough to stop him from killing the fucker.

When Gustav15 saw the Knights' leader on his feet, he aimed his weapon at the prisoner who knelt closest to him and stared at Hammerhand with cold disdain.

"He'll die next. Then her. Then him. I have fifteen rounds in here and I'll use them all on someone who isn't you, Hammerhand."

The brutal assurance in the man's tone was sufficient to ensure that he didn't take another step. The weight of the threat hung heavily, and he chafed beneath it. Slowly, he sank to his knees again and tried to ignore Gustav15's smirk.

There was nothing else he could do. His adversary had his measure perfectly. While he didn't much care if he lived or died, the people who were under his command were a different story. He would die for them but never let them die if he could help it.

But despite that, Tinker lay still a few yards away from him. The bleeding from his head had slowed to a trickle and most had soaked into the dust on which he was sprawled.

Hammerhand had expected the old man to outlive every one of the Knights. When they were all dead and gone, the immortal Tinker would have merely started over again somehow.

It seemed as hard to accept the loss of the idea as it was to comprehend the death of the man. He stared at the motionless figure of his friend and hoped and prayed that something would change. His rage buried itself beneath a cold numbness that half-convinced him that his mind was playing tricks on him. At any moment, Tinker would scramble to his feet and laugh at the tears that trickled down his cheeks.

Gustav15 turned to the other pilots. "Get the rest of them up. We'll head to FEMA City."

Hands grasped Hammerhand's shoulders and forced him to his feet. They shouted at him but he barely heard them and twisted for one last over-the-shoulder glimpse of Tinker. One last hope flickered.

It was impossible. Tinker couldn't be dead. He didn't notice that they shouted at him to move faster or that they shoved the butts of their rifles harshly into his ribs to force him forward as the light slowly flickered out behind them.

CHAPTER TWENTY-NINE

Dozens of people were called to the scaffold and every one of them was jeered and yelled at by the crowd who were kept barely under control.

Jessica13 wondered if the only thing keeping them subdued was the fact that every single sentence was the same.

Death by hanging. Death by hanging. Death by hanging.

They were all marched off the scaffold once their fate was announced. Mayor Jones possibly wanted to make it something of a display for them and so would kill everyone in quick succession once all the sentences were handed out. There would be no surprises, no mercy, and no possibility that any of them would come away with their lives.

The crowd seemed all too happy to watch dozens being led to the gallows and hung, but Jones had a flair for the dramatic and deliberately delayed the tableau he had planned. The last of the sentences was pronounced when the sun came out directly above them, the heat now almost unbearable.

"We'll take a recess," the mayor announced once he'd ensured that he had the attention of all present by thumping the table with the cup in his hand. "During that time, we will determine when to begin the hangings."

The crowd cheered as the tribunal stood and moved into one of the nearby tents, likely to escape the heat.

She paid little attention to the weather and had already sweated and trembled with every second that ticked by and every sentence announced. Watching the whole display presented by Mayor Jones told her there was little interest in his mind for justice. He, like the other people of Auburn and the woman in the tribunal, wanted revenge.

Wilbur seemed different, however, and he appeared to enjoy seeing the suffering in the eyes of the condemned more than any desire for vengeance. She noted each sadistic smile and every time he seemed willing to make the prisoner in front of him wait a little longer to extend their suffering as much as he could. Some inner instinct told her that he would want to put them through more punishment than merely a hanging.

"What are you thinking, Jessica13?"

Mini's ability to read her intentions could become problematic eventually but in this case, she was glad to have someone she could express her frustrations to.

"This isn't justice. I can't stand for this, right? How can I stand by and let them kill these people without any reason?"

"You mean aside from the fact that they attacked the town?"

"They followed orders under threat of their own death. At least, that's what Robert7 said."

"And you believe him? Trust him over Mayor Jones' judgment?"

"I think we should at least give them the chance to defend themselves properly instead of having everyone killed because of someone's lust for blood. And why are you trying to defend them? You said that whatever they did today was nothing like the justice Jones promised."

Mini stopped talking for a few seconds to give his processors enough time to engage with his core. "I know that, but I wanted to make sure you felt that way as well. It is interesting to see that you support your emotional response with at least a passably logical foundation. As I've said before, I do need significant upgrades to many things pertaining to detailed information. But if history is any indicator based on the data I do have available, your response is not as common in humans as one might think."

Jessica13 settled into her controls while she considered what he meant by that. It was probably something valuable—an insight she could glean and learn from—but she wasn't in the mood to be taught any lessons at the moment. All she had time for was to wrack her brain for how she could help.

"And so, I ask again—what are you thinking, Jessica13? I assume you will consider a plan to break the prisoners out of their confinement?"

"Unless you think there's any chance we would convince the tribunal to stay their execution until a proper court can be organized."

"Is that rhetorical or would you want me to run the odds?"

She didn't have time to respond as already, the people began to return despite the fact that the heat of the midday sun had barely begun to fade. Whatever she chose to do, it had to be soon. She steadied her tattered nerves by taking slow, deep breaths.

"I think it will be messy but it will be the best option that doesn't end with me on the chopping block as well."

"I can't help but agree."

Her gaze fixed on the gathering crowd, she allowed herself a few more seconds to calm, although a frown settled in when she considered the obstacles the people might create in her rescue attempt.

One of the townsfolk approached her where she remained in the mech. The Auburnites hadn't yet forgiven her for trying to help Robert7, and the only reason they hadn't been openly hostile was because she was a member of the Knights Mechanica. While the Minato was small in comparison to the other mechs that had been in the battles, they didn't have any themselves aside from a few repurposed specifically for agriculture. To regular humans, the Minato was more than enough mech.

"I thought you might be interested," the young man said and spoke softly and furtively while he glanced around to make sure no one saw him talking to her. "They'll bring the prisoners out for execution tomorrow morning. Mayor Jones wants the whole of Auburn to be present for them, and Wilbur's militia will make sure there are no further objections like yours."

"Why are you telling me this?"

He looked uncertain but simply shrugged. "Maybe you're not the only one who thinks our town is worthy of more than another oppressive regime."

Before she could reply or voice another question, he vanished into the crowd that began to grow more restless as the minutes ticked past.

"Well, I guess we have until tomorrow morning to find a way to get Robert7 and the other FEMA pilots out."

"What about the raiders?" Mini asked.

"What about them?" she snapped and immediately

regretted it. Maybe it wasn't quite the justice-centric outlook she had supported not minutes before.

She would have to find answers in the time she had available. There would be no time to second-guess herself once her plan was set and the chaos began.

CHAPTER THIRTY

Jessica13 still didn't have much of a plan in place when night began to fall. The crowd lost interest in waiting for the tribunal to return and gradually slipped away to their usual activities. The prisoners were herded to the stockade as a group, where they would spend the night.

Hopefully, her inner caution reminded her. She still didn't know if Wilbur would decide to simply drag them to a ditch or hole and execute them like he'd done with the others.

There was time to plan, at least, and if they were taken out of the stockade, her job would be much simpler if a little messier.

None of the men on guard appeared overly invested in their responsibilities. They left their weapons propped carelessly against a half-wall and were seated near fires that had been lit when the temperatures dropped and a wind began to whip around the town. Mini explained that the large fires that had burned had affected the weather and the results they now witnessed would only be temporary. It sounded interesting, but neither of them had time to explore it.

"I've been thinking," she said once she'd found something to eat and returned to the mech. "Getting the prisoners out of the stockade is only the first step, although it is important. The next will be to find some way to transport them. Did the Prophet's men leave any of their buggies behind?"

The AI conducted a quick scan. "No, they took those with them when they left. However, it would appear that the APCs they used when they tried to evacuate civilians from the city are still where they were abandoned. They might be a little damaged but are likely functional."

Jessica13 looked toward the section where the APCs had been left, which wasn't too far away. She wondered why she hadn't noticed them earlier but her mind had obviously been on other things. A few bullet pockmarks were visible on the armor, but they had been functional enough to drive the people into the town through the flames that had circled the edges of the town.

"Well, that gives us something to work on while we wait," she mumbled, guided the mech to the vehicles, and climbed out.

"What are you doing?" Mini asked. If she didn't know better, she would have thought the slight hint of an inflection in the AI's voice meant he was concerned.

"Keep an eye out and make sure there isn't anyone out there to see me working," she whispered and crouched as low as she could. Most of the people were in another area of the town, either involved in the work they hadn't done all day or preparing and eating their evening meal. Either way, she had the area to herself for the moment, but she could only imagine the inevitable problems if the militia found her mucking about there on her own.

They already didn't trust her, after all.

Even in the growing darkness, there was still enough light for her to examine the engines. They were a little dirty and grimy but three of them were functional enough for what she had in mind. The other two had bullet holes in the engines and she didn't trust them to hold up under a sustained race to freedom.

The fuel was still in their tanks, which meant no one had paid them any attention since the failed evacuation. It was an unexpected windfall and worked out perfectly for her plans. Their neglect would be her ally in this. A few other checks on the engines told her they couldn't expect the APCs to take them too far. Aside from the fact that the fuel stores were bound to be guarded, the dirt would probably cause them to overheat.

But they would get them clear of the town, and that was a start.

She climbed into the Minato again and moved cautiously toward the stockade, where the situation was the same as when she had left it. The guards now played what looked like cards and paid no attention to the prisoners or even patrolled the area once night had fallen completely. It seemed as though they believed guarding the gate was enough since the prisoners would not be able to break through the heavy logs that had been erected to keep them secured.

And in any other situation, they would have been right.

Jessica13 moved toward the back and away from the fires and the lights. Mini was able to help her navigate toward the edge of the stockade without raising the alarm.

Her fingers felt like they had never touched a mech's controls, and her whole body seemed to tick, alive with all kinds of sensations and not all of them good. She didn't like how this was somehow more nerve-wracking than going into battle. Maybe it was because she was on her own and without the support of the Knights, Hammerhand, and Tinker to help if it went wrong.

Or it could be that she was suddenly very aware of the consequences if she should fail. It seemed certain that the prisoners would die anyway, of course. However, she was as likely to be executed alongside them since that appeared to be the kind of justice Mayor Jones was determined to mete out.

There would be no leniency for her being a member of the Knights this time.

She studied the structure for a few seconds. The wooden stakes were set into the ground and buried almost a half-meter into it if she didn't miss her guess. Her heart thudding, she took a few steps back.

"Be ready to catch whatever falls," she said, aimed the grappler at the nearest log, and pulled the trigger. The dart buried itself between two of them. Something that was usually so quiet when compared to the gunfire and explosions of the battlefield suddenly sounded like it could be heard for kilometers.

Instinctively, she froze in place for a few seconds and listened for anything that might indicate that alarms had been raised. Fortunately, the militia guards were either too far away or too occupied with their card game to hear what was happening.

"Or maybe it's not as loud as I thought it was," she mumbled aloud and leaned the Minato back cautiously.

If she were on her own, it would take a fair amount of engineering to get the logs out of the ground. While not impossible by any means, it would be difficult and time-consuming. With the Minato, though, there was little need for that. The weight and power of the mech were enough to drag them down even with them partly buried.

They began to tip, and Mini took control of the mech smoothly to catch the others before they could thunder free. The mech strained under the weight, but after a few seconds, it lowered the load carefully to the ground. It was impossible to make no sound at all and the slight noise still seemed too loud, but the lack of any alarms once again told her she was in the clear, at least for the moment.

The prisoners inside stood motionless, not sure what to make of the fact that two logs had been dragged away from the walls that should have contained them. She climbed out of the mech and tried to identify faces in the darkness.

"Robert7?" she called, her voice a hushed whisper.

"Jessica13?" He stepped out from the group and looked confused. "What are you doing here?"

"Oh, I only came along to chat, see how you were doing, maybe have something to eat—what the hell do you think I'm doing here?"

"Oh, right. You're here to get us out of this place?"

"Of course. Now gather your friends and let's move. It's only a matter of time until—"

Maybe her luck had run out or someone had heard them talking, but her voice broke off when people shouted outside the stockade and the lights brightened beyond the gate.

"Fuck!" she snapped. "Get a fucking move on!"

Robert7 was only too happy to oblige. The group that was with him followed, while the rest seemed as determined not to be there to face execution the next morning and pushed through the gap behind them. Jessica13 didn't much care where those who weren't from Robert7's group were going.

They would provide a good enough distraction for her escapees to get clear.

She scrambled into the Minato and Mini had already put them into motion before she had even settled inside. Her group fell in behind her as more shouts were heard from around the town. All the others who had chosen to make their escape scattered quickly. It seemed none of them had any intention to stick together since they probably wouldn't manage to avoid their captors if they remained in a large group.

"I assume this isn't the full extent of your plan?" Robert7 asked as he jogged alongside the Minato.

"Of course not. Let's keep moving toward the APCs over there."

She didn't have time to explain the whole plan to him, which was for the best since she didn't have it all resolved yet anyway. There was no way to know how far they would get. Once they had managed to evade capture, they could decide where they would go.

The dirt around their feet kicked when gunfire erupted from behind them. The militia still had no mechs at their disposal. Most of those that were functional had been sent with Hammerhand and the Knights to help with the battle and the agricultural ones had little value in a combat situation.

The bullets would have difficulty breaching even the Minato's light armor, but the prisoners weren't similarly protected.

"Stay in front of me!" she shouted. "Mini, try to give them as much cover as possible."

They seemed to progress far too slowly, mainly because the pilots had to cluster in front of her to reach the APCs and avoid being shot from behind.

"More are coming," Mini alerted her. "They have circled and are ahead of us."

"Mount up now, Robert7!" Jessica13 yelled as they reached the vehicles. She turned and confirmed that a group of the militia remained in pursuit. "You get in there and drive."

"What about you?"

"Do as I tell you!"

He complied, scrambled into the drivers' seat of one, and started it.

"You might want to reconsider fighting back," Mini warned her as she began to advance on the militia.

"Why—"

"Despite everything, these people are still allied to the Knights. They were the victims of an oppressive regime and could simply be acting out because of it."

Jessica13 growled softly. She knew the AI was right, but running away didn't feel right. It wasn't in her blood.

She turned as the APC began to move again.

"Get in!" Robert7 shouted.

"You get going. I'll come in behind!"

Of course, he couldn't know how fast the Minato was but he would soon learn. The militia continued to fire and some seemed to have decided to board the other APCs and attempt to pursue them. Unlike the pilots, though, they didn't seem to know how to operate the vehicles effectively.

Or, at least, not in a trained and skillful manner. The prisoners were soon clear of the town and headed out into the open landscape.

"Jessica13, are you there?" Robert7 asked over the comms.

She didn't reply immediately but made sure no one would be able to intercept or overtake them before she shifted the

Minato into Bulletfoot mode and sprinted over the dried grassland toward the lonely APC. It could move at quite a pace, but the mech was considerably faster.

"I'm…fuck, going to have to fix that inertia dampener one of these days. Yes, I'm here, Robert7, coming up behind you."

"I was wondering where you plan for us to go from here?"

"Honestly? I hadn't thought we would get this far. I think you will probably be safer if you return to FEMA City."

"You know they'll only make us sign up and fight you again, right?"

"It's better than you all being executed in what can only be described as a war crime."

Jessica13 wasn't sure if she meant that and had a feeling she would come to regret it, but it still felt like the right thing to do. She could face the consequences for it later.

"There's something coming up in front of us."

Robert7 sounded panicked over the comms and the APC began to slow.

She peered into the darkness ahead and confirmed that there were, in fact, more than a few somethings waiting for them. They were mechs, and judging by the spikes that protruded from their armor, they were the Prophet's, although they seemed in poor shape compared to when she'd last seen them. Most were covered in dust and evidenced all kinds of damage to their armor and weapons. A couple were carried on the backs of those that were a little more mobile.

"Halt!" the familiar voice of the Prophet said. The man's Argonaut stood out in front, his slug launcher aimed directly at them.

Robert7 did as he was told once again and brought the vehicle to a stop almost fifty meters from the massive mech.

CHAPTER THIRTY-ONE

There was no telling how long he had been in there. The darkness made it difficult to tell time but it hadn't been too long. They had only fed him three times, which told him it could only have been three days at the most.

He hadn't felt hungry enough to try the foul-smelling meals, but that was no real surprise. Food was certainly not something he was interested in at the moment, not after seeing Tinker die in front of him.

Hammerhand once liked to think there would be no man in the world who would keep him from avenging the death of his friend, but that was no longer true. He knew there were a great many who would, and every one of them were the members of his beloved Knights.

The enemy had won.

Trust had brought him down in the end, exactly like the Prophet had foretold. Damned if the guy hadn't lived up to his name. He wondered if he was still around to deliver what would be a justifiably smug, "I told you so."

It was a hope, of course, and it would be more desirable if

the man himself came to deliver it while he performed something like a rescue.

Unfortunately, it wasn't a very substantial hope. The chances were that the Prophet had either been killed, captured, or had simply run away when things had turned sour.

Maybe not the latter. He didn't seem the type to run away from a fight, although Hammerhand had been wrong in his assessment of others before.

He clasped his hands together until he could feel them burn from the strain. It was a way to try to give his mind something to focus on other than the darkness he had wallowed in for who the fuck knew how long.

Suddenly, the lock on his door opened and his cell filled with enough light that it hurt his eyes that had become accustomed to the darkness after so long. He groaned softly and covered them with slow, sluggish movements.

"Prisoner 317 will stand!"

The voice wasn't familiar but the tone was. It sounded like someone who was used to giving orders and having them obeyed immediately. When Hammerhand didn't, two pairs of hands caught him by the arms and shoulders and forced him to his feet.

"Prisoner 317 has been isolated for incarceration in the prisoner population—"

"Who the fuck is Prisoner 317?" he asked. His answer came in the form of a fist in his gut, which forced him to double over and gasp for breath as his whole body exploded with pain. Breathing was difficult for a few seconds before he was straightened by a vice-like grasp and he could see the man who spoke a little better.

He was a soldier, that much was obvious, and one who

probably didn't spend too much time piloting a mech, judging by his neatly brushed hair and thick mustache.

"Prisoner 317 will remain silent," the man continued in a quiet, bored tone. "Prisoner 317 has been sufficiently acclimated to the prison and will be transferred into the general population forthwith. Do you understand these statements as I have stated them?"

Hammerhand looked at the two bruisers who held him up while the silence dragged on for a few more seconds. "Am I still to remain silent?"

"Do you understand—"

"Yes, I fucking understand."

"Then Prisoner 317 will be transferred to general population."

The men thrust him out of the cell and into the hallway outside. He was allowed to move on his own but only as long as he kept pace with them, and the pace was brisk. Unfortunately, he was sore and stiff from the battle and the subsequent sojourn in a cell that was a little too small so it took a few shoves to help him keep up.

After a relatively short walk, they reached the general population area, and one of the guards moved forward to unlock the solid steel door and let him into a chamber.

Although chamber wasn't quite the right word, he mused. It was easily one of the largest rooms he had ever seen in his life. It was a cavern, that much was clear, but the roof stretched almost a hundred meters above them. Nuclear-powered lanterns were visible at the top to simulate sunlight in the massive cave that looked, he decided, like a hangar bay, only many, many times larger than any he'd ever seen.

It almost felt like they were out in the open. He could feel a breeze, although that could only be the result of air being pumped in from outside. Even a place this large wouldn't have a natural source of wind.

The door closed behind him as he stepped into the general population area of the prison. A large group of inmates milled about. The secured area itself only took up a small portion of the larger cavern and it was directly adjacent to FEMA City itself. It was an impressive sight, even in the light of the lanterns above them.

Chain-link fences separated it into blocks and heavy assault mechs painted dark-blue patrolled between the fences. Escape wasn't really an option, not while they manned the area.

The prisoners, alerted by the door opening and closing, looked around to stare as Hammerhand walked toward them. He searched instinctively but could see no familiar faces among them. It was a little disheartening but he hoped it meant the rest of his people were in one of the other blocks and not that they still rotted away in a solitary cell—or worse, were buried under the city.

As he approached, he noticed all the signs that a scuffle was about to break out. Tensions were high already and thankfully, not directed at him.

A larger man with a scar that started at the crown of his bald head and ended under his jaw lurched forward. He was surprisingly fast for someone that size, and a smaller man tried to beat a hasty retreat.

He wasn't quite fast enough, and his adversary launched his attack. Protein-patty-sized fists drove powerfully into the smaller man's jaw.

Hammerhand sighed softly. Getting involved would only make things worse for himself, but it wasn't in his nature to sit around while someone was beaten to death.

"Enough of that!" he declared authoritatively and tried to use the tone of voice that usually drew the focus of his Knights.

Sure enough, it worked. He had the attention of the large scarred man, who straightened, fixed him with a glower, and uttered a low growl. "Enough of what?"

The situation struck him as decidedly odd. He was used to usually having at least a size advantage in any one-on-one fight. Still, he wasn't about to back down despite the fact that the man stood almost a head taller than him and rolled his broad shoulders slowly and with obvious menace.

"Why don't you fight someone your own size?" he suggested. He regretted his words as soon as they left his mouth as they appeared to trigger the huge fist to swing toward his head.

Thankfully, while the scar-faced man was fast on his feet, the punches were predictable and Hammerhand was able to take a step back and lean a little more to avoid a blow that could have dealt significant damage. His assailant attempted an uppercut next but put a little too much power behind it. When it missed, the prisoner stumbled forward a step or two but enough for his opponent to gain the advantage.

Hammerhand stepped forward and his foot flicked out to catch the other man on the instep and force him further off balance. He immediately pushed closer again but knew better than to hit someone in the face with a closed fist. Instead, he jutted his elbow out to catch the man on the cheekbone.

It was enough to draw blood, and he followed it by quickly putting one leg behind the man to flip him over his hip. The prisoner landed hard and kicked up a cloud of dust. The shouting and cheering prisoners around him fell silent and the large man looked a little dazed and winded. He stared at the distant ceiling.

"Had enough, big'un?" Hammerhand asked as his opponent wiped the blood from his cheek.

He nodded slowly and looked a little confused as the knight offered his hand to help him up. The smaller man scurried to the other side of the yard as his erstwhile assailant lumbered to his feet.

"Why didn't you finish me off?" the scarred man asked.

Hammerhand shrugged. "I assumed you had a reason to attack the other man but not enough of one to kill him—which, from what I saw, you could easily have done. I have no quarrel with you, so there'd be no point. Do we have a quarrel?"

The large man shook his head and gingerly touched where he had cut his cheek. "I don't think so, no."

"Excellent. I'm Hammerhand."

"Why'd they call you that?"

"Long story. What do they call you?"

"Scar."

"I guess I don't have to ask why they call you that."

The man chuckled and touched his scar lightly. It appeared he was a little self-conscious about it, and Hammerhand made a note not to make mention of it again.

Shouting from the other side of the yard instantly caught their attention and he turned as ten guards entered through the gate he had used earlier. They carried assault rifles and these didn't appear to be loaded with non-lethal rounds.

His theory was confirmed as every prisoner in the yard immediately adopted their best behavior, lowered to their knees, and put their hands behind their heads. Their reaction was one of instant and long-practiced compliance to an order they knew would come, even before it had been uttered.

It was clear that when the guards were in the yard, they were the primary threat and none of those present would cause any trouble.

Hammerhand didn't like it, but he settled slowly onto his knees and put his hands behind his head before the order to do it was shouted into his face with a gun barrel pointed between his eyes.

CHAPTER THIRTY-TWO

The day went about as well as Hammerhand had expected it to. The tense atmosphere among the prisoners remained. None of them appeared overly trusting of the others and they moved in well-coordinated groups that assiduously avoided one another. If one group came too close, they tended to fling insults but they never allowed it to reach actual violence at any time.

He assumed it was because they knew it would result in the yard being invaded again.

Otherwise, the prisoners were mostly left to themselves, although some of them were led out and put to work in some of the fields nearby, likely to grow food or clean drainage pipes. From what he could see, it was usually anything that would allow them to work with minimal supervision, as it seemed the prison was mostly self-sustaining. It made sense since he doubted they would all be held and maintained as a drain on resources that brought no benefit to the rest of the city.

For the moment, though, he wasn't given any work, which forced him to stay in the yard with a handful of others.

Despite his irritation at the forced inaction, he didn't particularly mind. He didn't want to work for the people who had incarcerated him and being out in the open, more or less, was something of a relief compared to however much time he had spent in the dark little cell. It was good to be able to stretch his legs, at least.

The lamps at the top of the cavern moved in a way that mimicked the sun's trajectory outside and drew across from what looked like east to west. He was interested to see the whole process play out. From the fact that they had them at all, he could tell FEMA City was unlike any other bunker he had seen. Maybe there were more of them out there.

The size of the city itself certainly played to the concept that there were too many people to feed from what they could grow. The other bunkers were rigidly contained and controlled and the population was strictly monitored for that very reason. Maybe they had decided to lift those restrictions.

When the replica suns reached the top of the cavern and hung directly overhead, the steel gate opened once more. A group of prisoners pushed a large wheeled table carrying a huge steel pot with a steaming liquid inside, likely the same kind of stew he had seen in every other bunker. Beside it was a stack of the protein patties and what looked like loaves of bread sliced for the prisoners who pushed forward to eat.

It seemed as though the people in FEMA City ate better than most of the other bunkers, most probably the benefit of their raids on the surrounding countryside for provisions whenever they needed it.

Hammerhand joined the others and collected his food on a tray. He wasn't surprised that it smelled much better than anything he had eaten in any of the bunkers he had visited in the past.

The table he had chosen appeared to be avoided by the other prisoners, some of whom elected to eat standing up rather than sit beside him.

Once again, he didn't particularly mind being left on his own. He wasn't really in the mood to interact. People who wanted him to talk usually waited for orders or something like that, and he couldn't help but think that he needed time to get back into that frame of mind.

Besides, he had a feeling that if he attracted too much notice to himself, people he didn't want to watch him would, in turn, pay more attention to him.

He wanted to be alone for the moment. It had been a long, horrifyingly bad few days. Hell, weeks, he supposed. Ever since they had abandoned their search for Citta Del Mar and decided to help the people of Auburn, things had gone from bad to worse. Every decision he had made for the Knights had ended with them in deeper shit than before.

"Are you all right?"

Hammerhand looked up and realized that he had been in something of a reverie. He turned, a little surprised that someone had joined him at the table. It took a moment for him to recognize the smaller man he had saved from being beaten by Scar.

Well, saved from a worse beating than he would have otherwise received. There were still bruises across his cheek and his left eye was a little swollen and darkening quickly.

"Yeah, I'm fine," he muttered. "Why do you ask?"

"Because you've sat here without touching your food and I'm fairly sure you've bent your spoon out of shape. The guards don't like that."

He looked down and sure enough, the metal spoon in his hand was bent into a ninety-degree angle. Quickly, he reversed the damage. "Huh. Right you are. I guess I must have been lost in thought."

"Well, you'll want to eat that food. If the guards see anyone wasting it, they take it out on the rest of us. Sometimes, they don't feed us for a couple of days."

He nodded and began to half-heartedly eat the mostly cooled stew. "Thanks for the tip."

"Given that you saved me from almost certain death, it's the least I could do. Hammerhand, right? I'm Luther17. You're one of the fighters they brought in, right? The ones they caught in the tunnels trying to attack the city?"

The Knights' leader narrowed his eyes at the man. "You sure know a lot about what happens around here."

Luther17 smirked. "That's me. I get my ass beat and I know things I shouldn't."

"Is that why you ended up here?"

"Well, that had less to do with my knowing things and more about me spreading them among the general populace. You know, back when people still used to have a problem with the coup that was carried out by the militant faction. After they started throwing objectors in here, they told the guards to be a little more violent than before. To the point of killing any folk who don't toe the line all proper-like."

"You didn't approve of the coup, I take it?"

"Nope, and they took offense to that. In fact, most of the fuckers you see between these fences are those who didn't approve of the coup. I'd say they account for over two-thirds of the current population. Folks like Scar were in here before and they didn't like to share their little kingdom with intellectuals."

"How long ago did this coup happen?"

Luther shrugged. "I'm not sure, honestly. It's been a while, though—long enough for folks to start accepting the status quo. Until you rolled into the area, that is."

"How is it that you know enough to be locked in here with the rest of us ignoramuses?"

The other man tried to keep a smug smirk from touching his lips. "I worked intelligence. Of course, that was back when it was mostly making sure no one took too much food or catching someone trying to score extra canteen by peddling fuel to the people who came to buy at our gates. I learned a thing or two about this place, and that knowledge helps keep me informed. It can be useful to stay a step ahead of trouble but sometimes, trouble has a quicker step. I never was much of a fighter."

Whatever else he wasn't, he certainly was a talker.

"And why is it that Scar wanted to beat the absolute living shit out of you?"

"I found out how he got his scar. He told everyone when he got in that it was when enforcement beat a confession of stolen goods out of him. Later on, though, when he was a little off his rocker, he mentioned that he actually got it long before. He drank a little too much stuff he was caught brewing, went to work, tripped on a shovel, and landed face-first on the blade."

"And you shared it?"

"Well, I told him I know and hoped to score some points by not spreading it to the other prisoners. He took it as a threat, though—like I tried to force him into something."

"You're not much good at this kind of thing, are you?"

"I usually only gathered the information. It was on others to use it."

"And you shared it with me because…"

"I feel I don't owe the fucker anything now," Luther17 said and scratched the brown bristle on his chin and ran his fingers through his long hair. "At the same time, I feel I owe you for keeping him from killing me. And I think someone like you might have a use for someone like me. I have ways to find information from the different blocks of the prison, given that's where the rest of your outsiders are being held."

He nodded. "I don't suppose I could cash in on that favor already and ask you to get word out to those folks who came with me. Maybe find out how many of them are still alive."

Luther17 nodded as Hammerhand began to eat with a little more enthusiasm. "I can do that. Is there anything else?"

"I think I'd like to have a word with Scar."

"You don't think he's likely to kill you after you put him on his back like that?"

After a moment's thought, he shook his head. "I think he's likely to think twice about making the attempt but he'll consider it unless I reach out to him first and make sure he knows there's no bad blood. Besides, I have to take a chance on a big lifer criminal like him having a little good in him someplace."

His companion stood, already finished with his food. "I'll see what I can do. But try not to get your hopes up too high."

Hammerhand didn't want to tell the man that he was already working from the dregs of his hopes at this point—from desperation, really. He didn't seem like the kind of guy to share something like that with. He wasn't Tinker.

CHAPTER THIRTY-THREE

As the suns moved toward the western end of the cave, they became a little dimmer and the odd effect of them lighting the roof gave the impression of a sunset as well. It was a strange sight, not quite as gorgeous as the real thing and definitely intentional but still beautiful in its own way. The people who had designed it had put in a little extra effort to give the people below a nice show.

Another table was wheeled out and the same type of food as before was handed to the prisoners. They were all eager enough to partake, and Hammerhand felt something like an appetite returning. He took a tray again and sat at the same table.

Once again, it looked like the other prisoners had no real desire to interact with him. They moved to the other tables and threw dirty looks at him as they passed. Or maybe it was their regular looks. He couldn't tell and honestly paid no attention.

At least this time, he noticed when someone joined him at the table, but it wasn't Luther17 like he had assumed it would be. The smaller man was nowhere to be seen. Instead, the considerably larger Scar now sat across from him.

"The little mouthy man told me you wanted to have a word with me."

Hammerhand took a deep breath. He certainly didn't want to keep talking to people. He felt like he needed time to himself to collect his thoughts. But people still needed to talk to him, and he still needed to talk to them. There was no time to gather himself, and there certainly was no time for him to settle in. He was in captivity, after all, and every waking moment needed to be spent trying to find a way out for himself and those of his people who had survived.

"I did. I wanted to make sure there wasn't any bad blood between us. I wouldn't want to make an enemy out of you if I can help it."

"You have no need to worry, Hammerhand," Scar replied in a subdued tone. "I know who you are now and the fact that it is in your nature to help the less fortunate. In fact, there is a great deal that I've come to learn about you. None of it was really what I expected, given how you fight, but I'm not the kind of man to judge too much."

He raised an eyebrow. The word had spread already, likely thanks to Luther17, although he wasn't quite sure how they would have heard of his reputation. While they had made a point to spread the word that the Knights Mechanica were there to help people in need and it had certainly come to this area, what were the chances that it would make it into a prison?

Either the word of the Knights Mechanica had spread more than he could have ever hoped for or the other Knights who had been captured with him had talked. He wasn't sure whether to feel annoyed or pleased.

"Well, I'm glad there's no intended violence between us," Hammerhand said, leaned forward, and rested his arms on the table. "I have the feeling that could end very badly for me,"

"You and me both," Scar muttered and chuckled. "I'll have the pretty little keepsakes you gave me for a while. And I'll wear them every day too."

"That was because I had surprise on my side. You didn't expect a fair fight from the likes of me. It seems to me that would change if we ever came to blows again."

His companion looked pensive for a moment before he nodded. "Sure, I suppose. It still don't mean I want us to come to blows, though. But no matter. I had the feeling you wanted more than to make peace between you and me."

"What gave you that feeling?"

"Honestly? Luther17 did when he approached me. I wondered where the little fuck grew his balls from all of a sudden and realized it could only be you. So, Hammerhand, tell me why you wanted to have this talk."

He rubbed his cheek gently, where he could feel bristle already beginning to grow. It would be a pain in the ass to shave it off if he ever piloted his Excalibur again.

When, not if, he told himself. When.

"I mostly wanted to discuss hypotheticals. You have men with you, yes? Those who would follow your actions should you need them to?"

Scar narrowed his eyes, his expression stern as he tried to decide where the conversation might go. "Sure. They're not quite as loyal as your people might be but they'll have my back. Why do you ask?"

Hammerhand leaned a little closer and lowered his voice as much as possible while still being audible to the other man.

"Would they have your back in the event of a hypothetical escape from this prison?"

The larger man finally realized what he was getting at. "Why would they be? What future would be available to them after? They'd only be rounded up and shot in the city."

"What kind of future would encourage them to support a hypothetical escape plan?" he insisted.

Scar shrugged, the gesture a little jerky due to the tension in his massive shoulders. "A chance at life without being criminalized. A real chance at freedom beyond the chain links, and the possibility of being more than what they were before they were locked up here."

Hammerhand nodded slowly. "I think that would be in the realm of possibility in this hypothetical escape plan."

"They'll not accept anything less, but if you can offer something like that—honestly offer it—then, and only then, would they help."

"I hope you know I'll hold you to that." He extended his hand to the man across the table from him.

Scar took it firmly. "Something like that would be in our interest too, you know. If it can be done, you can hold me to whatever the fuck you want. I could probably find other ways to help you too if you like."

"I might take you up on that too but for now, I think it best if all plans remained..." His voice trailed off when his gaze settled on one of the mechs patrolling the perimeter "Purely hypothetical."

CHAPTER THIRTY-FOUR

Jessica13 stood her ground for a moment and stared at the Prophet's men while she tried to decide what to do. It wasn't like she knew the man all that well, and what she did know about him had been gleaned when he was in a good mood.

From what she could tell now, though, the man was angry and so were his followers. They had taken losses, and those who were still mobile were in desperate need of repair.

"Wait," she said, climbed slowly out of her mech, and held her hands up.

"What are you doing?" Mini asked but she ignored him and moved forward to where the leader of the Desert Warriors could see her. He would remember her face better than her mech.

"If you all are here…where's Hammerhand? Where are the other Knights?"

A somewhat strained silence followed. From the way the mechs moved, she could tell they were discussing something they didn't want to share with her.

Robert7 and the other escapees climbed out of the APC as

well. They were careful to keep their hands raised to avoid any possible hostilities, which resulted in more discussion among the Prophet's forces.

Before too much time passed, however, the hatch of the Argonaut opened and the leader climbed out. None of the others did the same but he, at least, was willing to speak to them face-to-face.

As he approached, she could see the damage hadn't been restricted to his mech. He looked bruised and a couple of cuts around his eyes and mouth told of heavy impacts that had gotten through the mech's armor.

"What happened to you?" Jessica13 whispered and took a tentative step forward. "And what happened to Hammerhand?"

"I wish I knew," the man responded in a hoarse voice. "We were led into a trap, it seems. The tunnels were collapsed on me and mine. Some managed to escape, as you see, but many did not. Among those might be Hammerhand and his Knights. But enough questions from you. I would know why you are beyond the reaches of the Auburn township and escorting those who were clearly among the captured in the battle for the town."

Jessica13 could feel the full weight of the man's growing anger in his tone, even if the words themselves were fairly polite. She couldn't tell what he would do if she didn't answer the questions to his liking, but she was long past feeling ashamed for her actions. If she was killed for her choices, she would die with the knowledge that she had done the right thing.

"These men were going to be executed," she stated firmly and took a step forward. "They said that they were ecologists who were forced into combat by FEMA City and beyond that, they offered to help to lead us into the city in exchange for their lives. The people in the town refused them justice—or even a proper trial—or consideration for how they could help us in the long run and elected to simply kill them. I could not stand by and let it happen."

She wasn't sure where the barrage of verbiage had come from, but she certainly meant every word of it.

The Prophet studied her for a few long seconds and his piercing gaze felt like it could cut right through her and see into what she really thought. The rest of his men stood in silence and made no attempt to add anything to the conversation, but she had a feeling they would kill her and the pilots without a second's hesitation if their leader told them to.

Finally, he turned his attention away from her and strode to where Robert7 and the FEMA City pilots stood. The young man stood at the front of the group and therefore appeared to receive the brunt of his attention.

"Is what the girl says true? Are you all from the Hall of Ecologists?"

It wasn't a name Jessica13 had heard before but Robert7 appeared to recognize it, judging by his look of surprise.

"I am. And seven of the others too. The rest were gathered from the Gene Bank and other sections of the area."

"What happened to those who fought at the side of Lady Hoot or who came from FEMA City?"

"Most of their wounded were taken back. Those who weren't ran off with the raiders and tried to find another way to freedom. I wouldn't side with any of them if my life depended on it. Not anymore."

The Prophet nodded slowly and tilted his head in a challenge. "And why would we believe you?"

"I can't give you anything more than my word as well as a

hidden way into the city. I can also tell you the exact radar wavelengths the Artillery Company Omega uses."

"Which company is that?"

"It's the one that operates the Heavy Katyusha platoons at the top of the city to defend it from assault."

Jessica13's eyebrows raised. "Why didn't you say anything like that before?"

"Why?" the Prophet asked and looked quickly at her, a little confused.

"If we know the exact wavelength, we'll be able to design radar chaff strips to match it. If we could get above and shower them, they wouldn't have any way to aim their cannons. They would literally have to fire blind."

The man looked at the rest of his group. She could see two realization slowly touch him and fully engage his interest. "This would make a full-frontal assault on the city possible. Still difficult, I suppose, but possible. That doesn't answer the question of how we'd be able to get the chaff over them, to begin with."

"You captured one of the weather balloons that were launched to attack Auburn," Robert7 reminded him.

"We did?" he asked.

Jessica13 narrowed her eyes. "In the first battle, yes, we brought one of them down. Before you arrived to aid us."

"It would be simple to repair it and use it to blind them with the chaff," the young continued.

The Prophet paused for a few seconds, and she could almost see the gears turning in his head. Whatever happened that had left him and his mechs in such a terrible condition clearly hung over him, and he wanted to make another attempt to attack the city.

"Very well," he stated finally and loomed over the two

young people. "You two should go through this secret entrance, storm the central control facility, and open the city's blast doors. We can seize the spire and its elevators, but we may stall and fail if those doors hold."

Robert7 and Jessica13 shared a glance before she nodded. "I think that's possible. Difficult, but possible."

"I will have you know," he continued and shook his head, looking like he thought he might regret making this decision. "If this ends up a trap or a ruse, I will kill you, Robert7, and then you, Jessica13."

The man's steely gaze sent a chill down her spine. "I believe you."

CHAPTER THIRTY-FIVE

Hammerhand regretted any time he was forced to spend in his cell, but like the other prisoners, staying out in the simulated sunlight wasn't something he could enjoy all the time.

For now, he was in the tiny space that was a little too small to sleep in comfortably, and there was little he could do about it. The only option was to sit and wait in the hope that they wouldn't leave him there for too long.

There were plans he wanted to continue to work on. Besides, with the other prisoners around him, it was easier to let his mind drift and not focus on the issues that constantly plagued his mind. The echo of a single gunshot through a cavernous tunnel repeated relentlessly, over and over in the darkness around him.

He had learned how to keep himself in full control for most of his life, but this was something different. Nothing in his experience had prepared him for it and he had no idea how to handle it.

Tricks were all he had, at this point, and the reality was that he had very few cards up his sleeve.

His body stiffened when the door to his cell opened and he stood quickly to avoid being pushed and shoved into the yard again. Still, the intrusion seemed out of place. It didn't seem like enough time had passed for it to be daytime in the city yet.

His instinct proved correct. The light that streamed in was weaker and was provided by fluorescent bulbs, which told him it was still dark outside the prison. The light was strong enough to obscure the face of the person who stood outside and leave him with only a silhouette.

"Prisoner 317, you have a visitor," the guard said, stretched into the cell, and dragged him out. Hammerhand had almost anticipated this and cooperated as he was guided away. He soon realized their path wasn't toward the general population area but deeper inside the prison building. They reached an area built to accommodate visitors without allowing them any physical contact with those who were incarcerated. Laminated, tempered glass kept the visitors separated from those they visited, and an antiquated telephone line connected the two.

There was, of course, no mistaking who waited for him on the other side of the glass. Even though it had been many years since they had parted ways, Athena was as memorable as the day he had first laid eyes on her.

Her hair was secured in a tight braid that showed a few streaks of silver, although it didn't take anything away from the sheer presence she exuded. If anything, those streaks only added to it. Her clear, clean face was marred by a couple more scars than before too, and the lean look she had always possessed had carried over. She was a little shorter than him, although not by much, and a sinuous power in her arms and shoulders was still very apparent.

She smiled when she saw him, relaxed into her chair, and gestured for him to take a seat as well before she picked the handset up and motioned for him to do the same.

"It's been a while, Hammerhand," she said when he complied, her voice still a little raspy from when someone had tried to slit her throat and left his mark on her vocal cords. "Do they still call you that? Maybe you've gone back to your real name? What was it again?"

"It's probably better than Lady Hoot," he replied and raised an eyebrow. "Did you come up with that yourself or did you need help with it?"

"You are still so very droll," she muttered and shook her head. "Not that talking was ever your strong suit. You were always much better at throwing your fists and hammer around in the hope that it hit something. I say were, of course, because all that is very much in the past tense, isn't it? I've spoken to the warden, and he says you've been involved in fights. That doesn't last very long when you're in a place like this, or so I've been told. Your Knights aren't here to protect you and Tinker isn't around anymore to give you his sage advice."

Hammerhand stiffened in his seat and grasped the phone a little tighter. He tried not to let any of it show but from the gratified look on her face, it was apparent that she knew how far under his skin she was.

"They fought for what they believed in," he replied with an effort to keep his tone calm and measured. "I guess the same could be said for the crazed fanatics you surround yourself with. How do you justify such wanton destruction and violence?"

"Oh, Hammerhand." She sighed. "You always were too good for this world. You would have been right at home in the world-that-was, playing ancient knight, killing the guilty and saving the innocent in the name of country and...queen or something like that. But you never realized how those ideals have no place in the world we know and love. You were always a little too naive for your own good. Of course, you had the old man to pull you back when you were being a little too stupid. Well, so much for your attempt to stay pure in a world gone to shit. Your holding onto such antiquated ways of thinking with such stubbornness is exactly what got Tinker killed, and don't think I'll ever forgive you for that."

"He would be ashamed to see how you ended up, Athena."

His voice was a cracked whisper, and when she leaned forward, the smug gloating slipped for a moment. "You're a relic in a world that doesn't want you anymore, and I think it's sick of trying to kill you. You might as well do us all a favor by taking care of it yourself."

He had no answer to that and merely tried not to look into the icy gray eyes as he recalled his own words on the topic. They had discussed their place in the world many times, and he had shared a good deal about himself with her. He had thought she had done the same, but in the end, it was easy to see he knew very little about the woman now seated in front of him.

"Food for thought," she whispered and placed the receiver in her hand in its cradle.

Hammerhand stared into the glass long after she left until the guard came to pry him from his seat and guided him into the now comforting darkness of his cell.

She was right, of course. Athena always did have a way to look into the truth of matters when she put her mind to it. The world was shit, and there was nothing he could do about that. He could play the knight in shining armor, but all that would do was get himself killed in a world that didn't accept his type anymore.

And if he was any good at it, all it meant was that he would get other people killed before his death claimed him.

Time ticked past in the isolated darkness of his cell and his mind churned. It could have been minutes or hours for all he could tell. It felt like years.

The slot in the door opened to give him a brief glimpse of what was happening outside his cell. A guard pushed in a plate of food, but unlike all the others he'd been given, this was covered by a piece of cloth.

He leaned forward and pulled the tray closer. It was too light to carry any food, but something rattled on the metal tray.

It was difficult to make anything out as the only light that filtered in was from the small sliver between the floor and the bottom of the door. It wasn't much, but it was certainly enough to see what was under the cover when he lifted it off.

The small knife was well-made, judging by the balance and weight of the steel. The handle was wood and something had been carved into it. His fingers traced the inscription to make it out in the darkness.

Love, A.

He sat on the cold floor and stared unseeingly at the small weapon in his hands. It seemed like a lifetime ago that he'd told Athena he didn't want to live in a world where there was no goodness and no chance for him to fix it. She'd remembered and turned those words back on him. There was no goodness, he reminded himself again. They were in a world of shit where everyone he tried to save either turned their backs on him when he was no longer needed or actively tried to kill him.

There was nothing that even came close to goodness, and every attempt he made to change that was met with indifference or hostility.

What point was there?

Anyone would agree that he'd fought his fight. Was there really any reason to continue now that he was stuck in this prison cell? Even if it would be Athena's ultimate victory and prove that she was right in the end, why would he question her?

The knife felt comfortable in his hands. It wasn't the fanciest but it had been crafted by skilled hands, there was no doubting that.

"Courtesy for a gentleman," Hammerhand muttered and tested the edge on his thumb. The prick of pain and a small, warm wet spot told him how sharp it was.

It was more than effective for the task it had been sent for.

CHAPTER THIRTY-SIX

He wasn't sure how long he spent staring at the knife, even though it was too dark for him to see it clearly. It was difficult to tell time inside his cell but it probably wasn't morning yet since they were likely to take him to the general population section once more when the time came.

Numbness seemed to tuck itself around him. He hadn't seen something like this coming. Having deliberately chosen his kind of life, he had always known that he wouldn't die peacefully in his bed. Still, he had always thought it would come in the field of battle where he stood against impossible odds, fighting the good fight, as it were.

Not hiding in a dark hole with a knife to his wrists. One never really knew where one would end up, after all.

Hammerhand felt the prick of the blade against his skin. He closed his eyes and took a slow, deep breath. He would join his friend soon.

Tinker's face was the one he saw now. The man who had resisted the idea of surrender in the tunnels, who had thought they had the option of dying in battle instead of being slowly worn down by a life in prison. The man who would not stand for him ending everything simply because he didn't feel there was any hope to be had during a seemingly endless wait in a prison.

Without a doubt, his friend would outright slap him for that. He'd done it before when he thought he was being stupid and needed a little sharp reminder to wake him the fuck up.

He didn't know what he believed when it came to life after death, but if there was the smallest of chances for him to join his comrade, he wanted that reunion to come when the man wasn't likely to simply kill him again out of frustration.

The thought of Tinker possibly watching him from the afterlife allowed him to reach a decision, at least for the moment. Quickly, he tucked the blade into his sleeve. Out of sight and temporarily out of mind. His eyes closed and he leaned back against the wall of his cell and tried to put the thought of Tinker's death out of his mind.

It wasn't easy, but sleep gradually pulled him in. He had no way to tell precisely, but it seemed like only a few minutes had passed before footsteps approached his cell. His eyes snapped open and almost immediately, Hammerhand knew what he would do next. It seemed impossible not to act on the decision his mind had made of its own volition. His pulse raced and the thudding in his chest increased speed as he straightened, his body ready to act as the door was unlocked and swung open.

The false daylight was a little blinding but he adapted quickly. His eyes adjusted to the change in brightness in seconds, and as the two men entered the cell to yank him out, he surged forward. His shoulders collided with them both and with a roar, he drove them out of the cell.

One lost his footing, rolled, and struck the wall behind

him as the other tried to take hold of the prisoner, hoping to shove him back and find some way to stop him.

He twisted, ducked under the man's hands, and drew the knife from his sleeve.

There was nothing grand about this. He'd formulated no tactical plan and had nothing to fall back on if he didn't succeed. Failure was not an option at this juncture.

The knife flashed and sliced easily through the body armor the guard wore. It was designed to protect against bullets moving at high velocity and did little to stop the knife that slid easily into his gut.

The man groaned and clutched his wound as Hammerhand straightened, grasped the guard's hair, and jerked his head back to expose his throat before he slid the blade across it. The keen edge found the artery and red sprayed across the hallway and splashed the other man who struggled to stand and drew his attention with the movement.

He focused on the second man, who tried to retreat and wiped the blood from his eyes. In his haste, the guard tripped over his own feet and landed hard while still partially blinded, which opened him to a swift attack. The knife did its work cleanly and sliced into his throat, preventing him from shouting to raise the alarm.

In moments, his struggles ceased, although there was far more blood now than ever. Hammerhand wiped his hands clean and pushed to his feet.

Thankfully, it didn't seem that anyone had heard the struggle. The guards had been eliminated before they could shout for assistance, and the two dead men weren't wearing any radios that might have had a silent alarm on them.

Despite this, alarms started to ring in the distance and were quickly picked up by those in the prison and possibly the rest of the city too. Hammerhand paused only to wipe the knife blade clean on one of the fallen guards' sleeves before he straightened and readied himself to see this through.

It was time to see if Scar and his men were still willing to help with his escape. He retrieved the keys from the belt of one of the dead guards and made his way toward the other cell blocks.

CHAPTER THIRTY-SEVEN

"Do you ever get tired of being called Jessica13?"

She looked up from her work and narrowed her eyes at Robert7, who was digging beside her. "I… don't know. Do you ever get tired of being called Robert7?"

"I don't know either. Like, have you ever had a nickname that you use? Maybe in the middle of a fight when saying the whole name might be too time-consuming?"

"Well, Hammerhand and Tinker call me Jessie, but it always feels odd when I hear it. I was always Jessica13 to myself, so I got used to saying it quickly."

"Huh. I suppose that makes sense."

"Why?" she asked. "Do you think I should call you something else? Like…Bob7? Or only Bob?"

"I don't know. Maybe Rob? Something like that? I like my name, but I would like to have something shorter."

"So only Rob, or Rob7?"

"Just Rob."

"You two had better be working out there," the Prophet shouted from where he continued with the repairs to his

Argonaut. "I would be a little more concerned, if I were you, as I doubt our FEMA City friends are sitting around waiting to be attacked."

He wasn't wrong, of course. FEMA City hung over them as an ever-present threat and wasn't something to be ignored, and the Prophet knew he had no choice but to see if Robert7 had told the truth. The people of Auburn had similarly agreed to those terms and allowed the FEMA City pilots to remain alive after he had convinced them to do so.

Fifteen of them had come to the coordinates the young pilot had given him, including Jessica13 and Robert7, to dig for the secret entrance that would lead them into the city. The Prophet and two of his men had accompanied them but would join his main force once they had located it. While the young people used the tunnels to reach their target unde-tected, he would lead his Desert Warriors in the planned frontal assault.

The idea had at least seemed promising, although it was more difficult than anticipated. The knowledge of the loca-tion was all well and good, but when it was hidden under-ground, there was nothing else to do but dig until they located it.

And thus far, none of them had any luck. Jessica13 couldn't help the niggling doubt that her trust in Robert7 had been misplaced. She didn't believe he had intentionally betrayed them but maybe his memory of the exact position wasn't quite as good as she had hoped.

"There's nothing out here," she said, scowled, and looked at where Mini had put the Minato to work as well. They had discussed having her inside the mech, but time was of the essence. Letting him do the work with the mech and her doing what she could on her own would at least slightly increase their work rate.

It wasn't by much and at the moment, it seemed it wouldn't make any difference anyway.

"Are you sure this is the place?" she asked and grimaced when sweat began to soak into the pilot sleeve. "We have been digging around here for a while."

"They had the records of the secret entrance at the Hall," Robert7 explained. "These are the coordinates, down to the minute, but…I don't know. They put the damn things in over a hundred years ago before the Invaders. There could be a hundred different places by now. Or they could be fucking buried."

"That sounds suspiciously like you're having doubts."

"Well, given the stakes we're working against, I think I would be crazy not to have doubts."

He wasn't wrong in that regard. If there was ever a time to doubt oneself, it was when one's life was on the line.

Or maybe that wasn't quite right, but she had those doubts as well, so she couldn't judge him for them. All they could do was keep looking and hope they eventually stumbled on something. Their lives depended on it.

"Jessica13," Mini called from the Minato's position about twenty meters to their left. "I do believe I've found something."

"Wait…what?"

A hint of elation touched her as she jogged to where the AI stood over a group of bushes. He'd pulled them up from the ground and dug into the dirt less than half a meter before he discovered what could only be described as a steel hatch that led underground.

The AI stepped closer, grasped the handle, and spun it

slowly. The rusted steel groaned under the strain and left her fearful for a moment that it would break, but after a few long turns, it moved a little smoother.

"Nice work, Mini." She chuckled, unable to hide her relief.

"Your compliment is noted and appreciated."

"How were you able to find it?"

"I…" The pause was uncharacteristic since the AI was almost never at a loss for words. "Data not found. If I were to venture a guess, I would say I might have been here before. I will need to conduct further tests to establish for certain whether that is correct."

The Prophet approached as Mini worked the Minato to heave and pull the heavy hatch open and reveal the darkened entrance to a tunnel.

"Nice work. I began to have my doubts as to Robert7's trustworthiness."

Jessica13 shook her head. "You and me both."

"What was that?"

"Nothing. But I think that we should all wear the protective gear if we go down there. Bunkers usually only isolated these locations when they used them to dump the radioactive waste from their reactors back in the day, so the chances are that whatever is down there won't be healthy for us."

"That is a good idea, Jessica13," the man said and her team began to pull the hazmat suits on. It was slow work but eventually, they were ready to enter.

"May the sun guide you through the darkness," the Prophet said as Jessica13 adjusted her protective gear. "And may we see each other on the other side."

She couldn't help a small smile. "Right back at you. And thanks. You know, for believing in us."

"I will thank you when you complete your mission."

CHAPTER THIRTY-EIGHT

__Ten minutes prior to the prison break__

She had heard of places like this in the past. Most of the bunkers had them for when they needed to flood the reactors. Maintenance was usually an issue since it was almost never needed, which allowed most of the locations to fall into disrepair over the years.

While she'd never paid the information much attention, she'd never thought it would be like this. The fact that there were branches of tunnels was already a little alarming. It meant these led to a variety of reactors that would lead them to more than one entrance into the city.

Only a few meters in, Jessica13 could already hear a cacophony from the Geiger counters they'd brought. That alone told her their decision to descend while already wearing the protective gear had not been in error.

"Mini, why don't you run scans into the tunnels to see which one is likely to bring us out closer to the central control facility of the city?"

"I could, but...the radiation interferes with the scans. These passages lead in various directions. We should head into the second tunnel from the left."

"Wait, I thought you said you can't see that far?"

"Once again, data is not found, but we should head down that tunnel anyway."

She had never seen the AI act like this before. Then again, he had never talked about having been somewhere before either. There was no reason for her to trust this sudden impulsiveness from him.

Then again, there was no real reason not to. Who was she to say he didn't know what he was doing?

It seemed more sensible to trust him, so she walked in the front of the group and directly behind Mini as they continued through the narrow passages. Hammerhand had been right, and if they ran into any defenders in this area, Mini's ability to get her and the rest of them out of trouble would be severely hampered.

What had happened to Hammerhand? And Tinker? And the other Knights? The Prophet had said he and his warriors had been led into a trap which they had barely escaped but that the Knights hadn't come out either. They'd been separated, and there was no telling whether they were alive or dead.

There wasn't much in the world that could kill Hammerhand, that much she knew. Tinker was a tough fucker too. If there was any way they could get out of whatever trap had been arranged for the Knights, they would have found it and gotten clear. The only question was whether they had tried to retreat or had pressed forward and attacked the city as planned.

Jessica13 shook her head. Her mind needed to be

grounded in the present and there were enough dangers out here for her to deal with. The tunnels themselves were neglected and the arches had already begun to decay and fall apart. The coolant liquid seeped through the cracks, dripped onto the floor, and covered it in a light film that already started to steam. This, in turn, made clear vision almost impossible the deeper they went.

The clicking from the Geiger counters accompanied the unceasing drips of the coolant fluid in a way that made her skin crawl with every step. The suits they wore were effective against radiation, but there was always a chance that something would go wrong or the suits would reach a point where they soaked in too much.

She wanted to get out of there as quickly as possible.

All they had to go on were the metaphorical gut instincts of the AI that piloted her mech. She had trusted Mini with her life in the past and there was no real reason to doubt him at this point. Nevertheless, a hint of concern pushed at her, a nagging feeling that something was wrong.

They were already a considerable distance from their entry point when she realized that the pools of coolant liquid had become steadily deeper as they progressed. Jessica13 scowled and shifted her gaze to where it was leaking, while the faint nag of concern steadily became a demanding alarm at the back of her mind.

"What's the matter?" Robert7 asked when he noted her distraction.

"This is way too much coolant fluid to be missing from the reactors. Something's gone wrong—and I mean very wrong."

"How do you mean? Have you worked with these reactors before?"

"No, but in my bunker, they drilled us in emergency

procedures that had to be implemented if there was ever a reactor meltdown. The first problem that always arose was when the coolant fluid evaporated too quickly or leaked out. That led to the containment starting to melt."

"You would think they would know about it," Robert7 said, but his eyebrows raised in full realization after a few seconds. "Unless a whole group of them were arrested during the coup and left unqualified people to simply keep pouring more liquid in."

Jessica13 shrugged. "I guess the bright side to that is they don't have anyone guarding these tunnels. On the downside—"

"We can expect there to be far more radiation here."

She knew for a fact that she preferred dealing with guards than the radiation, but there was no way to change anything.

They continued through the underground labyrinth and to confirm her misgivings, the fluid beneath their feet grew noticeably deeper. She was reluctant to complain about it yet and possibly stir the others to panic, but the counters grew noisier with every step forward. Her feeling was that they now approached one of the cores, and she wasn't sure it was a place where they wanted to be.

Mini stopped suddenly and raised a hand to make sure everyone could see him in the mist that thickened around them.

"There is a cave-in ahead," the AI alerted them. "We must find an alternate route. Calculating now."

Jessica13 approached the mech and placed her hand on the armor. "How are you doing in there, Mini? Is the radiation affecting any of your core functions?"

"Not as yet, and your concern is appreciated. All my core

functions have been thoroughly shielded from radiation and other calamities that might damage them. There is always room for error, of course."

"We'd better not stick around and wait for that to happen. Let's find our alternate route."

CHAPTER THIRTY-NINE

The radiation spiked even higher as they pushed on and Jessica13 couldn't help the rising feeling of anxiety with every click from the counters. Sweat traced rivulets down her spine, rather like an insect crawling down her back with every step.

"Mini, are you sure this is the right way to go?" she asked as he led them forward and the team waded cautiously through pools of the coolant.

"It is the only path I can detect that gets us into the city at the assigned location, but we might face difficulties as we get in closer."

"You mean we'll be swimming through this fucking liquid before the end?"

"That is unlikely. But we do appear to be approaching the source of the radiation in these tunnels and the reason why it appears to be spreading."

She wanted to know more but assumed Mini probably didn't know more than what he had told her. They would have to find out personally.

They reached the end of the tunnels but instead of a cave-in, the section was intentionally walled off with a solid concrete slab blocking their path. Thankfully, there was a steel stepladder that led them to a small yet heavy steel door. They needed the Minato to pull it open, and she noticed that rust had begun to form on the hinges.

When the Minato opened it, they stepped cautiously into a small control room. She could make out more than a few different control features, all of them antiquated by well over a hundred years. The reactor and the control room had likely been put in place many, many years before the Invaders—probably before their first attack.

"Well, that explains why they haven't maintained this place," she commented and moved closer to the controls. They were a little beyond the mechanical engineering she understood, but the basics were the same. From there, it wasn't difficult to tell what the controls were for and what the gauges measured. They had all been made by the same hands, after all.

"What are you looking at?" Robert7 asked and peered through the sealed and laminated windows of the control room. The steam outside made it difficult to see anything in particular, but a deep blue light source remained out there and cut through the mist.

"Temperature measures," she replied, cleaned a few of the gauges, and tapped them to loosen the needles from the dust that had collected inside. "And I think there are some old-fashioned Geiger counters to measure what's going on inside."

"Do you know what's happening?"

Jessica13 scowled at him. Maybe his Athena genes had been more focused on giving him ecological knowledge than mechanical. Or maybe that wasn't how it worked at all.

"The temperatures in there are too high for safe passage.

That light you can see is the core already exposed from the coolant fluid. The container has melted away on the top part and it's heating the rest of the room. Right now, it's almost a hundred and fifty degrees."

"Shit."

"These suits we're wearing aren't designed to take that kind of heat. If we stay in there too long, it'll damage the containment material and we'll be flooded with radiation. Mini, is there any other way into the city?"

"Sadly, this is the only way I can find. We'll have to get across that walkway to the other side of the chamber."

"How long would our suits be able to be in that room before they lose their containment?" Robert7 asked.

She turned to face the mech.

"The suits will maintain containment for about eight seconds while in the chamber. It should be enough time if you move across quickly," the AI explained. He was better at running the calculations than she was.

"About eight seconds doesn't sound very exact," one the Auburn rebels pointed out.

He was right. When dealing with something as lethal as the amount of radiation that flooded the room, even one second was too large an increment to deal with. And that was based on the assumption that the suits they wore were in top shape.

Given how long they had languished in the Beast from when Tinker had acquired them, it wasn't the safest assumption to make.

"Couldn't you take us across there, Mini?" she asked. "It would take a while, but we would be more isolated from the heat inside the Minato."

"I could take one person," Mini pointed out. "But the

weight of the mech would be too much for the walkway. I would have to be the last one across to avoid risking the lives of the rest."

Jessica13 scowled and shook her head. "One at a time, then. And eight seconds. Every one of you keep that in mind. I'll go across first."

"Is that wise?" Robert7 asked.

She shrugged. Heading through a room flooded with radiation probably wasn't wise, to begin with. It would be better if she went across first and into the isolation chamber on the other side to make sure everything was working correctly. "You decide who goes across in the Minato and we'll keep moving. Good luck."

"And to you," Mini replied.

Robert7 could only offer a small nod as she stepped into the isolation room between the control room and the chamber. The design for the main area was older, intended for the larger fission reactors that were used to power cities back in the day. It explained why it was in such a poor condition. They had built the bunker around it, which caused cracks in the foundation and from that point, it had only been a matter of time. Over a hundred years, small cracks had grown larger and leaked the coolant fluid to the point where the erosion simply gained momentum.

Her calculations said that a terminal meltdown would probably happen if no action was taken, but only in about twenty years if no efforts were made to stop it.

Maybe if they weren't successful, she would go ahead and warn someone about the impending disaster anyway to make sure innocent lives weren't lost.

She took a deep breath, peered into the open area, and

tried to determine the quickest path across the walkway through the steam before she pulled the door open.

The heat struck her like a wave and immediately fogged her visor. Even so, with her route through already plotted, she summoned the courage to sprint forward. The steam made everything farther than two meters almost impossible to make out, but at only five meters in, she could see the room she needed to reach.

Sweat streamed from her skin and pooled inside the suit as she yanked the door open and shut it again hastily. The sudden change in temperature was drastic as the room instantly went through the decontamination protocols.

She'd made it somehow. It seemed almost impossible for something to go right at this point.

"Mini, I'm across," she said over the commlink. "Send the next one."

All she could hear on the other side was static for a few seconds before a couple of words came through. "Robert7...coming..."

The radiation would be hell on their comm lines, but the idea was transferred well enough. A few seconds later, Robert7 raced across the walkway, almost ran into the door, and scrambled into the isolation chamber.

He looked as shaken by the experience as she was, but it wasn't time to celebrate yet. They focused on the next one to come across and he traversed the distance as quickly as he could.

Her stomach clenched painfully when he tripped and stumbled forward, his arms flailing as he tried to regain his balance while he covered the final few feet to the door.

Jessica13 stepped into the isolation chamber, shoved the

door open, and grimaced when the heat swept over her. She hauled the man inside and closed the door behind him.

"Th-thank you!" he gasped as the decontamination kicked in.

"Don't mention it," she replied and tried not to show her reaction to seeing him trip. They moved out of the small space and Robert7 signaled for the next one to come through.

Another dash followed and this man seemed steadier on his feet than the last one. The team followed one by one, and she was almost ready to explode with tension as they reached safety without mishap.

The third to last stepped out and broke into a sprint. He stopped abruptly and twisted to see what had caught him and now prevented him from moving forward. Jessica13 leaned to pull at the door.

"No!" Robert7 snapped, caught her hand, and dragged it away. "He's…he's already dead."

She looked up, her eyes wide. The man's suit had snagged on a protruding piece of the walkway that had begun to fall. The constant traffic of each person crossing had put additional pressure on its eroded mooring on the wall and it had gradually worked loose. He dropped to his knees and raised his hands to his face.

The suit was torn and the radiation would be swamping his body. It might take a few hours, but he was already dead.

The rest of the team crossed quickly and Mini brought up the rear. Jessica13 tensed when the walkway shuddered under the weight of the mech, but it moved quickly. The AI already had the grappler ready to use if the walkway fell and he paused to help the compromised man from his knees and all but carried him the final distance.

Thankfully, the structure held, and it wasn't long before the two stood in the isolation room being decontaminated.

The man had already begun to show the effects of the radiation sickness. He removed his helmet and immediately threw up as he walked out of the room. His skin was clammy and pale and he shook uncontrollably.

"I'm so sorry," she whispered as he moved past her.

"Speak no more of it," he whispered, and while he looked weak and uneven on his feet, he managed to walk. "I still have a little while. I'll help as much as I can until the time comes."

CHAPTER FORTY

Once they were through the chamber with its lethal radiation levels, the tunnels provided numerous options for the way forward. They could have made much faster progress if they hadn't had to worry about the man who had been affected. He was, however, deteriorating rapidly and Jessica13 wondered if it wasn't better to simply leave him.

She pushed the thought aside immediately and let Mini carry him on the back of the Minato. The chances were the dosage of radiation he had received was higher than they had calculated, and he might have less than an hour left.

The group needed to push on and for now, they would take him with them.

Radiation levels decreased steadily as they moved away from the core, to the point where the clicking had reduced to regular, survivable levels. Even so, she wasn't ready to abandon their suits yet. They appeared to do their jobs, despite the beating they'd taken, and there was no guarantee that they wouldn't run into another exposed reactor.

The chances of that diminished as they drew closer to the

city. Coolant liquid no longer dripped from the ceilings and they were able to see the kind of architecture that had gone into the construction of the labyrinth. She had expected to see the same kind of minimalist work that had defined the building of bunkers, but this was altogether different. The ceilings were supported by arches that had been intricately carved, and the pillars were all similarly designed and sometimes made to look like ten-foot-tall men and women who held the ceiling up.

It was impressive and she wasn't the only one to notice it. The entire group slowed and couldn't help but appreciate the workmanship involved in creating the pillars and arches.

"I guess they had more time and talent for this kind of stuff back in the day," Jessica13 muttered and traced her fingers over a column that had been carved to look like a school of fish swimming upward.

"I think this was where many people hid while there was fighting in the sky," Mini explained as he came to a halt beside her. "These tunnels were where they took refuge from the possibility that something would destroy the world above. In the end, it became a statement that they would survive, if through nothing else than the work of their hands."

A small smile crept onto her face. "I like that."

Regrettably, the group knew they couldn't linger and continued their journey until they reached a set of stairs that led into what she could only guess was the town. They wouldn't wait for whatever the Prophet planned to do from the outside with the army he led. Their small team needed to accomplish their mission as quickly as possible.

She led them up the winding steps and by the time they were halfway to the top, she could already hear movement above them. Everything remained fairly muffled but what she could identify didn't seem like normal activity. Klaxons blared to indicate some kind of emergency and she imagined the troops being mobilized to address the emergency.

"I guess the Prophet's already started his attack," she muttered and raised her voice to the rest of the team. "We need to pick up the pace. Everything needs to be open out there for this attack to succeed."

Her words galvanized them and they all but ran up the steps until they reached the door at the top. It was, predictably, locked.

"I think I can help," Mini suggested and moved carefully through the group until he reached it. The Minato yanked it from its hinges with little difficulty. Everyone covered their eyes at the sudden bright light that streamed through the aperture.

It looked like sunlight and her assumption was that they were only a few steps away from being in the open again.

They stepped out into a somewhat disappointing reality, although Jessica13 couldn't help but stare and marvel at the sheer feat of engineering the chamber represented. A massive ceiling arched above them, and what were clearly nuclear-powered lamps provided the light for the cavern. These were drawn on tracks to mimic the movement of the sun across the ceiling-sky.

Whoever had put this much work into the construction had left little to chance. They wanted a society to flourish while they remained in hiding.

Jessica13 pushed forward while the others in the team appeared to be similarly awed by the massive cavern they had entered. They needed to remain focused if they wanted to succeed in this, she reminded herself brusquely, and there would be little room for error.

"Come on, we need to get out of these suits and looking a little less like outsiders," she snapped, dragged her headpiece off, and removed the rest of the suit. Her teammates hurriedly followed her example, while she turned to Mini and Robert7.

"Do you know where we're supposed to go? Where is the central control facility?"

The pilot took a few deep breaths. "It's one of the tallest buildings in the city. They wanted to have unimpeded access to all sectors in case of an emergency, kind of like what we see here."

"I am constructing a map of the city now," Mini stated. "The tallest building in the city is about three hundred meters to our left, although there are significant urban barriers between us and it."

"Well, there's no time like the present," she muttered and took a moment to survey their surroundings. The alarms that blared demandingly were a little less disconcerting than the constant clicking of the Geiger counters, but barely. Fortunately, the constant racket seemed to focus the attention of the residents elsewhere, and the resultant chaos might prove an advantage. Everything in her wanted to push toward their target immediately since the Prophet and his people waited for them to succeed and expected them to come through.

Of course, the man wouldn't be able to deliver on his threat to kill her and Robert7 from where he was, but it was still an effective motivator.

"Jessica13, my sensors detect incoming mechs," Mini alerted her. "I would suggest you climb in and prepare for hostilities."

She didn't hesitate or even think about it before she scrambled in through the hatch. The heavy footsteps of assault mechs approached. The Minato wouldn't have much of a chance against them, but it was still better than they would have without it.

Three mechs came into view and she froze and grasped the controls of the Minato tightly. The adrenaline surged in her body and made her blood pump faster than before. They were big mechs, altered Lancers with heavier armor and likely more firepower to the assault rifles they carried. A hasty scan of the surrounding area showed no obvious terrain advantages. She could always outrun them, but that would leave the rest of her team to the mercy of the enemy.

Windchime's suggestion that she save herself rang in her ears, but she shook her head. She wouldn't leave anyone behind, not if she could help it.

The mechs came to a halt in front of the rebels, who stood stiff and silent, not sure what they should do next. The Lancers, all painted dark-blue, formed up around them, although it didn't seem to be a containment formation. It looked more like they intended to attack.

Jessica13 could see why they would choose to do so. They were in the middle of a fight for the city and intruders wouldn't be treated lightly.

She looked around and tried to find a way through the group. Maybe she could distract them or persuade them to pursue her and leave her team alone. While she considered the odds—none of which seemed to be in her favor—the mech in the center stopped moving. The hatch opened and a head emerged.

Dumbfounded, she stared and gave herself a moment to confirm who she was looking at. The short growth of hair and a beard were a little off-putting, but she couldn't mistake Hammerhand's movements and his demeanor was unmistakable as he pulled himself out of the mech.

"I think I'd know that Minato anywhere," he rumbled and a broad, uncharacteristic grin played across his face.

She pulled the hatch of the Minato open and exited as well, sprinted to the man, and all but tackled him in a hug. "Hammerhand! I didn't know if you'd made it out alive. The Prophet said there was a trap but he had no way to know if you and the Knights managed to escape or not."

"It's good to know that bastard made it out alive." He chuckled and after a few awkward seconds, chose to return the hug stiffly. "I assume he's the one we have to thank for the mess of alarms we hear? I initially thought they had been triggered by our escape from prison but realized after a while that there must be some kind of external threat."

"I think it's him," Jessica13 replied and finally released the man. "He did have an attack planned, so it can't be anything else. What happened—no, there'll be time for that later. Where are the others? The other Knights? Windchime and Tinker?"

She received her answer from the way his expression dimmed almost instantly.

"Windchime is organizing the rest of the Knights and prisoners who have thrown in on our side. Tinker… Tinker didn't make it."

A hard, painful lump settled in her throat. She had thought she'd made her peace with losing the Knights when the Prophet delivered the news of what happened, but the thought of the group without the old man felt incomplete somehow. They were missing a vital piece.

And she could tell that Hammerhand felt the same way.

She cleared her throat, although it did little to dislodge the lump that had appeared there. "We need to keep moving. There's time…time to think about…" She cleared her throat again and nodded firmly. "We need to reach the central control facility of the city and open the access to the cavern for the Prophet's arrival."

"How does he plan to attack the city itself?"

"We found a way to neutralize the artillery defending it, so the plan is an all-out frontal assault. But it won't work if the cavern isn't open. Can you help us?"

Hammerhand turned as a mixed group approached them. Knights, either on foot or piloting the same dark-blue Lancers he had been in, had been joined by the Auburn rebels who had survived the battle as well as a group of men who looked like the dangerous kind. These were led by a man with a large scar across the side of his face.

"I think we can," the Knights' leader replied with a small, manic grin.

CHAPTER FORTY-ONE

Ten Minutes before Hammerhand Broke out of Prison

There were few things in the world that were worse than waiting for something to happen or for things to fall into place. Patience was a virtue, or so the old writings went, and the Prophet sometimes wondered if the only thing that made it a virtue was the fact that it was so difficult to do.

Night had fallen a few hours before and the sky was full of clouds that partially obfuscated the light of the moon and stars. It still wasn't quite as dark he would have preferred, as the full moon traced the grasslands here and there with a dull blue light, but it would have to be enough.

He turned to look toward the open plain where they had set the salvaged blimp. Until now, their main focus had been to make sure no one could see what they were doing and to a large extent, they'd been able to use the landscape to their advantage. They wouldn't have to charge into the teeth of the massive artillery shells, which changed the odds of success considerably.

"The time has come," he said, pushed up from where he had laid prone, and jogged to his mech that he'd left in a crouched position. "Release the blimp."

Once he'd climbed into his Argonaut, he kept it low as he advanced to the hilltop once more. This section of mountainous terrain had shielded their advance thus far, but it was the last cover they would have until they reached the spire.

Which, of course, was the purpose of the Zeppelin and the reason why they'd put so much time and effort into it. They needed it to create cover where there was none.

The Prophet looked into his scanners and scowled. "I said to release the blimp. Why is it still grounded?"

There was no immediate answer and he glanced at where it was buffeted by the wind.

"We can't release it under these high winds," someone finally shouted. From their accent, it was one of the Auburn rebels. "Otherwise, it'll drift out into the open and could take hours to bring on track again."

They were right and that would be disastrous. It didn't mean he had to like it, though. Waiting for conditions to become favorable wasn't how he was built. He had always advocated the benefits of a speedy assault and the ability to maintain the speed and agility required to advance and retreat continually to sting the enemy a hundred times until they died.

But that wouldn't work against this enemy.

"Patience…is a virtue," he muttered aloud in an effort to calm himself.

The wind gauge on the Argonaut confirmed that they were dealing with gusts that blew at almost a hundred kilometers an hour. With the open grassland all around them, they wouldn't find any advantage to it until it shifted to blow from the direction of the rock formation they used for cover.

"Come on, come on," he whispered.

"What was that?"

The Prophet realized his comm lines were open and cleared his throat. "Nothing. What's the status on the blimp?"

There was no response again, but he was more than able to judge the situation for himself. The group comprised at least two dozen—some in mechs and some not—but all now struggled to hold it in place. They had set up a series of ropes and anchors in the ground to facilitate this but even so, they fought an ongoing battle against the gusting wind.

He turned his mic off but continued to listen to the communication between his people. They were all anxious to enter combat but once they initiated their final march, they would have to impose radio silence during their attack. It wasn't likely, but the possibility that the people in the artillery mechs at the top of the spire would be able to triangulate their position despite the chaff release was too high.

Coordination was key, and they had spent hours running over the details during the day to plan their assault as meticulously as they could.

With that done, all that remained was to hope that nothing went wrong.

He studied the wind gauge with barely harnessed impatience. The speed didn't decrease but the angle shifted slowly to finally reach a trajectory toward the spire.

Surprisingly, the velocity slowed and seemed to settle into a steady and fairly substantial drift toward the target with none of the unpredictable gusts that would have caused significant interference.

He turned his mic on. "The winds are down. Release!"

His team released the mooring ropes and the balloon elevated smoothly. When it reached its optimal altitude, the rotors engaged to work with the wind and it began to surge forward. It looked almost impossibly slow but gained speed and advanced steadily toward the spire.

CHAPTER FORTY-TWO

While a clever idea, it remained an enormous gamble. The artillery guns would have no problem eliminating the blimp in mid-flight if they wanted to, and that would massively stall the assault while they tried to find another way to neutralize the defenses. The absence of an existing alternative plan was a reminder that they had no other options, to begin with.

But, as Robert7 had pointed out, the defenders believed that the blimp had been destroyed in the battle and therefore that they were the only ones who possessed any. It might seem a slim advantage, but not when added to their inevitable assumption that their trap had worked and no more enemies were left to defy their dominance of the area. Together, these would lead them to think there was no way someone would attempt a frontal assault.

They had good reason to believe that, obviously, and therein lay the gamble. One single question as to why a blimp had appeared on their radar, even in the strong winds, would lead to a challenge and that would be the end of it.

But the Desert Warriors and their allies would find a way

through. They had to. He would not allow failure to plague him, not again.

The Zeppelin continued its progress and its speed increased as it glided a little higher as well. He had previously considered the possibility of using the cloud cover to hide its advance, but that would have delayed their attack further since they would have needed to start from kilometers away to allow it to gain sufficient altitude. Besides, cloud cover wasn't something they could rely on.

The Prophet pushed these futile what-ifs from his mind and focused on the fact that the die was cast. The people manning the guns could see it by now, and if they intended to fire, it would happen soon. He tensed in his Argonaut's cockpit but try as he might, he couldn't see any way to calm himself. His body and mind had been ready for a fight for what seemed like hours and he'd chafed during the long wait for the right conditions.

The seconds ticked past and the balloon continued to move. He could discern no sign of the cannon barrels moving to engage their new target or that any kind of alarm had been raised about an attack.

He could barely believe that their plan seemed to have fallen so easily into place. Of course, it wasn't complete yet and all he could do was hope—and maybe pray—to push the blimp a few hundred more meters into its firing range.

His mouth was dry and the blood thumped in his ears as it finally moved into position directly over the spire.

The seconds ticked past and its speed decreased when the rotors turned off. It was time to fire.

When the expected response failed to materialize, he scowled.

"Why haven't you fired?" he demanded over the comms he opened to the people who controlled it.

"We're trying," one of the pilots answered. "There's something wrong with the trigger."

He cursed his fucking luck. Had they not checked the trigger mechanism beforehand, or had something been destabilized during the short flight?

"Shit," he snapped while he tried to think of some way to drop the chaff despite the technical failure. It would need to happen soon since the wind had already begun to push against the side of the blimp and force it to the left and away from its attack position. "I think if we maybe have someone who can shoot that far..."

His voice trailed off as a small cheer erupted from his people. There was enough of a response to indicate that something positive had happened, and he turned quickly to identify the reason for their jubilation.

The blimp had been pushed slightly out of position but it didn't quite matter at this point. The cloud of chaff had already been released over the spire. He had talked to the people who controlled it and they would turn it to try to deliver weather damage. The reasoning was that even if it was shot down, it would draw fire away from the real attack.

Speaking of which, it was time for the Desert Warriors to act.

They chose not to use their horns this time. As much as the Prophet appreciated the psychological effect it had on their enemies, it was simply a bad idea to announce this particular assault. The cannons could still see well enough, even if their radars were down.

He delivered the order on their commlinks and made a dual statement to command them to advance as well as initiate radio silence from this moment forward until they engaged fully with the defenders.

The Prophet moved out first and his lieutenants fell in beside him while the others assumed battle formation behind them and they began the charge. The troops included a mixture of the mechs the Desert Warriors were known for, the colors reminiscent of the desert and spikes jutting from their armor. A number of rebels had joined them as well. The mechs they used were mostly those that had been recovered from both sides after the battle in Auburn. The Knights had left a few functional mechs behind and a few others that needed minor repairs.

It was, he decided, an army. There was no other word for it, and he could appreciate the support as they raced forward. The larger Argonauts couldn't run properly, but the longer strides did allow them to keep up with the smaller, lighter mechs, at least over the open ground.

Their numbers and sudden movement were enough to capture the attention of the people who manned the defenses. When they were about five hundred meters from the spire, he could hear that alarms had been triggered inside. The cannons at the top began to swivel to aim at the attackers, but they looked uncoordinated and leaned to the side and almost intersected with the others. They would no doubt open fire, but they would effectively be blind.

Despite that assurance, it was still daunting given the sheer size of the weapons and the devastation they could deliver.

Even from a significant distance, the grinding whirr was clearly audible as each cannon powered. This was followed by a thump as the five-kilogram rounds were launched with enough force to make an impact that shook the ground all around like an earthquake. The warriors already knew to remain in a wide, loose formation, and the first volley missed. They overshot the attacking mechs and only one shot landed inside their ranks. Fortunately, it was too far from any of them to deal any real damage.

The sheer impact was still a sobering thought, and the Prophet pushed his mech a little faster.

The next volley seemed a little more coordinated. They had abandoned trying to aim by sight and now focused on suppressing fire in selected locations in an effort to disrupt the charge.

They were still firing blind, however, and the signal went up among the warriors. The mechs at the back fired flares that arced into the sky and slowly descended as the second volley was launched. The bait was taken, at least partially, and most of the rounds were aimed much higher than they should have been to be effective.

A few struck home, however. The Desert Warriors drew back from a crater that had suddenly materialized in front of them, and one of the Auburn rebels was all but obliterated when one of the rounds found him.

The Prophet hadn't expected to reach the spire without taking casualties, but every man or woman lost would be painful to watch. He steeled himself and pushed forward. It was foolish to even imagine that they could accomplish their assault without losses but at the same time, he was also forced to acknowledge that each and every fighter was needed if they expected to break into the city.

Their plans had been partly based on the reasoning that their group would be practically unreachable by the mechs above the spire when they came too close. At a certain distance, the cannons wouldn't be able to swivel enough to target them.

It appeared that the defenders agreed. The firing slowed as they continued to advance and when they were about fifty meters away from the entrance, the gates opened slowly and mechs rushed out to set up defensive positions.

"So, it begins," the Prophet stated. He lifted the radio silence, let his warriors form up a little closer, and pressed forward.

CHAPTER FORTY-THREE

It occurred to him that they would miss Hammerhand's shield in this assault. With it, they would have been able to push in behind the barrier and time their volleys for the few moments when it dropped. The Knights had shown how effective the tactic was time and time again.

But there was no point in crying over missing tactical necessities. They would have to make do, something the Desert Warriors were extremely capable of.

The mechs that had brought up the rear suddenly rushed to the front. They carried heavy loads on their backs, and as the defending forces opened fire, they dropped their burdens in front of them. A couple more moved in on either side, pulled out what looked like large steel bars, and opened them into massive steel sheets.

It wasn't the same as Hammerhand's shield, but at least it would protect more mechs as they surged forward. The smaller rounds all ricocheted off the newly constructed shields, but the larger shots powered by the Guardians in the defense left dents and even broke through, although they also fired blind at this point.

Tinker had, fortunately, left a wide variety of interesting weapons and gadgets in his Beast, and with the help of Jessica13, they had been able to determine what each was for or at least what it could be used for in a fight.

The distance between the two lines diminished and finally, the shields pressed into the defending mechs. They weren't pushed back but they didn't need to be. The Desert Warriors, equipped with swords and buzz saws, shoved through the gaps of the shields or, with help from the support mechs, were able to vault over them. Showers of sparks erupted as the warriors unleashed a determined assault.

The defenders tried to withdraw from their outer defensive position and retreat behind the gates where they could work from cover as well.

The Prophet and his two lieutenants thrust closer to the shields and two of the support mechs shifted the barriers to create an opening for them to push through. They opened fire and the depleted uranium slugs punched easily through the armor of the assault mechs that attempted to pull back.

The defenders retaliated, but the Prophet barely felt any of the rounds they used. All were unable to penetrate the heavier armor he and his troops wore.

Those Desert Warriors who had melee weapons converged on the heavy mechs that had remained to try to hold the outer defense. They looked like ants crawling over the heavier mechs as they sliced and hacked chunks of their armor off and dragged them free before they struck at the vital sections.

It was accomplished quickly, the kind of work the Desert Warriors were more than capable of performing. They were in their element now and their coordination and skill definitely outclassed those who hadn't been prepared for the attack.

The order to retreat became obvious when those who had survived turned and withdrew behind the gates they had emerged from. It was clear that they hadn't expected someone to breach the defenses that had been set up. There was no other explanation for how unprepared they were.

Fortunately, their unreadiness worked to the warriors' advantage. The Prophet reloaded his rifle and continued to fire at selected targets among those that had already turned away from the fight. He maintained a slow but steady rhythm to add to their casualties as much as he could in the time he had available to him.

The defenders retreated into a larger chamber that was already protected by the spire structure. A number of mech-sized elevators would most likely allow them to return to where they had come from. From the way they ignored the damage and focused on pushing clear of the battle, the Prophet knew it was in his army's best interest to prevent them from reaching their destination.

He highlighted the location while the support mechs retrieved the shield to allow their full troop to attack as one. They surged forward and pounded into the lines of the mechs that had defended the gate. He was at the front, together with his lieutenants, and they drove hard into their lines and punched holes in their armor for the buzz saw fighters to take them apart for scrap metal.

The lack of coordination among the defenders was their downfall. The Desert Warriors decimated their ranks in a concerted push toward the back lines. They eliminated the support mechs as they churned over their fallen comrades in an effort to get over them. Most failed, and the carnage slowed the retreat to the point where the invading force was able to defeat them all.

A small cheer of victory issued from the group as the last enemy mech fell from the group they had engaged. The Prophet and his forces knew this wasn't the last of the defenders. They were probably only the first wave, the immediate response while the others prepared better defenses.

Still, a partial victory was better than what they had endured on their first attempt.

"Gather the wounded!" he shouted, anxious to resume his men's formation lest they be caught unawares. "Reload and make what repairs can be done quickly."

Those who needed to remain behind did so while the rest entered the elevators. He knew it wouldn't be quite as simple as walking into the city. The element of surprise was long gone, and all they could do was steel themselves for what was likely being prepared for them below.

The larger mechs pushed forward and the shields were placed at the front to provide some cover to work from. The elevator doors slid shut and they began to descend.

It was a long and slow journey into the earth. Robert7 had said that it was almost a hundred meters and the elevators couldn't cover that distance in the kind of speed he would prefer.

Still, they seemed to move more sluggishly than expected. He looked at the mechanism and scowled as the system seemed to slow even further until eventually, they ground to a halt about thirty meters down the hundred-meter drop.

"They've done something to the mechanism from down there," the Prophet surmised and tapped his foot on the door in front of him. "We'll have to find another way down. Buzz saws, you know what to do."

Those who had the weapon in hand immediately worked together to cut a hole in the elevator large enough for the mechs to climb through. Another group opened sections of the top and used grapplers to provide cables to climb down with. It was quick work and something they had done before. It wasn't long before the first group of five proceeded down the cables.

They moved quickly and only slowed once they were close to the bottom. When they did, they were fired upon immediately. A couple were dropped and their mechs caught fire.

The others managed to take cover in the small chamber, while more of the Desert Warriors followed with shields held level to support their attack. The Prophet elected to move after the next group, clamped hold of the cables, and rushed to the bottom where his troops rallied and positioned themselves to allow space for more of their numbers to enter the next level.

He looked forward to seeing the best that FEMA City had to offer in a fair fight.

CHAPTER FORTY-FOUR

His boots touched the bottom of the shaft and he shifted aside a little more as the rest of his men carved into the mechs that tried to hold the elevator area against them. They wore the same kinds of mechs and colors as those they had fought on the surface but there were fewer than the Prophet imagined there would be.

This close to the city, he would have thought they would have put more numbers into the defense, especially as the chambers grew smaller and tighter.

Thus far, the Desert Warriors experienced little difficulty. They thoroughly outnumbered the group they were attacking. The defenders struggled to retreat and assume defensive positions, but they weren't given any room to maneuver. Swords and buzz saws shredded their armor and spat showers of sparks that illuminated the chamber they pushed into.

"I really thought they would put more resistance down here," the Prophet grumbled and scanned the surroundings as he reloaded his assault rifle.

Of course, Robert7 hadn't known what they could expect

with these defenses, which was perfectly reasonable. The young pilot hadn't been privy to the strategic planning and tactics, after all. It merely meant that whatever they encountered this deep into the city's defenses, they would simply have to find a way to push through or around it.

For now, they waited for Jessica13's team to make their impact. Not that he expected them to make it this soon but a part of him had hoped they might. He would have preferred to maintain the momentum rather than have even a few moments to think.

The last of the fighters of the company that had been the first to engage the Desert Warriors were taken apart, prevented from retreating, and killed. They didn't even try to surrender, of course, which left his troops with no choice but to kill them to a man.

He wasn't sure where his sudden doubts about the decision came from. Maybe he had spent too much time around Hammerhand and his Knights and their morality had begun to rub off on him. It was all well and good in this area in the world but it would get them killed in the desert when they returned.

If they returned.

The Prophet steeled himself as they worked to get the elevators functioning once more. The last of the Desert Warriors were allowed to descend, which gave them the chance to fully repair and put their mechs together again before they turned their attention to the massive gate that now impeded their passage.

He couldn't help the feeling that they had merely cleared the chaff from the wheat, the scraps from the larger force they were about to face when they pushed through the barriers.

They could only be described as gates and stood almost

three times as tall as his mech and wide enough for ten mechs to march through shoulder to shoulder. Grapplers were fired into and attached to the gates, and the groups combined their efforts to pull them open.

There was some resistance as the magnetic locks tried to keep them closed, but the strength of dozens of mechs was enough to accomplish their goal.

His eyes narrowed, he zoomed in on the group that had already assumed formation on the other side of the chamber revealed behind the gates.

The cavern looked natural, although it was supported by massive columns. Lighting appeared to come from the ceiling by way of nuclear-powered lamps.

The Prophet had never seen this much space that wasn't out in the open. Whoever had built it had likely found these caverns already formed and made use of them. Otherwise, he couldn't begin to imagine the amount of work that would go into the excavation required for something of this magnitude.

The troop they faced looked a good deal more formidable than those they had encountered earlier, even though they were far inferior in number.

For one thing, they looked more organized.

Four companies of four Quadrupeds each were formed up in front of another gate. They were massive, larger even than the Excalibur Hammerhand piloted. They were painted all in black, and from what he could see, they carried more armor than most Quadrupeds did—which was saying something since they were the heaviest mechs ever produced.

A couple of assault mechs and two heavy mechs that supported them almost seemed tiny by comparison.

A few other modifications were discernible but he couldn't make out the details. Still, the attack had come this far and he had no intention to stop now. They would find a way through them.

"Form up, you sons of bitches!" the Prophet called to his troops and leveled his assault rifle at the mechs opposite him. The Desert Warriors moved in beside him and set their shields up for an advance. They stood about fifty meters away from their adversaries, which meant a short charge. Once they were in close enough, his men were better prepared for melee combat than the huge Quadrupeds.

Something groaned behind them, and he turned quickly as the gates they had opened now closed again behind them with a heavy thump.

It appeared that they were trapped in the chamber with the defenders, an interesting proposition although not something he'd expected.

He turned to face the enemy when they began to beat mechanical fists against something positioned at their sides. Low, deep chants emitted from the mechs themselves as they took a step forward and set themselves into place.

One by one, they pushed the heavy metal plates that were at their sides out in front to act like shields. They were a good deal thicker and taller than those the Desert Warriors carried. The mechs shuffled a little closer and sections of the shields interlocked to form a perfectly solid barrier between the attackers and the gate behind them.

The Prophet suppressed a hint of trepidation. Even with those shields, they were still at a disadvantage when it came to melee combat. Once his troops closed the distance, gaps would be found or made as necessary and they would break through the lines.

"My warriors!" he called, raised his rifle, and lowered it slowly to point at the opposing shield wall. "Give them hell!"

A low roar issued from the men as they began their advance without horns or fanfare. They could almost taste victory.

He'd no sooner thought that when the Quadrupeds tightened their formation and adjusted their shields. Gaps were created around ten meters from the ground and once they appeared, huge barrels emerged.

A strong sense of foreboding swept over him, but he steeled himself and continued the advance with his warriors.

The first volley felt like an earthquake ripped through the room and clouds of dust puffed loose from the ceiling.

The rounds savaged his group. Their shields offered little resistance and huge holes allowed the ordnance to plow into the mechs that were behind them. Chunks of metal exploded from the impact, and mechs fell to pieces, unable to withstand the force.

"Shit!" He growled his frustration and fury. The reason for shutting the gates behind them now made sense since there was no cover between them and the attackers. Their shields wouldn't do them any good, and all they could count on was their mobility to avoid complete annihilation.

The Prophet scowled and hastily scanned their surroundings as another volley of rounds obliterated their shields and felled a group of his warriors. The floor shuddered beneath their feet in a series of aftershocks.

"Evasive maneuvers!" he shouted over the comms, and his men were only too glad to comply. They immediately broke formation and separated to make use of as much room as the cavern gave them while they advanced.

The fact that there was no retreat available to them was known to every member, so the only way was forward and through. Of course, there was no way through, not unless

Jessica13 and Robert7's team did what they had been sent to do.

"Don't you dumbasses let me down," he muttered and hoped they would somehow hear him. His heart heavy, he pushed his Argonaut forward to attack.

CHAPTER FORTY-FIVE

There was no other place for the central control facility to be. It stood at the dead center of the city and its structure rose like the spire directly above it. Although considerably less impressive, of course, it was still extremely effective.

It was likely in place to control the spire and would be exactly what the Prophet needed to aid in his assault.

Jessica13 slipped into the Minato and moved them toward the entrance. They had expected defenses but the sight of a couple of assault mechs standing at the ready at the front of the building made her take a quick step back.

"Do you have any suggestions?" Mini asked.

She shook her head. "Nope. How about you?"

"I do, but I didn't want to step on any metaphorical toes in case you had something in mind."

"The mech is yours."

"That is appreciated."

Mini took control and guided the Minato into the open street ahead of the control facility. He kept to the shadows as the two mechs appeared to be very much on the alert thanks to the shrill alarms that continued to blare through the city. All the citizens had apparently been drawn into their homes for safety, which made this maneuver far simpler.

After a moment, she had an idea of what Mini attempted to do. He snuck in closer to the tall building and deliberately added enough stealth to the movement to make sure the two guards would see them.

They wouldn't ask questions, not when a strange mech with no known markings appeared while the entire city was on high alert. They immediately swung their weapons, aimed quickly, and opened fire.

Mini was already on the move. He darted to the right and immediately to the left before he shifted seamlessly into Bulletfoot mode and bounded off the wall with all four limbs and landed in front of the two defensive mechs.

They fired where the Minato had been rather than where it had gone, and most of their rounds missed. A few connected but deflected off the armor. The AI had brought them in a little too close for comfort, but she already knew what her role was. She disconnected the dart from their grappler, waited, and braced herself inside the cockpit.

He shoulder-charged the closer of the two mechs, shoved it to the side, and resumed the Minato's bipedal stance as she immediately aimed the grappler's air gun into the chest of the other mech and fired.

It was enough to make them stagger a couple of steps and hopefully make the enemy assume that the tiny support mech had rethought the concept of attacking the assault mechs.

The Minato turned tail and sprinted away while it lowered to all fours and remained mobile enough to make sure they couldn't land any solid strikes. Mini moved quickly and constantly to prevent their opponents from finding solid aim while he forced them to immediately begin pursuit.

Both of them obliged and she reminded herself it was a good thing. That was the aim, after all.

As they circled into the dead-end street where they'd started, Jessica13 clutched the controls of the mech a little tighter—not to take control but to keep herself from being thrown around the cockpit when Mini punched up and forced them into a vertical leap.

The two mechs rushed in and opened fire as soon as they were around the corner. They stopped shooting immediately, however, and seemed confused by the lack of a target in the street that supposedly had no exit.

"Well played." She chuckled and felt a little breathless.

"Your compliment is noted and appreciated."

As the assault mechs moved deeper into the alley and tried to determine where the Minato had disappeared to, another two assault mechs clambered down the sides of the building using the cord she had sacrificed from her grappler. They moved fast so stealth wasn't an option, and the two assault mechs turned quickly but were unalarmed by mechs wearing their colors.

More descended from all sides, and it wasn't long before the two guard mechs were captured and forced slowly to the ground. Their weapons were removed and handed to some of the other mechs.

Hammerhand stood over them and aimed his assault rifle into their cockpits.

"You have two choices," he told them briskly. "Climb out yourselves or be carried out as corpses."

It wasn't much of a choice, and both pilots were quick to follow the man's instructions. They scrambled through the open hatches and slipped out and were quickly overpowered by a group of convicts. A couple of the prisoners climbed into the recently vacated mechs and added to their numbers of effective fighters, and Jessica13 moved out from the alley toward the control facility. She doubted they only had a couple of mechs in place to defend it but getting inside was a vital first step.

"Hammerhand," she called over their newly created comm channel. "Head back to the Knights. I have the feeling the Prophet will need your help."

"Do you think his attack is going well?"

"I'll take the fact that the alarms are still blaring as a good sign."

"Fair enough. Good luck, Jessie."

"Right back at you."

CHAPTER FORTY-SIX

More than anything, Jessica13 wanted to join the Knights. She felt like she had been apart from them for far too long, and when Hammerhand headed away to liberate his people and lead them into combat again, it didn't feel right. Everything in her said she should be with them but instead, she had to continue to sneak around the damn place.

She hesitated for a moment and watched from a distance as he broke through the fences that kept the prisoners contained. The captives themselves either expected something like this or were simply quick to take advantage and the few guards that remained were quickly overwhelmed.

They did call in for help and a group of mechs began to advance, but those mechs led by Hammerhand overwhelmed them efficiently and easily. He clearly had capturing the mechs in mind, and those under his command grappled the newcomers to the floor, disarmed them, and once again offered them the chance to exit their mechs peacefully or in pieces.

"What are you waiting for?" Robert7 asked when he noticed her hesitation.

"It's only—nothing. It's nothing. Let's get this over with."

The conical building looked like it had been one of the first set up in the city, given the Cities-That-Were type of architecture, not unlike how things had been in the tunnels. There was a uniformity to it, however, and it was certainly better maintained than the subterranean passages had been. Sculptures of angels were carved into pale white marble and circled toward what appeared to be the only way up—a flight of stairs.

The walls were painted with a variety of angelic beings, from tall ones with swords and large wings to smaller ones that looked like babies with tiny wings and bows with arrows tipped with heart-shaped heads. All were illuminated by the light that streamed through stained-glass windows that added extra color to the whole structure.

They were all artistically decorated and for some reason, they were all naked too. She didn't quite understand that part, but who was she to question the artistic preferences of the people who had built it?

They moved rapidly up the steps, although it was almost instantly apparent that this was the only route to the top and there was a long, long way to go.

"Why don't you hop on the back?" she suggested and her companion complied with no small sense of relief.

The paintings and sculptures were less prolific the higher they went, although they didn't vanish completely. It seemed like it somehow depicted an ascent that not all these angelic beings were capable of making. Whether it was intended to be a metaphor about the difficulty of reaching the top of the spire or not, it seemed fairly relevant.

"I detect more mechs ahead," Mini said and brought up a highlighted section of the steps where she identified two of the same kind of assault mechs standing guard at the top of the staircase.

Jessica13 scowled deeply. "Let me guess—you have a plan for this one too?"

"I think I have the same kind of plan you would have had," Mini replied. "We could use the windows."

"It seems a shame to break them. They're beautiful."

He had no response to that. Either he had no concept of what made art beautiful or he was focused on how they could use the windows to their benefit in the fight.

Either way, they needed to get the job done. The defenders most likely already knew someone was coming up the steps and would already have trained their weapons in anticipation of their entering range.

"You might want to dismount," Mini suggested to Robert7 and once again, he did as he was told. The mech shifted to all fours and surged up the last rounds of the steps.

As they came into view of the two mechs, Mini bounded onto the wall above one of the windows and shifted to regular mode in midair. He had timed the leap and already had the grappler primed and ready. It fired and launched its dart to catch the mech on the right. When it embedded itself securely, the AI twisted the mech's torso, pulled the captive, and yanked it down the steps.

It stumbled and tried to regain its balance before it tumbled down three more steps and shattered one of the gorgeous stained-glass windows before it spun out of the building and plummeted.

Mini twisted to land on all fours again as the remaining mech opened fire at them. Bullets punched chunks of marble from the structure around them as the Minato bounded up the remaining steps, leapt over their adversary, and kicked off from the wall above it.

The AI twisted again and launched the Minato against the defending mech while it still attempted to pivot to reengage. The smaller support mech managed to squeeze between the assault mech and the heavy wooden door it defended and used its legs to launch the heavier one down the steps and through the same window his comrade had fallen through.

Momentum and the same push had reduced the door behind them to splinters and they launched through to the other side and landed a little awkwardly. Fortunately, they regained their balance quickly.

They stood in a large, circular room surrounded by a huge, single-paned window that gave it a full view of the city below.

Below the window and in a single line, a vast array of different digital and analog controls followed the entire circular wall. The center of the room was the most interesting, as a handful of panels connected to controls that were directed into the antenna in the spire.

About a dozen men and women in white coats were busy there, all surprised to see the small mech suddenly appear in their workspace. None of them were armed and they seemed unsure of what to do.

Jessica13 had a few ideas. "Get the fuck out of here or I'll drag you out. Choose now!"

They still looked a little confused.

"Now, dammit—now!"

The shout snapped them out of their shock and they sprinted toward the door, where they wisely avoided Robert7 as he made his way into the room.

She climbed out of the hatch of the Minato, stiff from being knocked around in the cockpit.

"You're a little terrifying, do you know that?" the pilot pointed out as they moved toward the central panels.

"Mini did most of the work."

"Well, yes, I was referring to your mech's AI, but you have much the same effect too."

She couldn't help a small smirk as they situated themselves in front of the controls.

Most of the time, machines and controls simply spoke to her. There was always something about them that made it easy for her to interact with them, but these controls were different. Nothing about them seemed familiar and even the readings displayed on the screens around her felt completely foreign.

"Shit," she muttered before one particular control caught her eye. It certainly stood out. A switch flanked by two marble angels had that kind of effect. She approached it and after a moment of hesitation, pulled the switch down.

Unfortunately, nothing happened.

"No, not that one," Robert7 said and waved her toward one of the smaller panels. Only a few screens were connected to it and the board held three switches.

He flicked all three at the same time. "There we go."

"Are you sure?"

"Fairly."

Jessica13 sighed, having expected something a little more emphatic. Her gaze drifted to the angel-flanked switch. "I wonder what that one did."

CHAPTER FORTY-SEVEN

"Mommy, Mommy—the world is ending! The world is ending!"

The mother looked up from her work and wiped a bead of sweat from her forehead. It was an uncommon claim, but a child's fanciful thoughts didn't lend themselves to common occurrences.

A loud, metallic groan from above made her drop the steel pail of water she had carried and her gaze turned to the ceiling. She froze when she registered movement up there.

Massive gears turned in a mechanism that had rusted with age. They resisted every cycle forced by the machine but continued to move anyway. The entire contraption shuddered and shook, but there was nothing to prevent or hinder what was to come.

Large steel cords were suddenly strained, tugged, and pulled as the gears continued to turn. Some of them broke and whipped wildly under the pressure as the wheels moved. Redundancies kicked in and the cavernous chamber was filled with the noise of centuries-old machinery being awoken and set to task.

The gears began to throw sparks as they were driven against the rust that had set in. They spun slowly and worked what had settled on them loose to jettison it all in a shower of dust that poured over everything below.

People screamed, dropped whatever they had in their hands, and hastily took cover in the nearest buildings to avoid the apparent mayhem around them.

Suddenly, a crack appeared in the ceiling. The nuclear lamps that had acted as their sun for so long extinguished and descended to where they had been recalled into a night phase prematurely.

The darkness that filled the cavern was almost palpable as the sound of thousands of voices rose in terror greeted the inevitable. Nothing could halt the inexorable outcome. The world was ending.

While those trapped tried to come to terms with their imminent demise, a light appeared. At first, it was only a single beam with a blueish sheen that cut through the darkness like a knife and illuminated the ground like a spotlight. A few other sources were soon dotted around it, although none were quite so intense as the singular orb that floated over the ceiling of the cavern.

No, not on the ceiling—far, far above it. A disk of blue light was revealed as the ceiling itself was drawn away. The gears began to spin faster now. The rust had been removed and oil was pumped in automatically so everything worked in unison. Every gaze turned to see their world change rather than end.

It looked like a flower suddenly in bloom being drawn up and away from above them to slowly display more and more of the sky above. The moon—yes, that was the name on everyone's lips. They'd all read the instructional texts of the world above.

Thousands of stars were spread across the sky in tiny yet iridescent pinpoints of pure light. They glimmered against the velvet backdrop and made the darkness a little less dark and even then, it only seemed to emphasize the majesty of what was revealed above them.

"No…not ending," the mother murmured in awe and gathered her child in her arms. "Not ending, I hope."

"What's happening, Mommy?"

She shook her head. "I don't know, dearest."

CHAPTER FORTY-EIGHT

Most of the surviving Knights were now mounted in the captured prison mechs. There had been a small warehouse full of them, so their numbers were bolstered by a group of prisoners who wanted to be involved in the fighting too.

Hammerhand still felt a little naked without his Excalibur. The inability to deploy a shield to cover his people and sweep around it with his hammer was annoying, but for the moment, he was happy to be inside a mech and have the chance to carve out his own destiny. He would search for his mech again once the battle was over.

They wouldn't have destroyed it, right?

Suddenly, as the Knights and their new recruits gathered in the prison yards, the floor of the entire structure began to shudder. Loud, metallic groaning and rumbling echoed through the cavern and deafened the whole team to the point where conversation was impossible.

Something was changing around them, although he couldn't quite make out what it was.

"Is it an earthquake?" Windchime asked from where he had used the quiet moment to adjust to his new mech.

"I don't think so," Hammerhand said with a small smile as the cavern began to open slowly. "I think Jessie came through for us. Not that I ever doubted her."

It was an interesting view, and as much as he wanted to continue to watch and study the handiwork that had gone into making the city work, the loud rumble was quickly replaced by the unmistakable sound of a firefight. Loud booms from cannons, repetitive cracks of smaller gunfire, explosions, and other signs of fighting seemed located not far from them.

If that wasn't the Prophet, he would give up piloting his Excalibur for the rest of time. He turned to address the group assembled. They weren't all Knights and they weren't all in mechs, as some of the prisoners had taken possession of the weapons the guards had carried.

"Knights Mechanica!" he roared through the external speakers of his mech. "To me! The time has come to prove your valor, your mettle, and your worth. This battle will define our legacies and show the world that there is still goodness and brotherhood left in it. For our brothers, we will not fail in this fight. For Tinker, we will show that his death was not in vain. Unto the breach once more, my brothers!"

The Knights, whether they had been among the ranks before or not, roared and rushed through the streets of the city toward the battle. He was at the front and ached to get into combat. Playing at chipping away at the inside of their enemies was all well and good but getting out into the open and into a real battle felt right.

They soon reached the area where a fight was in progress. A

gate had been opened and a group of Quadrupeds, painted black, had locked together and formed what appeared to be a shield wall to repel an outside attack that was still ongoing. He raised his assault rifle as he had identified that four smaller mechs—two assault mechs and two Guardians—held the back line.

They opened fire in an attempt to slow the advance of the Knights who attacked their rear ranks. Hammerhand wove his mech forward and tried to keep it in motion while making its movements difficult to predict. A couple of rounds impacted and three of his Knights faltered in their charge, but the rest remained undaunted.

The four were no match for the dozens that suddenly swarmed their position, and a hail of bullets brought the two Assault mechs down. The Guardians tried to back away to find cover among their heavily armored comrades, but one lost control of its left leg. The hydraulics had been compromised, and he reached it first. The vibrosword had never been one of his favorite weapons, but it was more than effective to hack through the armor and into the Guardian that attempted to pull back.

The Quadrupeds tried to turn to engage the new threat, but it was painfully apparent that while they had been adequately set up to stop any attacks from the front, they were unprepared to deal with those coming in from behind them. They were all locked into position and therefore unable to move unless the entire shield wall turned.

They began to disengage the interconnected barriers and a couple managed to maneuver somewhat awkwardly to face the new enemy, but there was little point to it. The gaps in their shields were suddenly swamped by those who had attacked from the outside, while the Knights, wielding the weapons they had allocated from the reserve held by the prison guard, began to operate as a unit to pull them down.

It was a slow process, as the massive cannons the Quadrupeds carried were still dangerous. A couple of the prisoners were caught in the fire while the Knights continued to press them.

"Be careful, you sons of bitches!" Hammerhand roared through the comms. "There is no point in rushing in when we can wear them down. I'll personally murder the next dumbass who gets himself killed because he's in too much of a rush."

They did as they were ordered, even the newcomers, and advanced but acted carefully to simply feint at the edges of the larger mechs until an opening was found. The Desert Warriors were more reckless, and he could see why. Without a doubt, they had taken severe losses by engaging the heavily fortified enemy and now looked for revenge. They demolished the mechs and hauled the pilots out, kicking and screaming, and tossed them aside.

He couldn't say he approved but at least the pilots were left alive, captured quickly, and bound to be dealt with later.

The last of the Quadrupeds—five of the sixteen had survived the dual-pronged onslaught—dropped their weapons. They had no way to raise their hands to indicate surrender, but the pilots climbed out slowly to show that they had no further desire to continue the fight.

Hammerhand paused for a moment and let the adrenaline from the battle continue to wash over him.

They'd won? How the hell did that happen?

He looked around at the mechs that milled around the entrance and realized they were as shocked as he was. Somehow, even with all their efforts and planning, the concept that they might survive this had never settled in as a definite possibility.

In a battle, that kind of thinking didn't come to the fore until the end.

A familiar if heavily battered Argonaut marched through the group toward him and he opened the hatch to his mech and climbed out.

It came to a halt in front of him and after a few seconds, the cockpit opened to reveal an even more familiar face as the pilot scrambled out to greet him.

"I bet you didn't think you'd see us again, eh?" Hammerhand asked with a small smirk and an extended hand as the Prophet approached him.

"No, and I'll concede that your timely help came as a surprise," the other man admitted, ignored the hand, and moved closer to embrace him instead. "But I did not think nature would allow for an imbalance to exist between us, my friend."

The Knights' leader stiffened at the hug but returned it awkwardly before both men parted again. "I'm fucking glad to see you survived those tunnels."

"And the same to you. Not that I ever doubted your ability to survive the impossible, but—"

"You did doubt. That's understandable. I had some of my own."

"It's good to see them thoroughly expunged, then."

The conversation ceased when the rumbling above them finally registered again and this time, they were able to take time to see the effects. Slivers of the cavern's ceiling had opened and peeled out to slowly reveal the sky above.

Hammerhand couldn't help but stare at the slightly cloudy

sky peppered with stars and with a hint of gray to suggest that morning wasn't too far away.

At the far right, a blimp moved slowly in the wind and fought to turn.

"What—"

"It is best not to ask until we have time to explain in detail, my friend. And there are a great many details to share. For now, let us enjoy the first sunrise this city has seen in its entire history, most likely."

He nodded. "That sounds like a good idea."

CHAPTER FORTY-NINE

There would have been a time when she would have paused to marvel at the gorgeous sight of the sun rising in the east. It cast a bright red hue across the sky as it slid above the horizon. If one paid heed to the old proverbs, it would probably rain.

Today, however, she had no time for it. The sight of the petals opening from the spire to expose FEMA City told of a story that would not have a happy ending for her if she remained.

Athena climbed into her Excalibur and activated it as quickly as she could. She even took the chance to push all the startup engines into a red line to make sure they wouldn't remain for longer than was necessary.

Her raiders were woken by the noise, and when they realized that their leader was mounted up, moved quickly to enter their assorted mechs and vehicles. They had been with her long enough to know that when she was raring to go, she wouldn't wait for anyone.

"Fucking asshole," she muttered when she finally brought

the Excalibur online. "If he'd only taken to the knife, he would have saved all of us a whole ass-load of trouble. But what does he do instead? Throw a fucking coup!"

"Oy!" one of the FEMA City guards shouted when he saw the raiders mounting up. "Where the fuck do you think you're going? We're to stay here until further orders."

There were only five of them assigned to oversee the raiders and report to their superiors in the city. It was adorable that they thought the orders meant anything at this point.

"We're leaving," she announced loudly and clearly. "No one will give you orders anymore, so if you want to come along, you'd better pick up your step."

"We won't go anywhere until there's confirm—"

His voice cut off quickly when Athena charged her spear and stepped closer. She thrust her hand forward to drive the weapon through the cockpit, ruin the mech, and kill the man inside.

She stepped away, yanked the spear out, and spun it to catch a second mech that rushed to help his comrade. The tap alone wouldn't have done much damage, but the electrical charge the spear shaft carried was more than enough to over-come the isolators of the Lancer and fry all the circuits inside as well as the pilot.

The rest of the FEMA City mechs froze in place, cognizant of their vulnerable position as the raiders were all mounted, armed, and ready to fight at the behest of their leader.

"Come or stay, I don't give a shit which," Athena snapped. "But if you come between me and where I want to go, you're dead—understood?"

It was an easy decision. They all knew that, against all odds, the city had fallen and they wouldn't be accepted with open arms. The three remaining men quickly joined ranks with the raiders and the group headed west, away from the city and into the grasslands.

The entranced look in the eyes of every single citizen as they opened their windows to look at the sun for the first time was awesome to witness. Jessica13 remembered feeling the same way when she had seen her first sunset, and it was a feeling that would never fade. It was funny how being trapped inside for one's entire life made one appreciate the Outside so much more.

She was settled on a small seat beside the Minato. There was something final about watching the petals open to reveal the sky, but there was still considerable work to be done. The Knights and the Desert Warriors had their work cut out for them to isolate the last few pockets of resistance and make sure no further skirmishes would break out. Peace was the idea, and it was long past time that the FEMA City assholes accepted that.

There seemed little that she could do at this point, though. Most of the work was carried out by the assault mechs that could actually bully other assault mechs into compliance, which left her with little to do until Hammerhand found something that needed repair.

Likely his Excalibur, if and when he ever recovered it.

In the meantime, though, she was content to go through the repairs the Minato so desperately needed. Even so, speakers across the city called for all FEMA City soldiers and fighters to surrender and turn their weapons over, mechanized or not, to the Knights Mechanica for appropriation. He was very insistent that while this was most definitely a coup, it was done so the people of the city could decide who they would have governing them.

An election was in the works too.

"I guess that's what the switch did," Mini commented as she pulled the back panels open. "What are you doing there?"

"I want to try to find that damn inertia dampener. This is the last damn time that I'll nurse bruises from being knocked around in the cockpit all day long."

"Follow the red wiring until you reach a small control panel. It'll light up."

Jessica13 grunted. "Thanks. I would have found it myself, you know."

"Clearly, but efficiency is the idea, is it not?"

She couldn't help a small smile and patted the shoulder armor of the Minato. "Yeah, I guess so."

CHAPTER FIFTY

Three Weeks Later

People had only now begun to take those damn posters down.

Jessica13 had absolutely no idea how much work would go into an election for a city this large, but sure enough, people had come out of the woodwork to decide who would be in charge of rebuilding the city now that the old regime had been overthrown.

Hammerhand had insisted that he and the Knights would only remain for as long as it took for the people to establish their own government and would have no part in how the city was run beyond what he had already done.

She wasn't sure how much people believed him, but it was nice to remain in the same place, at least for a while. Sleeping in an actual bed and being able to work with people to rebuild their homes while enjoying real food had been a treat as well.

Now, however, the election was over, and she basked in the sunlight and enjoyed a cool drink of something sweet and orange.

Robert7 dropped into the seat beside her, carrying a plate of food that had been served after the election finished.

"Do you want some?" he asked and held it out for her.

With a smile, she shook her head. "I already had my fill and was enjoying a quick break before I get back to work. People have offered me food all day since Erica8 was elected as the mayor."

"Suit yourself. It means more for me. But you might want to rethink that. Hammerhand announced that he and the Knights will move out as quickly as possible now that everything's settled and the reconstruction is underway. Maybe he feels staying here for three weeks is a little too long."

She nodded. "I suppose. He doesn't like to remain in one place for too long, and I have a feeling he won't want to stay in this one place in particular for any longer than he has to. There are too many bad memories for him, I expect."

"Being in prison?" the pilot asked around a mouthful of what looked like meal cake.

"I doubt that memory will haunt him. Tinker was one of his oldest friends and the loss impacted him more than he'll ever admit. I think he'll be on a revenge path from this point forward unless the Prophet can convince him to keep hunting for Citta Del Mar."

"But Lady Hoot's raiders weren't responsible for any of the deaths as far as I heard. They weren't even involved in the fight."

"No, but he'll still hold her responsible, I wager. Still, not much in the world can predict what he'll do next."

Robert7 nodded and placed his plate on a small table next to his seat. "What about you? What do you think you'll do next?"

Jessica13 straightened and narrowed her eyes at him. "What do you mean?"

"Do you think you'll head out with the Knights too or have you thought about staying? I know the folks around here wouldn't mind having someone of your skills to help get this city into working order."

She pursed her lips. "I've thought about it, but... Well, the Knights may be a hokey bunch but they're my hokey bunch. I've come to believe in what they fight for and I think I belong with them, at least for now. There will be other FEMA Cities out there—other Auburns and other raiders. They'll need to be stopped, and if the Knights want any chance to succeed, they'll need to have me around. Especially now that—"

While she didn't want to think about it, she also knew it was necessary, especially since it was likely that she would take over running the Beast now that Tinker wasn't there to do it.

He nodded slowly. "I think I understand."

"Besides, I've spent most of my life holed up in a bunker and I don't think I would ever be able to do it again, not since I've tasted the freedom of living Outside. How about you? Would you consider joining the Knights, wandering around and doing good deeds?"

The pilot shook his head. "I don't think so. I was never a violent person, even before I was drafted. My place is holed up in a bunker doing research. That's my way of helping people, I guess."

"And it's perfectly valid too," she assured him.

"I think I should thank you again," he said and looked away. "For saving my life. Back in Auburn, you know? Just... Yes, I think that needed to be said."

"Well, consider it repayment for you not shooting me while I tried to help you heal your leg."

He laughed and Mini drove the Minato closer to them from where it had stood a few meters away.

"Human humor dictates that I request the two of you to find a room," the AI stated firmly.

"I…what?" Jessica13 asked and frowned. "What is that supposed to mean?"

Robert7's face turned bright red and his eyebrows raised as he once again looked away. "I have no idea."

CHAPTER FIFTY-ONE

It had been a long three weeks of dodging the Knight patrols and staying away from where people had gathered in large groups to debate the next mayor.

Electing someone like Erica8 meant that the previous regime was certainly dead and gone, and they had been more than willing to turn the keys of the city over to the invaders. Whether it was because they were the first ones to break through Alpha Company's shield wall or not was up for debate.

Or it would be, once they were gone and some semblance of normalcy returned.

All he needed to do was wait until the Knights were gone and he could rejoin the new society. People always needed the hard types like Gustav15 to get the more difficult and tougher work done. He had lost his position among the Gene Guard but that didn't mean he needed to settle for being a farmer.

There were a few people in the city who were still willing to house him, and he could stay with them until it all blew over. It couldn't take that long, right?

After a furtive glance around the alley, he moved into the open but remained close to the wall as he moved toward his new home. Or temporary home, at least.

He didn't need to turn to notice the two men following him. They hadn't moved much until he crossed into their line of sight and after that, they had walked at a matching pace with him through the streets and made sure not to lose him while they acted like they weren't following him.

They weren't very good at it and losing them would be simple. A couple of alleys connected ahead of him, and he could use a door to hide and let them pass before he resumed his journey.

Gustav15 timed his movements and slowed until they had almost passed him before he circled and slipped into the narrow street. He caught their sudden change of direction out of the corner of his eye. They were too far away and it wouldn't be difficult to hide and let them run past.

When he twisted to make sure they were still following him, he ran into what felt like a wall. His speed didn't help and there was no give to the obstacle, and the impact knocked the breath out of him as he dropped on the cobbles.

A large, powerfully built man stared at him. His shoulders and arms were massive and his head looked like it had been recently shaven. A long scar stretched from the crown of his head to his jawline.

He couldn't help a small shiver when he looked into the man's steely eyes, but even more chilling was the sight of a small knife in his right hand.

"You want to rethink this," he said and pushed quickly from the ground. The man was large but he didn't have the training of one of the Gene Guard. All he needed to do was get that knife out of his hands and that would be that.

Someone grasped him suddenly from behind and held his arms back as the scar-faced man advanced on him.

"You should have thought twice about betraying the Knights Mechanica," Scar stated simply.

Gustav tried to evade the thrust but was unable to move as the sharp blade drove into his stomach. A hand clamped over his mouth to prevent his scream as the knife continued to savage his abdomen and splashed blood over his attacker's hands. The assault seemed endless and he couldn't scream into the muffling hands. It became too difficult to breathe.

He felt like he was held up by the two men when Scar finally brought the knife to his neck and slashed across it.

It was almost a relief and the pain ebbed slowly. He didn't feel anything when he was flung onto the street before the men walked away.

The world had already begun to go black when the weapon that had killed him clattered on the cobbles in front of his eyes.

Love, A, had been inscribed into the wooden handle, barely visible through the blood.

CHAPTER FIFTY-TWO

The train had long since left the rich green countryside. The terrain changed to look more like dry shrubbery that revealed the lack of moisture in the ground or perhaps only the lack of fertilizer. The heat grew more intense as well, indicative of the long trip south they were taking.

It moved quickly. The nuclear-powered trains were capable of moving at high speeds over the longer journeys the New York Western Railroad Company preferred. Slow-moving trains were those usually caught by bandits and raided.

Which was a little ironic, given their current circumstances. Levi Stone chuckled softly as he took another sip of the tea that had been prepared for him. There weren't many raiders who were effective enough to take on an armored train like this one, but there were many stupid enough to try. It was better to keep it moving quickly and avoid the hassle and paperwork.

The shrubbery began to thin and all that was left were vast sand dunes almost as far as the eye could see. The only break was the mountains to the west, capped with snow. It had been a long time since he'd seen snow. Maybe he could talk his superiors into sending him to inspect their holdings there.

He pulled the radio up from the table and keyed into the comm line. "This is far enough, conductor. Why don't you pull us to a stop?"

"Will do, Mr. Stone."

The train began to slow, gently at first to avoid damaging any of its cargo. Eventually, he could hear the brakes bear down on the wheels.

Stone jerked his hand out to keep his tea from sliding across his table until the train rolled to a complete stop.

Quite honestly, he had dreaded this part of the trip. The heat out there was scorching beyond words, but it was part of the deal he'd struck.

With real reluctance, he climbed out of the passenger car he rode in and kept an eye on the workers who had already begun to open the cargo cars at the far rear of the train.

He sighed and opened an umbrella to shield himself from the worst of the sun as he walked down the track.

These weren't people he enjoyed spending time with, but deals had been struck and they needed to be observed by a certified auditor of the New York Western Railroad Company.

The first one out of the cars was a large Excalibur mech. Unlike the others that he'd seen of the same model, this one had traded the rocket-powered hammer and ozone shield for an electrical spear. Abandoning defense for offense really did seem to fit Athena's type.

"Are you sure this is it?" she boomed through her mech's external speakers as her men climbed out of the other three cars that they had been riding in.

"Of course. We at the New York Western Railroad company pride ourselves in mapping these abandoned areas," he stated and gestured with his hand across the barren landscape around them.

"Why did you help us? I thought you were on Hammerhand's side?"

"The New York Western Railroad Company takes no sides in internal power conflicts. We do, however, remember our friends and those who have helped us and assume the same courtesy will be extended in turn."

"Sure." Athena grunted and turned away. "We'll be sure to remember who helped us."

"Please do. Have a pleasant journey."

The Excalibur led the raiders away from the train and Stone let the fake smile slip from his lips as he turned to head to his car. Hopefully, they had increased the cooling inside to make up for the doors opening. Otherwise, he would need to have another chat with the train's conductor.

He climbed inside and keyed into the comm line. "We are ready to move again."

"Right away, Mr. Stone."

The train advanced once more.

The End

If you enjoyed this series, you might also enjoy Steel Dragon from Kevin McLaughlin and Michael Anderle. You can pick up book one in the series by clicking the link below.

Get Steel Dragon and Amazon or through Kindle Unlimited.

Marshal Rust was born in Boulder, Colorado, where he still resides to this day. His parents - both hard-working blue-collar folk - made sure he got a good education and ensured that included reading as many books as he possibly could. And it's no surprise he came to absolutely love science fiction and fantasy. He cut his teeth on the works of Heinlein, Asimov, Tolkien, and more. He later progressed to the works of Robert Jordan, Terry Brooks, David Brin and Cormac McArthy, and many of their contemporaries through and over the years. He's worked in his father's trade as a welder, moonlighted as a delivery man, sold computer hardware, and done a brutal stint as an animal massage therapist (yes, it's a real job), and has even had to chase a goat that made off with his paper bagged lunch, but nothing makes him happier than clear skies and a blank sheet of paper to write on.

Bulletfoot Series

Origins (Book 1)

The Auburn Rebellion (Book 2)

At Athena's Gates (Book 3)